Kiss Now,
Lie Later

KISS NOW, LIE LATER

Copyright © 2020 by C.W. Farnsworth

Cover design by Mary Scarlett LaBerge

CONTENTS

"My only love sprung from my only hate."

WILLIAM SHAKESPEARE, *ROMEO AND JULIET*

CHAPTER ONE

MAEVE

End of Freshman Year

Some things are set in stone.

The length of a second. How many days fill each month. If you're from Glenmont, then you're obligated to hate anyone from Alleghany.

But even stone can be altered. Some seconds feel hours long. August passes too quickly; March drags too long. And a girl from Glenmont could hate how much she *doesn't* hate a boy from Alleghany.

I've lived in Glenmont my entire life. I know the tiny town better than the grooves of my own palm. Its small downtown area where my mother's real estate office is located; the wooded running paths that surround the high school; the stretch of sandy beach that encircles our half of the lake. And I say "our half" in acknowledgement of Glenmont's single most defining characteristic: its hatred of the town that owns most of the remaining lakeshore, Alleghany. The town of Fayetteville has the misfortune of being sandwiched between us on one side.

I have no idea how the rivalry with Alleghany started, only that it's been a divisive force for longer than I've been alive. My father grew up in Glenmont; he was the hometown football star here before going on to play at nearby Arlington University, and then eventually to coach there.

Based on the stories he's told to my twin brother Liam and me, tensions ran just as high then.

At least until last September.

This past fall, the scales tipped. The tides changed. And not in the direction of being one big happy family singing around a campfire.

Things changed for one reason, composed of two words: Weston Cole.

The rivalry between Alleghany and Glenmont has never been ordinary, or normal. It's always been petty and vicious. We compete for everything, but there are striations to it. Some victories are worth more than others.

At the top of the hierarchy? High school football.

The two teams and their respective hometowns hate each other just as much on the one Friday night they clash as on the other three hundred and sixty-four nights of the year. For several consecutive seasons, Glenmont won. Starting the very first year my father left his coaching job at Arlington University and became Glenmont High's head football coach instead.

This past fall was meant to be different. Better. It marked the start of Liam and I's high school careers.

I entered the halls of Glenmont High as an afterthought, but Liam entered as a legend. The heir to the Stevens football dynasty. Glenmont's golden ticket to another four years of victory.

In what seemed like a perfect twist of fate at the time, the first game of the regular season was against Alleghany. Nothing like beating your mortal enemy to start the season off right. Instead? Liam stepped on the field as the starting quarterback, but so did another freshman, who had just moved to Alleghany over the summer. Weston Cole.

And we lost.

Badly.

Weston Cole stepped out onto the field and ruined the start of what was meant to be a four-year legacy. That one game would have been bad enough, but as a freshman, he led the Alleghany Eagles to their first state football championship during my father's tenure as head coach.

His name is uttered reverentially in Alleghany and with hatred in Glenmont; no more so than in my house.

Liam has always been serious and focused, especially with football, but this past season pushed him beyond his normal bounds. I spent the remainder of my freshman year after his first clash with Weston Cole being woken up early each morning to the sound of clanging weights on the other side of the wall we share. Not the most pleasant way to start the day, but I've never said anything to him about it.

Liam and I rarely discuss the rivalry or its repercussions. I know Liam feels like he let everyone down last fall: our dad, our town, and our school. But his personal rivalry with Weston Cole goes beyond football. Liam tends to be quiet and reserved. Football is where he's always excelled.

I know it gets to him that Weston is rumored to have the cocky swagger characteristic of most quarterbacks. That he's known to be popular and charming and manages to do so with little effort. He may be hated in Glenmont, but that doesn't preclude him from the high school's gossip mill. If anything, he features more prominently because of it. And the rumors are far from limited to just football.

The ceaseless lights of Glenmont's football stadium flash by on the right, and I add being on the track, running sprints, to the list of things I would rather be doing right now.

I was the only freshman to make Glenmont's varsity girls soccer team, and I'm determined to do more than just ride the bench sophomore year. I have a training plan for the entire summer already mapped out, even though the last day of school was only yesterday.

When my best friend Maggie saw it, she rolled her eyes so hard I was worried they'd fall out of her head. But I can't help it. Like Liam, I tend to be serious, steadfast, and predictable. I'm a rule follower. A planner. Some would call me boring. Maggie did, until I agreed to tag along on this outing.

That's why I'm currently in a car with Maggie and her older sister, headed to a party in Fayetteville.

I make the safe, responsible choices so that other people can make stupid ones. Which is the main reason I'm spending my night attending this Fayetteville party. Some sophomore guy Maggie met outside her dance studio invited her, and I refuse to let her become a crime statistic. Our other two best friends, Brooke and Sarah, left this morning to be camp counselors in Maine for the summer, and I knew if I refused to go, Maggie would forge ahead alone.

Apparently, I'm a naturally cynical person since Maggie doesn't seem to have any similar reservations about meeting a random guy at a stranger's house. But I've always been guarded with anyone unfamiliar—likely a result of growing up sheltered in a small town.

Or maybe it's because I'm a Stevens. Known to everyone in the county as Coach Stevens' daughter and Liam Stevens' sister.

I always know any misstep I make will reflect on them.

"Come on, Maeve!" Maggie's voice pulls me from my musings. I glance outside the car to see a small cabin next to a stretch of trees. Hordes of teenagers mill about. Rap music pumps through invisible speakers.

We've arrived. *Wonderful.*

"You're sure about this?" I hedge as she opens my door like a chauffeur. "We could just head to my house for a sleepover…"

I'm not antisocial by any stretch, but I much prefer the company of my friends, or at least familiar faces, to that of drunk strangers. And since Fayetteville is considered neutral territory, there could even be Alleghany students here.

"You already agreed," Maggie sings.

I groan as I climb out of the backseat of her sister's car.

"I'll be back at midnight!" Maggie's sister calls before driving away, taking my only escape route with her. This party is on the very outskirts of Fayetteville, alongside the small stretch of lakeshore not owned by Alleghany or Glenmont. As we draw closer to the cabin, I can see the moonlight reflecting off the glassy surface of the lake through the trees ahead. It's beautiful, but the scenic view also means I'm stuck until Maggie's sister returns. It would take me at least two hours to walk home from here.

Maggie drags me over to the largest crowd of people, correctly surmising it's where the alcohol will be located. I raise an eyebrow at her as she fills a red cup with the malty liquid enclosed inside the metal keg.

"This is all I'll have," she promises me. "They used to give beer to little kids, Maeve!"

I scoff at her reasoning as I flip open the top of the red and white cooler resting on the dirt next to the keg. It's filled with more beer, this time bottled, and some cans of soda as well. I grab a cola and take a long sip. The carbonation tickles my throat, and the cold liquid chills my esophagus.

I set the can down on a nearby tree stump so I can unknot the flannel shirt tied around my waist. I shrug it on over the thin tank top I'm wearing, glad I opted to wear jeans. Most of the girls here are dressed in skimpy skirts or dresses, acting as though it's already mid-summer rather than barely June. I'd be surprised if the temperature is above sixty degrees.

Maggie gives my worn cotton shirt a disdainful glance, but I can see goosebumps on her arms thanks to the glow of the cabin's floodlights.

"Do you see him?" Maggie asks, glancing around the crowd anxiously.

"That would require knowing what he looks like, so no," I respond dryly, picking up the can of soda and taking another sip.

Maggie rolls her eyes. "I told you, he has blond hair and brown eyes."

"Maggie, half the guys here have blond hair," I inform her as I glance around. "And I can't tell what color anyone's eyes are."

Maggie sighs. "Well, it's not quite 10:30. That's when he said he would be here."

"Here's hoping you found the only punctual teenage boy to ever exist." I raise my can in a mock cheers.

Maggie checks the time on her phone again. "Would it kill you to be a little more supportive?"

"Mags, I'm here. That's as supportive as you're going to get. I could be asleep right now. You know I'm running with Becca at six."

"I can't believe you're actually sticking to that insane training plan you made."

"That's the point of a training plan. You stick to it," I reply. "You have a schedule for dance, right?"

"It doesn't include getting up when it's barely light out!" Maggie contends.

"Don't you have cheerleading camp this summer?" I ask.

"No, did I forget to tell you? Samantha's parents bought a beach house in North Carolina. She's spending the summer there and canceled camp."

"Of course she did." I roll my eyes. The cheerleading team is by far the most popular girls' sports team at Glenmont High, which I can only surmise is based off the uniforms they wear since they put very little effort into anything else.

"You're wearing your judgy face, Maeve," Maggie teases.

"I know I am," I grumble. "Do you know the average number of attendees at our games last season? Fifteen! After twelve hours of practice a week! You guys gossip for one hour at most, and the whole school shows up for the cheerleading competition. It's infuriating!"

"Hey, I was one of the fifteen spectators," Maggie reminds me.

"I know." I sigh. "Rant over."

Maggie laughs. "Just ask—" She abruptly stops talking. "He's here!"

I follow her gaze, and sure enough, a blond guy is walking over to the cabin with two darker haired boys. He's looking around anxiously the same way Maggie's been doing ever since we first arrived.

"How do I look?" Maggie asks, fiddling with the hem of her light pink dress.

"You look gorgeous," I assure her.

"Okay, wish me luck!" Maggie says before taking off in the guy's direction. I watch as she approaches him. As soon as the blond boy spots her, he gives her a bashful grin of greeting before introducing Maggie to his companions.

Satisfied he's not a serial killer, I pull my phone out of my pocket and send Maggie a quick text, letting her know I'm walking down to the lake and to text me if she needs me. I skirt the assembled partygoers and slip between two large maples into the wooded stretch separating the cabin from the lake.

A carpet of moss covered with years of decaying leaves muffles my footfalls as I head deeper into the woods. The shouts, loud music, and laughter start to fade away.

I stumble down what seems like it was once a path, but years of neglect have left it overgrown and gnarled. I'm grateful for the worn sneakers I'm wearing as I navigate the uneven terrain.

A sigh of relief escapes me when I spot a fallen log up ahead, just before the growth begins to recede in response to the less hospitable, sandy soil surrounding the immediate lake.

Quickening my pace, I almost fall when my foot gets caught on an errant tree root. Finally reaching my destination, I plop down on the dead tree, looking out at the calm, dark surface of the water. The thick canopy of leaves above only allows a few small patches of moonlight to filter down to the forest floor.

I balance the red can of cola on my denim-clad knee so I can pull my blonde hair out of the messy ponytail I've had it in all day. It tumbles down around my shoulders in a comforting curtain, and I take a sip of soda, finally relaxing for the first time since we arrived.

It's not until an unfamiliar voice speaks that I realize I'm not alone. "Are you drunk?"

I almost drop the can I'm clutching as my eyes dart to the right, trying to peer through the darkness that surrounds me. A shadowed figure is barely visible on the opposite end of the log. It moves closer to me, and I tense, wondering if I should run. Scream.

A beam of moonlight illuminates the silhouette, and I immediately recognize who it is.

Weston fucking Cole.

I'm sure he has an actual middle name that's not profanity, but that's how he's known in the halls of Glenmont High.

This is only the second time I've seen him in person, and the first time up close. His light brown hair is windswept, and his white teeth gleam in the darkness. Even though he's sitting, I can tell he's tall. Imposing.

He's also staring at me expectantly, and I realize he's waiting for me to answer his question. "It sounded like a herd of elephants was coming through the forest," he elaborates.

I hold up the can of cola. "Not drunk. Just clumsy."

He nods, looking relieved, although I can't help but notice he's clutching a beer bottle himself. I hate hypocrites.

I'm about to stand and leave when he speaks again.

"I'm Weston. Cole." His voice is deep and confident but absent of the arrogance I expect to hear based on the stories I've heard about him.

"I know," I admit. "I'm Maeve." I pause, tempted not to share my last name. Reluctantly, I add, "Maeve Stevens."

Weston's eyes widen slightly, giving me a better glimpse of their distinctive cerulean shade. "Ah."

I sigh. "You know who I am." It's a meaningless statement; of course he does.

"I know who your father and brother are," Weston confirms.

I look over at him and smile slightly. "Not many people make that distinction."

"That you're your own person?"

I nod.

"Seems like a pretty easy one to me."

"Well, I've never met a guy—or anyone, really—who doesn't care about my last name. That I'm Coach Stevens' daughter and Liam Stevens' sister," I tell him. I'm slightly embarrassed by my admission, so I quickly shift topics. "What are you doing out here?"

"My dad's having an affair."

"Oh." The syllable hangs awkwardly between us. I'm unsure of what else to say. I assumed he was going to say he needed some quiet, or the party was lame. "I'm sorry. I didn't know," I finally add.

"Why would you have?" Amused blue eyes meet mine.

"Uh—people talk?" I offer awkwardly. Surely he knows about the efficiency of our towns' gossip mills. Especially when it comes to him.

Weston laughs once. Humorlessly. "Yeah, people do talk," he acknowledges. "But they can't talk about things they don't know."

It takes a moment for his meaning to sink in.

"Why did you tell me, then?" I can't help but wonder.

"You asked," he replies simply, taking a sip of beer. I watch the tendons in his throat contract as he swallows.

"I'm sure plenty of other people ask you things."

"If I want a beer? If I want to hook up? If I'm ready for the season? Sure."

I'm not sure how to respond to that, so I take the final swallow of my soda and begin playing with the metal tab on the can.

"Do you want some?" Weston holds the beer bottle closer to me.

"No, I'm good."

"You don't drink?"

"Nope," I reply.

"Bad experience?"

"My dad's an alcoholic."

I don't know who's more surprised by the admission: Weston or me. I've had the same three best friends since kindergarten, and I've never told any of them the real reason I avoid alcohol.

Blurting out the truth to one of them would be understandable.

Entrusting Weston Cole with the knowledge is unconscionable.

He looks over at me, and I'm oddly comforted by his serious expression. "People can't talk about things they don't know, right?" I say, half-shrugging. He nods once, acknowledging he's not the only one spilling secrets tonight.

Honesty must be contagious.

"Are your parents getting divorced?" I finally ask.

"Nah, everyone thinking we're the perfect family is too important to them. And this isn't the first time. It's why we moved here last summer."

The speculation regarding why the Coles moved to Alleghany from the city has been the subject of many a conspiracy theory in Glenmont, mostly due to the timing of their arrival, but none that I've heard mention a past affair. I take this to mean Weston has just shared another secret with me.

"That sucks," I finally say, unable to think of anything else to reply with. I'm confused, and it's muddling my thoughts. Weston Cole is nothing like I expected him to be. It's disconcerting.

"Yeah, it does suck." Weston takes a swig from the bottle he's holding.

I look down and study his hands. A bead of condensation rolls off the neck of the bottle and along his tanned, calloused skin before dripping silently to the dirt ground. His hands look older. Mature. Masculine. I imagine what it would feel like to touch them, and an unfamiliar heat spreads through my entire body.

"I don't think I could ever forgive cheating." I blurt the words to distract myself from the unsettling direction my thoughts have taken.

Weston studies me for a long moment. I take the opportunity to scrutinize him back and am unnerved to realize I understand what some of the girls at school have been going on about. I judged them at the time, so I guess I'm the hypocrite now.

"Me neither," Weston eventually says. He takes another long drink from his bottle of beer, draining it entirely. "I'd better get going."

The rush of disappointment is unexpected.

He stands, and he's even taller than I thought. Definitely taller than me, which is more than most of the boys in Glenmont can say.

"See you around, Maeve."

I'm not sure, but it seems like he uses just my first name on purpose.

"Bye, Weston."

He disappears into the darkness, headed back in the direction of the partying taking place around the cabin.

I replay our bizarre conversation in my head, lingering on Weston's admissions about his parents. I remember them from the game last fall. Cheering loudly opposite a sea of shocked, silent Glenmont fans. His father was wearing a suit, and his mother's appearance was carefully put together.

Like Weston said, they're clearly the type of people who care what others think of them. Who wouldn't want rumors of adultery swirling around. They moved from the city to escape speculation, and in our two towns? One whisper would ensure the conjecture never ended.

Weston Cole just handed me the means to eradicate him. And

I'm not the least bit tempted to do so. Not because I'm a moral, upstanding person, although I'd like to think I am.

Because I don't want to ensure I'll never see him again.

And that right there should have been my first clue.

Weston fucking Cole still applies, just for a different reason.

CHAPTER TWO

MAEVE

Summer Before Senior Year

"This is too weird, Maggie. They're not even going to let me past the front door."

"Of course they are. You look *hot*." Maggie surveys the short green dress I'm wearing—her short green dress—with a satisfied smile. I caved after ten minutes of her complaining about the worn jean shorts I showed up at her house in.

A new record for her; a new low for me.

"That's not what I meant. This is not like the Fayetteville ones we've gone to. We are literally in enemy territory!" I whisper the last sentence to her, since we're rapidly approaching the brick path of the stately house that's our destination.

Or at least Maggie's destination. I'm still considering fleeing.

"Are you forgetting I live here now?" Maggie asks. Her parents' divorce was finalized three weeks ago, and Maggie's mother opted to erect the iron wall known as the Alleghany-Glenmont rivalry between herself and her ex-husband in celebration.

Meaning one of my best friends is now a resident of the town I was raised to hate.

Not the way I envisioned starting the summer before senior year.

"I'm trying to," I reply honestly.

"It's not like I had a choice in the matter, Maeve," she responds, and I feel a fresh twinge of guilt. Cheering Maggie up is the only reason I agreed to go out with her tonight in the first place, since Brooke and Sarah have already left on their annual trip to Maine, and I know she's having trouble adjusting to living in Alleghany. She just neglected to mention our destination happened to be in her new hometown.

"I'm a Stevens, Mags," I plead. "If anyone here realizes that, it's not going to make your life any easier, and I'll probably be run out of town with pitchforks close behind."

Maggie rolls her eyes. "Don't be so dramatic, Maeve." An ironic statement coming from her. "You've never even talked to anyone from Alleghany. And everyone's probably drunk by now, anyway. It started two hours ago."

"Well, that's comforting," I tell her. "Because drunk people never do impulsive, stupid things." I know that better than most. "And I've played against their soccer team. We had to talk during that."

There's one other person I've spoken to from Alleghany, but I've never told anyone about *that* encounter.

Maggie snorts. "I doubt saying 'Good game' a few times a year has created such a lasting impression you can't show your face."

"Ugh, fine," I acquiesce.

"Plus, I doubt anyone from the girls' soccer team will be here. Natalie said the guest list is super exclusive."

"Well, if *Natalie* said so…"

"Maeve, I'm serious. Be nice."

"You're the one who's spent the last two weeks complaining about her."

"Because she's made my life a living hell so far. But if I get on her good side, she also has the power to make my senior year somewhat bearable. Being on the Alleghany cheer team is my only prayer of resuscitating my currently dismal life. You, Sarah, and Brooke are the only people from Glenmont even still talking to me!"

We reach the front door. The thick wood does nothing to muffle the pounding bass reverberating inside the enormous house.

"Okay, your guilt trip worked," I inform her. "But if anyone recognizes me, we're leaving immediately, okay?"

"Fine," Maggie agrees, smiling widely. "Honestly, I didn't even think you would get out of the car."

I groan.

We walk inside the house and veer left into the living room. It's loud and hot and exactly like every other high school party I've attended. But there aren't any glares or insults being hurled my way, so I temper my expectations. No one gives me a second glance, and I'm relieved.

One girl in a group huddled in the far corner of the expansive living room waves at Maggie, and she pulls me over to them.

I study the modern, expensively decorated room we've just entered as she yanks me along. The interior is just as nice as the exterior was, which is hardly a surprise. Alleghany has always been the more affluent of the two towns.

I'm distracted from studying the framed oil paintings that adorn the stretch of wall next to the fireplace when Maggie stops walking.

"Hey, girls," she greets.

The one who waved at her smiles, but the rest merely appraise us silently.

"Maggie. You made it," one girl finally says. Unenthusiastically.

"I did!" Maggie responds, keeping her tone upbeat. "And my cousin Mae is visiting, so I brought her along, too. I hope that's okay."

"The more the merrier," the same girl replies, in a tone that suggests the opposite.

I'm tempted to roll my eyes.

"Okay, well, we're going to grab some drinks! We'll see you all later," Maggie tells the group, before turning and pulling me away.

"Warm reception," I note.

Maggie sighs. "I know."

"Was that Natalie?"

"God, no. Natalie's way worse. That was Madeline. Her second in command. Hopefully she'll have found some football player to hook up with by the time we get back out there. Everyone else is way nicer when she's not around, I promise."

We enter the kitchen, and it's not as crowded as I thought it would be. Maggie was right about the guest list being exclusive, apparently.

She strides confidently toward the assortment of alcohol spread out on the kitchen island, and I trail after her. She grabs a cup and begins splashing the contents of various bottles inside. I open the fridge, only to discover it's filled with nothing to drink besides beer.

Sighing, I take a plastic cup and fill it half-way with water from the tap. I was hoping for something with caffeine. I've been up for—I check the clock on the stove—sixteen hours, and I'm supposed to be up in another seven.

I contemplate the odds of getting more than five hours of sleep as I watch Maggie chug a generous portion of the liquid in her cup. She swallows and meets my gaze.

"Come on, *Mae*," she teases, linking our arms to pull me back toward the living room. "Lighten up. It's a party!"

"Yeah, thank you very much for the adorable nickname," I grumble. "I thought you said—" I stop talking when I realize Maggie's not listening to me anymore. I follow her gaze and promptly lose my train of thought when I see who has just entered the kitchen.

Weston fucking Cole.

I knew—hoped—he would be here. If I'm being honest with myself, it's the primary reason I walked through the door once I realized we were in Alleghany. Glimpses of him on the field during his sophomore and junior year victories over Glenmont are all I've seen of him since the brief, revelatory conversation we had at the very end of our freshman year.

The past two years have been kind to him. One could say overly generous. All traces of boyhood have left his face.

He was attractive before.

He's devastating now.

His cheekbones are prominent and pronounced; his eyes sharp and assessing. Light brown hair falls in a careless disarray across his forehead, and he's sporting a light layer of stubble. I think back to the sight of his hands clutching that beer bottle, how mature they seemed for a boy his age. The rest of him has caught up. A faded navy t-shirt does nothing to hide his powerful, lean physique and broad shoulders.

But more than anything, it's the condescending expression that's different from the last time I saw him up close.

He looks colder now. Aloof and detached. Like a conquering hero.

Although villain would be more accurate, since his victory means my defeat. My family's defeat. Liam didn't talk for two days after we lost to Alleghany for the third time in a row last fall.

Weston's face is lofty, but his eyes are piercing. I hold his probing gaze as I wait to see what he'll do.

"Cole!"

Weston looks at someone behind me. Then, he simply walks past me.

I'm shocked by how much his indifference bothers me.

Annoyed I can't tell whether it is feigned or genuine.

I've spent an embarrassing amount of time wondering what he would say or do if I ever ran into him again. Blatant disregard was not a scenario I hoped for.

Maggie giggles beside me. "Holy shit, that was Weston Cole. He's so hot."

I glare at her, unthinkingly.

She rolls her eyes. "I live in Alleghany now, okay? One of the few perks—actually the only one so far—is that I'm allowed to appreciate an Eagle. *The* Eagle." It's unsettling to realize the petty rivalry wasn't why I was glaring. "Plus, you know most of the girls in Glenmont think the same. They just won't say so in front of you anymore."

"What? Why?" I ask.

"Because Liam's your twin," Maggie replies. "And whenever Weston Cole comes up around him, he looks like he wants to punch something."

"Oh, right," I respond, taking a sip of my water as we walk back into the living room. I have to resist the temptation to look back behind me as we do.

Maggie gives me a strange glance but doesn't say anything else as we head over to the same group of cheerleaders. The one who spoke before, Madeline, is missing, and just as Maggie predicted, we receive a much friendlier greeting this time around. I mostly tune out their conversation as I continue to take sips from my cup, bored by their conversation about people I've never met and never will.

I only tune back into their gossiping when Maggie responds to a query about where a girl named Abby is. "I don't know. I stopped paying attention to anyone else in the kitchen when Weston arrived."

"He's here?" the girl who asked about Abby squeals.

"We definitely saw him," Maggie replies. "Right, Mae?"

"Uh-huh," I confirm, taking another drink of water in the hopes it will preclude me from contributing anything else to a conversation about Weston Cole.

"Forget it, Jess," the girl who waved at Maggie when we arrived says. "I'm sure Natalie already has her claws in him."

"But they're not exclusive," Jess argues. "Weston doesn't date anyone for real. You know that."

"Doesn't matter. You remember what she did to Amanda after she hooked up with him last year."

I shift awkwardly, uncomfortable with the direction the conversation has taken, and annoyed with myself for feeling this way. Weston Cole's sex life shouldn't be of any interest to me aside from hoping he contracts chlamydia. I can't force my ears to tune out their continuing commentary, though, so I set my now empty cup down on a nearby side table and whisper to Maggie that I'm going to the bathroom.

She nods, but doesn't even glance at me, too absorbed in the ongoing speculation.

I wander out of the living room and through the massive house, finally finding the bathroom. Along with the line of eleven girls waiting to use it.

Since it was more an excuse than a necessity, I pass them and head outside through the first exit I come across. It's a sliding door that opens onto a stone patio. I close the door and walk over to the perimeter of the stones, next to a wrought iron couch with a thick cushion. The weatherworn fabric is still saturated with rain from the downpour earlier, so I continue further into the backyard. Several plastic Adirondack chairs sit around an empty fire pit. They've all dried, but I remain standing as I stare at the black hole where the fire would be.

A voice startles me, and I experience a flash of déjà vu.

"Good night for some stargazing."

I still at the sound. It's been two years since I heard the deep timbre, and yet I immediately know who it belongs to. Even more concerning? I'm thrilled to hear it. Elated he's not upstairs with a girl the way the cheer team suggested.

I glance up at the swirling remnants of vapor still dancing angrily overhead.

"Yup. Hardly a cloud in the sky."

I feel rather than see him come stand next to me.

"Never seen you at an Alleghany party before," Weston says. His voice is casual, but there's an undercurrent of something else. I'm tempted to look over to see if I can discern it in his expression but choose to keep my gaze on the overcast sky above us instead.

"One of my best friends moved here a few weeks ago. She forced me to show up." I wince internally as soon as the words are out. I don't owe him an explanation. Worse, I sound lame. Boring.

Should I care what Weston Cole thinks of me? Absolutely not.

Do I? Apparently.

"Huh," Weston replies, and I stand there, completely stupefied.

What the hell does one respond to that with? I desperately

grope for something funny or clever to say. I come up with nothing. My wit has entirely abandoned me when I need it the most.

"So, what's your name?" he asks after a long pause.

Fiery embarrassment burns through me. Of course he doesn't remember me. Of course the indifference in the kitchen wasn't an act.

A wave of humiliation engulfs me as I recall all the wasted minutes I've spent reliving our encounter in the woods over the past two years. He's done the opposite.

I turn to head back inside, absolutely disgusted with myself. Suddenly, listening to Maggie gossip with her new friends doesn't sound bad at all.

I'm stopped by the feel of a hand on my arm that sears through the denim jacket I'm wearing over Maggie's dress.

"I'm fucking with you, Maeve."

I meet Weston's eyes for the first time. The startling shade of blue seems especially vivid in contrast to the shadowed yard and stormy sky.

"I don't share secrets very often. Ever—as a matter of fact." His words hang between us. "It's not something I'm likely to forget."

I swallow. I'm simultaneously rejoicing he remembers who I am and pissed he purposefully pretended like he didn't.

"Did you ever meet him?" Weston asks. I arch an eyebrow, confused. "The guy who doesn't care?"

I'm shocked he remembers my exact words from the woods. Even more surprised he's asking about them. I start to wish he actually *did* forget our last encounter. Admitting to him most people don't pay attention to anything about me, aside from my last name, was one of my more vulnerable and less flattering moments.

I shake my head wordlessly.

"That's good to know," Weston replies. And then he leans down and kisses me. Every muscle in my body freezes. I stop breathing. Even the flow of blood through my veins seems to slow to a trickle.

I'm being kissed.

A boy is kissing me.

And not just any boy. Weston fucking Cole.

His kiss is sweet, almost hesitant. Not at all what I expect. Or rather, what I would have expected if I'd had any premonition this moment might happen. Which I didn't. I'm too shell-shocked to do anything but imitate a statue and savor the tingles.

Until his hot tongue traces the seam of my lips, and he tugs me closer.

I gasp, allowing him access to my mouth, and he doesn't hesitate to take full advantage. Every sensation intensifies. I'm drowning in the best way, overcome by heat and exhilaration and lust. My hands wander into his soft hair, and he groans. His mouth becomes even more insistent, and I finally let my tongue tangle with his.

Weston Cole conquers me. And I let him.

I try to remember why this shouldn't happen. That's he's part of the enemy. That he leads the enemy. But his lips are demanding and persuasive and warm against mine, and I can't muster the willpower to string a coherent thought together, much less leave them.

He's the one who breaks our kiss, and we stand there, both taking greedy gulps of the damp night air.

I'm dazed. Delirious. Drunk. Dizzy. Disappointed. That wasn't my first kiss, but it's the first time I've cared one's ended.

Weston half smiles when he looks at my face, and I wonder what he sees there. He produces a red cylinder and holds it out to me.

I grasp it automatically.

"See you around, Maeve Stevens." This time he not only says my last name, he also emphasizes it slightly. It's a reminder; I'm not sure whether it's one meant for me or him. I survey his expression, but there's no hint of the cockiness or derision he displayed in the kitchen. Is this his way of telling me *he* doesn't care about my last name?

Weston turns and heads back across the grass toward the patio, leaving me staring down at the can of cola in my hand.

I eventually wander back inside the house. Maggie's still standing in the same spot by the fireplace.

"Hey, I was just about to come look for you! What took so long?" she asks when I reach the group of cheerleaders.

I can't tell her the truth. That Weston Cole kissed me like his life depended on it and then I stood in the backyard for ten minutes in a daze because I'm pretty sure kissing him is what the aftermath of several shots of liquor must feel like.

"There was a long line for the bathroom. And then I grabbed this." I hold up the can of cola.

Maggie nods, accepting my answer without hesitation. "We can leave soon," she promises. "I just want to hear the rest of Skyler's story about her college visits."

"Okay," I respond, opening the can of soda and taking a long sip. I don't bother listening to the narrative being told, barely cognizant of the *ooohs* and *aaahs* from Maggie and the other girls.

I have more pressing problems than where an Alleghany cheerleader is planning to continue her education.

Weston Cole kissed me.

And I want him to do it again.

CHAPTER THREE

WESTON

B eads of sweat roll down my forehead as I force my shaking arms upward again.

"Did you hear Maeve Stevens was at Josh's house last night?" Chris asks as he's spotting me. My fingers tighten around the hard metal as I straighten my elbows.

"Nope." It's not a total lie. I didn't think anyone else would realize who she was.

"Caroline recognized her from soccer. I wonder if she reported back on how much better our parties are than Glenmont's. I can't believe she actually came to Alleghany."

"Why the fuck did she?" Charlie asks from the next bench, setting his own weighted bar down with a loud clang.

"Josh said there's a new girl who moved here from Glenmont a couple weeks ago who she was with. Still can't believe the Glenmont golden girl dared to be seen with us. She had to know we'd all be there," Chris replies.

"What are you guys talking about?" Adam joins the group that's huddled around me, discussing the one topic I really don't want to hear about.

I still can't believe I fucking kissed her. I've made a litany of excuses for what I confessed to her our freshman year. How I couldn't get the look on my mother's face out of my head when she realized my father hadn't gone to the office like he told her, the two beers I'd drunk, the fact that she stayed on that log long after she realized who I was. I don't have any such excuses for last night.

I kissed her because I wanted to. Because when I saw her in Josh's kitchen, I forgot there were other people in the room.

But I can't figure out why she kissed me back.

"Maeve Stevens." Chris replies to Adam's question.

"Coach Stevens' daughter? Why?"

"She was at Josh's last night. Blonde hair, killer body, I think she was wearing a pink dress?"

It was green.

"Holy shit. That was Maeve Stevens? She's hot." Grudging appreciation fills Adam's voice.

She kissed me back. And I can't make sense of why. I've done nothing over the past two years since we first spoke but continue to shred apart her family's football legacy, and she fucking kissed me back. I got the sense when she talked about her dad's drinking they aren't close, but I know she and Liam are. Maeve came out onto the field and hugged him after our game against Glenmont this past fall while I watched like a creeper.

"Is she dating anyone?" Charlie asks. "Doubt any Glenmont guy would be happy about his girl hanging out at our party."

I do four more reps and then set the heavy bar down with a loud rattle, sitting up and wiping my face dry with a towel.

"Who cares?" Adam scoffs. "But probably. The guys in Glenmont are jerks, but they're not blind."

"Let's get out of here," I finally interject, grabbing my stuff and heading toward the door that leads out to the gym's parking lot. I know they'll all follow me, but I don't expect them to still be discussing Maeve Stevens when they do.

I grit my teeth with annoyance as I open up the trunk of the brand-new Range Rover my parents bought me as a bribe and toss my gym gear inside.

"Caroline said she's good?"

"Yeah, but I don't know what that means. Hell, I didn't even know Caroline played soccer until sophomore year."

"Jeez, Adam, don't mention that to her. No wonder you're single."

"You guys are *still* talking about Maeve Stevens?" I ask, making sure my tone conveys I think their fixation is ridiculous. Advice I should take myself.

"Charlie just told me she plays soccer. Figured Liam took all the athletic genes in the womb." Adam is the only one who laughs at his lame twin joke.

"She doesn't just play, she's the team captain," I inform him. Adam, Charlie, and Chris all look at me with surprise. "What?" I ask.

"How the hell do you know that?" Chris questions.

"I read it in an article about how Stevens was selected as Glenmont's," I reply. I'm not sure why they bothered writing a news article about it; everyone knew it was a forgone conclusion Liam Stevens would be selected as Glenmont's football captain this year, the same way everyone knew I would be Alleghany's.

The only reason I even read the piece was because I was curious if it would mention Maeve. It did, but only in a cursory sentence that insinuated her athletic success was merely an extension of her brother's. It bothered me more than I expected, and not only because I'm far from Liam's biggest fan. I wonder if I even would have noticed if she hadn't already flat-out told me people only see her as her father's daughter or her brother's sister.

27

"You can read?" Charlie jokes.

I flip him off.

"We're meeting at Baylor's place, right?" Chris asks, unlocking his own SUV.

"Yup," Adam confirms. "Everyone else is already there."

"I've got a meeting with Coach Blake. I'll see you guys there," I say before climbing into my car.

It's a short drive to the main building of the high school, where I park outside the entrance closest to the football field. One of the many perks of being chosen as captain is the metal key that allows me to enter the locker room even when it's technically closed.

I unlock the heavy metal door and push inside the empty, quiet locker room. I've never been in here without my boisterous teammates before. The normally noisy room feels hallowed and empty without their loud presence. I bypass the gleaming rows of lockers out into the hallway that leads to Coach Blake's office. Despite its proximity to the belongings of sweaty teenage boys, it's actually a location of honor. Every other coach's office is relegated to the separate sports building I just came from.

His door is closed when I reach it, so I knock before I hear his booming voice call out permission to enter.

"Hey, Coach," I greet, dropping into one of the familiar folding chairs across from his cluttered desk. The metal squeaks underneath the weight of my tall frame, but I know better than to suggest he swap out the cheap seats for a nicer option. The rickety chairs are perfect for making football players squirm, which is Coach Blake's favorite pastime. Every uneasy movement elicits a creak he wears like a badge of honor.

"Good to see you, Cole," he replies, giving me a genuine smile.

Despite Coach Blake's stoic exterior, I've grown to respect

him for a lot more than just his uncanny ability to draw the best out of his players. He embodies many of the principles my father is sorely lacking. Like integrity, for instance.

"There are a couple things I want to talk to you about. First off, your training plan for the summer."

"Training plan?" I echo.

"You've got heaps of natural talent, Cole, but that's no reason not to work extra hard. We ended last season with three straight losses. Now, I know everyone is going to be focused on a full sweep against Glenmont, but I'm more concerned with making it to the state final this year. Prepare for that and facing Glenmont won't pose a problem. If you work on your conditioning this summer, we'll be poised to add some new running plays, and your throwing technique could also use some refinement. Thompson and Fields have gotten good at reading you, but you'll be a stronger quarterback if you can improve your accuracy. Clemens was a good captain last year, but you're the one the whole team has always looked up to. Use that to your advantage."

I nod.

"Good. Here are some specific drills to start on before preseason." He hands me a piece of paper. "Now, I also thought we should discuss your future plans. I've gotten a lot of calls from colleges about you, and I want to check and see if there are any particular schools you'd like me to ensure you get to play for. I've got connections all over the country."

"My father has always wanted me to go to Lincoln," I say. "That's where he went, and they're one of the top football programs in the country."

Coach Blake studies me. I didn't exactly give the university a ringing endorsement from my own perspective, which I doubt he missed. "They've expressed interest, as I'm sure you know."

"Yeah, I do," I respond. "I'd like to keep my options open, but there's no place in particular I'm considering instead."

"Let me know if that changes."

"I will, Coach."

"All right then, go enjoy the rest of your summer. I'll see you for preseason in a few weeks. Just keep in mind what we talked about."

"Yes, sir," I say before heading back out into the hallway. My car's still the only one in the lot when I emerge outside, and I climb in and head toward Baylor's.

I park in the open spot that's been left for me in the driveway and head into the backyard, trying to shake off the residual stress my talk with Coach left behind. I know my father will be happy if I continue playing football in college, but it's not a priority for him. He just wants me to go to a school that's competitive enough he can brag to his business partners about it.

Most of Alleghany High's senior class seems to be in Baylor's backyard. The lawn and pool are overflowing with hubbub and hormones. Everyone I pass calls out greetings to me, but I only respond to a few.

There are almost three hundred people in the senior class, and I doubt I could name more than fifty of them. I stick to socializing with the football team. Not because I'm a snob, but because anyone I talk to outside of my immediate friend group tends to either gab nonstop or lose the ability to speak at all.

Chris calls it the "Cole Charm." I call it annoying.

I grab a cold can of beer from the cooler set out on the patio and then head over to the deck, where I can see Chris and Charlie leaning against the railing. They greet me with hand slaps as I settle in the one open chair.

"How'd it go with Coach Blake?" Chris asks.

"Fine," I reply. "He just wanted to go over the plan for the season."

"What's the plan, O Captain?" Charlie wonders.

"Win," I tell him before opening the can and taking a sip of beer.

Chris laughs; Charlie rolls his eyes.

"Hey, boys," Natalie greets, sauntering over to us in just a bikini. It's an impressive sight, and neither Charlie nor Chris bother to hide their appreciation for it.

"Hi, Natalie," I reply.

"Never saw you at Josh's last night," she tells me.

"I was around," I respond vaguely. "Sure you weren't just too busy micro-managing the cheer team?"

Natalie laughs. "You know I like to keep people in line."

"Oh, I do," I assure her. Natalie's known for a lot more than her looks at Alleghany High. It's no accident the cheerleaders comprise the most organized, disciplined team in the school. And I'm well aware it's due to a lot more than the sugary sweet side she shows me. Madeline's the only one who was brave enough to venture up on the deck with Natalie. The rest of the cheer team remains in a huddled mass by the pool.

I scan the group of cheerleaders and am surprised to spot a girl with dark brown hair I've never seen before.

"Did you invite underclassmen?" I ask Natalie.

She follows my gaze, and her pretty features twist in displeasure. "No, that's Maggie Burchard. She's a senior like us, but she just moved here. From Glenmont."

Maeve's friend, I realize, and Chris comes to the same conclusion. "She's the one who's friends with Maeve Stevens?"

Natalie's glossed lips purse. "Maeve Stevens? As in Liam Stevens' sister?"

"Yeah, she was at Josh's last night," Charlie replies, then glances at Caroline. "Right, Caroline?"

Caroline ambles over from the patio, with Josh right behind her. "You guys always make me regret telling you anything. I don't know why people associate girls with gossiping."

"You're sure it was her?" Chris wonders, ignoring her dig.

"Yes, I'm sure," Caroline assures him. "Not sure why you boys care so much, though."

"Are you kidding?" Charlie asks. "She's a Stallion *and* a Stevens."

"So? She doesn't play football. If anyone should be holding a grudge, it's me. She made a mockery of us last year."

"You guys lost to Glenmont?" I can't help but ask.

Caroline looks at me with surprise. I'm not sure if it's because of my question, or that I'm the one who asked it. "Yeah, we did."

"I didn't hear about that." Normally, I don't pay attention to anything involving Alleghany's athletics that doesn't directly affect football. But since our encounter freshman year, I seem to have developed a sixth sense for Maeve Stevens' name. If someone had mentioned that victory to me before, I would have remembered. She's the only Stevens that's beaten Alleghany, something that stupid article didn't mention.

Caroline laughs. "Well, if you didn't know, soccer is during the same season as football. We aren't exactly the headline news."

"Losing to Glenmont usually is," I reply.

She shrugs. "The boys' team didn't. We rank even lower on the interest scale."

"I thought our boys' soccer team is terrible?" Chris asks.

"They are," Caroline responds. "We've beaten them in scrimmages before. But they didn't have to play against Maeve Stevens."

"She's really that good?" Surprise colors Charlie's voice.

"We're seriously going through this again?" I ask irritably before Caroline can answer. "I already told you she's their captain this year."

"He's really hung up on that," Charlie explains to Caroline, Natalie, and Josh.

"It must be a captain thing," Adam contributes, strolling over to join our conversation. "Like if you insult one of them, you insult all of them, or something."

I roll my eyes at them both. "That has nothing to do with it. But since you brought it up, the captain is typically the best player on the team. Which explains why neither of you two were selected."

"Start looking for a new wide receiver, Cole," Adam threatens as everyone else laughs.

"Please. If you're worried about having a tough captain, go join the cheerleading team," I tell him, winking at Natalie.

"Or the Glenmont girls' soccer team," Caroline adds. "Rumor is Maeve Stevens has her team training at six every day, plus she runs at the Glenmont track every night."

"Are you serious?" Charlie gapes at her.

"Why do you think we lost?" Caroline asks. "We train hard, but she's crazy dedicated. The warm-up drill they did before our last game against them was more intense than most of our practices."

"I can't believe a girls' team…" Charlie's voice trails off in response to the hard stares Natalie and Caroline give him. "That's impressive." He wisely opts to abandon his first statement.

The conversation finally changes to a topic entirely unrelated to Maeve Stevens, and I sit back and sip my beer as my friends plan a trip to the lake later in the week, nodding along to anything I'm asked without really registering what I'm agreeing to.

My thoughts are a million miles away. On shared secrets and scintillating green eyes and scorching kisses.

I thought meeting Maeve Stevens freshman year was an inconsequential blip.

I thought kissing her would allow me to forget her.

I was wrong about both.

CHAPTER FOUR

MAEVE

I reach the finish line, sucking greedy breaths of cool air into my desperate lungs. Sweat trickles down my face as I reach for my phone to check the stopwatch.

"You were faster that time."

I freeze, then stand straight and spin around. Weston Cole is walking across the Glenmont track toward me.

"I'd guess fifty-four seconds," he adds.

I glance down at the phone in my hand. Fifty-three. "Have we met before?" I ask grumpily.

Weston grins. "Touché, Stevens."

I take a long swig from my water bottle. "What are you doing here, Weston?"

"It's Wes. And I wanted to see if the rumors are true."

"What rumors?"

"That you run out here at night."

"There are rumors about me?"

"You have no idea, Maeve." Wes laughs but doesn't look very amused.

I wait, hoping he'll elaborate, but he doesn't.

"What are you actually doing here?" I finally ask.

"Nothing else to do tonight."

I eye him skeptically. "I know that's not true. My friend Maggie said there's a massive party at the same place as last night."

Wes doesn't deny it. "Yup."

"So…why aren't you there?"

"There are a few girls I'm trying to avoid."

I wait, but that's all he says. Is he trying to make me jealous? Did he actually just end up here randomly? I'm completely out of my element when it comes to Weston Cole.

"Huh," I spit back his same non-answer from last night, and I think I catch a ghost of a smile in response.

"You don't believe me?"

"Just not sure if I see the appeal."

Wes takes a couple more steps closer to me. Only one lane remains between us.

"Really?" He quirks a brow.

I'm usually full of false bravado with boys. I flirt, I quip, I tease.

Because I know I'll never have to follow it through with a Glenmont guy. There's a certain stigma that comes with being related to two integral parts of the beloved football team, despite the fact they both couldn't care less who I date. My father actually asked me why I went to prom last year with a basketball player from Fayetteville rather than a guy from his football team.

I have no protection or assurances when it comes to Weston Cole, however. Because I think he would follow through. Hell, his suggestive smirk all but promises it.

It's a thrilling prospect. It's also a terrible idea.

I break eye contact to wipe my damp face with the light jacket I brought and shed when I started sweating.

"So...do you need a sprint buddy?" Wes takes my subtle rejection in stride.

I eye him uncertainly. "Are you serious?"

"Did you find my offer funny?" Weston asks. I roll my eyes in response. "I lifted earlier, but I should do some cardio too. I've broken forty-seven on this drill before."

"You have?" I don't bother to hide my surprise as I bend down to set up a second set of cones for him.

"What? You thought the only thing I'm good at is kissing?" I knock over the cone I just set down and hear a low chuckle in response.

I straighten the orange plastic and stand. "I thought the only thing you're decent at is throwing a football," I reply evenly.

"Is that a compliment, Stevens?"

"I've seen your stats, Cole. Unfortunately, I'm just stating facts."

"You looked up my stats?" He gives me a cocky grin.

I snort. "As if. They're a frequent topic of conversation at the dinner table. Drives my mother crazy."

"Not how you've broken two school records?"

I look over at him in shock. "You looked up *my* stats?" I echo his question.

"Yup," he replies, unabashed.

"*Why?*" I can't help but ask.

"I was curious. Glenmont's heaping the athletic adulations on the wrong Stevens twin, if you ask me."

"I doubt anyone will." I try to tamp down the warmth his words elicit. No one aside from my teammates or close friends has ever complimented me about soccer before. "You sure your assessment has nothing to do with the fact I'm the Stevens twin who *doesn't* play the same sport as you?"

"I'm sure," Wes replies confidently. "I've beaten Liam at football. I'm not sure if I could beat you at soccer."

My eyebrows rise in surprise. I'm impressed by the way he states his record against Liam so matter-of-factly, without the slightest hint of gloating, and startled by his last sentence.

"Do you want to try to?" I challenge without thinking.

Wes grins. "Do you have a ball?"

"Not with me. But"—I waver on the precipice between what I should do, and what I want to do—"we could meet tomorrow?" I let myself topple where I want to, and I'm shocked that I did.

"There's a field in Fayetteville that's usually empty. I can meet you there tomorrow afternoon?" Wes's words are casual, as though he meets girls from Glenmont to play soccer all the time. I'm grateful he's being so cavalier because I'm freaking out enough for the both of us.

"Okay," I reply. My heart is racing, and I try to convince myself it's just anticipation and panic I'm experiencing. Those are certainly both present, but the dominant emotion is excitement. About how I'm going to see him again.

Wes holds out a hand. "Give me your phone."

"Why?" I ask, handing it to him cautiously.

"So I can text you, Stevens. Do you prefer to receive handwritten notes delivered by pigeons?"

I scoff at his heavy sarcasm.

Wes types something into my phone, and then hands it back to me. I smirk when I see what he's entered his name in my contacts as.

Good at one thing.

He grins in response. "I'll let you decide what that is."

I set my phone down on my gym bag and move next to the first cone for my third set. Wes copies me.

I count down as soon as we're both in place, and then take off.

The strain of my muscles alerts me to the fact I'm pushing myself even harder than before, and the tall, lean figure keeping pace next to me makes it impossible to forget why. I'm running drills with Weston Cole. It's an absurd thought.

As soon as we cross the final line, I check the stopwatch on my phone.

"Well?" Wes asks, quirking a brow.

"Fifty-one," I inform him. My best time of the night.

We run it five more times, and then move on to the next drill. Wes mirrors my movements exactly, only asking for a couple of clarifications as we work our way through my entire routine.

The longer we spend together, the more I'm able to appreciate I'm consistently running my fastest times ever, and less on the fact Weston Cole is the one running beside me. It's a relief to focus on the motions of the familiar drills rather than the confusing emotions he elicits with every encounter we have.

Finally, we finish the last sprint. Wes flops on the grass of the Glenmont football field, and it's a strange sight.

"Damn, Maeve. You do that every night?"

"Every other," I correct, grabbing my jacket to wipe at my face again. Not that it makes much of a difference; I'm soaked with sweat.

"You should seriously train our football team. Coach Blake is tough, but man, his practices are nothing compared to that." I feel myself blush in response to his praise. Wes sits up. "Of course, I'm slightly less motivated to impress him." He sends me a charming, crooked grin that prompts a fresh wave of warmth to wash over my already overheated body.

"It's probably a waste of time to try and impress anyone from Glenmont," I respond.

Wes isn't deterred. "Is it?"

I don't answer because it should be an obvious response—but it isn't. Not for me. Not when it comes to him.

"I should go," I tell him, fiddling with the zipper of the jacket I'm holding and avoiding his gaze.

"Do you want to go swimming?" He completely disregards my half-hearted attempt to leave.

"What?" I finally look at him.

"Swimming. You know, when you enter a body of water and flap your arms and legs about to keep from drowning?"

I smile despite myself. "That's your definition of swimming?"

"Yup." Wes smiles back. "You interested?"

I am, and I hate that I am. Hate the fascination that's taken root and made me amenable to anything Weston Cole suggests.

For once, I do the stupid, irresponsible thing. "Yeah, I am."

Wes's answering smile is blinding. "Okay, let's go." He grabs my gym bag and swings it over his broad shoulder before heading toward the parking lot.

I gape after him, surprised again. I didn't peg him as a gentleman.

Grabbing my water bottle and phone, I follow him. I open the trunk of the sedan I share with Liam, and he drops the bag inside. The jacket gets tossed in as well, since I'm still too warm to put it on despite the cool night air.

"Do you have somewhere in mind?" I ask. "Someplace no one will see us?" I tack on.

The clandestine element of any joint outing should be an obvious one, but we're standing in plain sight in the parking lot of Glenmont's football field right now. It's probably the rashest thing I've ever done.

"Let's go to the Fayetteville shore," Wes replies. "Since you're afraid to be seen with me." He winks.

I nod in response to his first sentence; it's the logical choice.

The closest thing to neutral territory we have. Then his second sentence registers. "I'm afraid to be seen with you?" I laugh. "I doubt the Alleghany football team would be pleased to know you're hanging out with me. Anyone seeing us together would be more like mutually assured destruction."

"You asking me to trust you, Stevens?"

"I'm telling you I'm trusting *you* on this," I reply.

Wes nods. "You can."

Oddly, I believe him.

"I'll follow you." I head toward the driver's side of my sedan.

He nods and walks over to the shiny black SUV parked a few spots down. It looks brand-new, and I'm not surprised. I know the Coles are well-off.

I follow Wes to a driveway I'm surprised to realize I recognize. He parks beside the same cabin that hosted the Fayetteville party I attended at the end of freshman year. The first time I talked to him.

I climb out of my car. "Are we trespassing?" I ask, glancing around nervously.

Wes grins. "No. My uncle owns this place. We're good."

"Your uncle? So freshman year, when we—that was your party?"

"Nah, my cousin's. He just asked me to show up."

"Huh."

Wes smirks. "Interesting word choice."

"It's catchy," I admit.

"Come on." Wes holds out a hand, and I grasp it, finally fulfilling my freshman year fantasy. The rush of heat I experienced imagining this then was nothing compared to the fire racing through me now in response to the sensation of his rough palm rubbing against mine. Because now I know exactly what actions those impulses are pushing me toward. Dangerous ones. But I don't pull my hand away.

The ground is shadowed and uneven, and I had plenty of trouble navigating it last time.

I also just don't want to.

We take about five minutes to emerge onto the sandy stretch of beach past the woods. This is further than I ventured before, and I glance around the peaceful lake, noting the pinpricks of light surrounding it on both the Alleghany and Glenmont sides.

Wes drops my hand and pulls his sweaty shirt over his head.

The fire turns into an inferno.

"What are you doing?"

"Do you normally wear a shirt swimming?" Wes asks, smirking.

I didn't think this through, which is extremely unlike me. Because now I'm faced with a new dilemma. I'm wearing a sports bra under my shirt, which is less revealing than my bikini top, but I'm wearing a thong underneath my running shorts.

I can either leave my shorts on or show Weston Cole a lot more of me than any other guy has ever seen.

He reads the indecision on my face. "I won't look, Maeve. I'll go in first."

Once again, his thoughtfulness surprises me. But I'm not hesitating because I don't want him to see me in my underwear.

I'm stalling because I do.

And the same thrill that propelled me to say yes to this excursion, to keep our palms pressed together, causes me to whip my spandex tank top off in one smooth motion.

My black sports bra doesn't reveal much, but it shows off the toned abdominal muscles I've worked hard for. Wes glances at the defined planes of my stomach a couple of times, and I can't help but relish each peep, especially considering the fact his own carved physique makes it clear he spends plenty of time in the gym.

Summoning all the courage I can muster, I pull off my running shorts as well. Sure enough, I'm wearing a hot pink lacy thong. The satisfaction of watching Wes's astonished expression is enough to make stripping worth it.

I kick off my sneakers and sprint toward the dark water, submerging myself in the freezing depths.

"Fuck, I feel like I'm taking an ice bath," Wes complains as he follows in after me.

"You get used to it," I tell him. I can already feel my muscles loosening, numbing in the cool water. I float on my back, staring up at the stars. Unlike last night, I actually can see the bursts of light scattered across the heavens.

"I saw your parents sitting together. At the game last fall," I tell Wes, keeping my gaze on the stars twinkling overhead.

"Were you surprised?"

"More sad, I think. After what you told me—that they were acting like everything was normal…"

"They both care too much about appearing perfect. Doesn't matter what the truth is; it's all about what people think."

"That's why you act like you don't," I observe. It's one of my brother's most common complaints about Wes: how he always appears unflappable and relaxed on the field, even in the final minutes of the game. Whereas Liam has a two-hour pregame ritual he keeps consistent to the minute.

"Who says it's an act?" Wes raises an eyebrow.

"Isn't it?" I challenge.

"The fact that you can't tell says a lot." Wes smirks slightly.

"Who says I can't tell?" I refute. "But if this whole football thing doesn't work out, you could have a future in acting."

"There's an old saying that applies to me: 'you can't lose a game if you don't play the game.'"

"I don't think Nike has actually been around for all that long," I respond.

Wes laughs loudly enough to startle a few birds from their perches in the trees surrounding the lakeshore. "It's Shakespeare, Stevens." I eye him dubiously, and he chuckles again. "Look it up. I didn't think there was a single high schooler in the country who managed to escape the sad fate of reading *Romeo and Juliet*."

"I read it; I didn't memorize it."

Wes just laughs again. Silence falls between us, but it's a peaceful one. The only sound is the occasional splash or swash as we displace the surface of the lake.

"What's your middle name?" I ask abruptly.

Wes eyes me apprehensively. "Why?"

"I'm just curious."

"About my middle name?" Wes smirks.

"Yes."

"Tell me the real reason, and I'll tell you."

I sigh. "Most people in Glenmont insert a profanity."

Wes grins. "I'm flattered." I roll my eyes. "So, you're wondering if my initials really are W.F.C.?"

I scoff. "Forget it."

There's a pause, then he answers. "Thomas."

"What?"

"My middle name is Thomas."

"Weston Thomas Cole."

Weston cringes. "Don't say my full name. My mom only uses it when she's really mad about something. Not a lot of great memories there."

I laugh. "Okay, your secret is safe with me."

"I know," he replies simply.

"You also know I'm a Stallion, right?" I'm only half-joking.

"Does it bother you?" Weston asks. "That I'm from Alleghany?"

It should be a ridiculous question, but somehow, it's not.

"Not as much as it should," I respond truthfully. "Does it bother you? That I live in Glenmont?" *That I'm a Stevens?* I silently add.

"Not for the reason it should," Wes answers. I wait, but he doesn't elaborate further. Instead, he asks me another question. "What's your middle name?"

"Elizabeth."

"Maeve Elizabeth Stevens?"

I chuckle. "Okay, I get it. Calling someone by their full name is weird. I feel like I'm either in trouble, or you're about to propose to me."

Wes snorts, and I blush.

Who mentions getting engaged on their first quasi date with a guy? Me, apparently.

"You get one," Wes informs me.

"One what?"

"Chance to call me by my full name. I do, too."

"Okay, deal," I tell him.

We're both silent again, and the quiet gives me a chance to catalog an array of subtle details: the way his light brown hair looks black now that it's wet, the freckle on his right collarbone, and the enticing curve of his lips as he watches me study him.

"We should, uh, we should head in," I suggest. My arms and legs are getting tired from treading water, but I'm more concerned about what might happen if I stay in this lake with him. I feel flushed again, despite the chilly water we're submerged in.

Wes nods, and we swim side-by-side back to shore. The air

temperature feels warmer than the water did. Wes sneaks a few peeks at me as we walk back over to our small heaps of clothes, which I only catch because I'm doing the same thing to him. Since neither of us are wearing actual swimwear, the water has done nothing but make our scanty outfits even more revealing.

My shorts slide back on easily, but it's no easy feat to pull my tight tank top on over my soaking sports bra. I think I hear Wes let out a low laugh as I do an awkward shimmy to slide it back on, but it's impossible to tell over the sound of the water lapping against the shore. His face is serious when he holds his hand out to me again and leads me back through the woods.

We're both silent, but it's not an awkward silence. It's a comfortable one. I don't feel this at ease with guys I've known since kindergarten.

We pass the cabin and arrive back at our cars. It's an odd sight, seeing an SUV with an *Alleghany Football* bumper sticker parked next to mine with a *Glenmont Football* one.

"Parting is such sweet sorrow," I quote as we stop between the two parked cars.

Weston smirks. "You making fun of me, Stevens?"

"Yes I am, Cole," I respond shamelessly.

His smirk deepens. "William would be proud. See you tomorrow, Maeve."

CHAPTER FIVE

WESTON

I 've spent more time thinking about Maeve Stevens than I would ever admit to anyone.

I've told her things I'd never told anyone else. Prior to learning any of the basic information you typically acquire about someone *before* confiding in them.

I've fantasized about the way she looked at me on that abandoned log, while other girls were begging for my attention.

I've kissed her. Because I wanted to the entire time I first spoke to her in the woods—both before and after she told me her last name.

She's an epically bad idea.

I know it.

But it hasn't kept me from considering it. Hasn't kept me from doing a damn thing, to be honest. Last night was supposed to get her out of my head.

Instead, she got more under my skin in the two hours we spent together than I thought possible. I'm not a sharer; I don't open up to people. Especially girls.

I'm tempted to blame my uncharacteristic vulnerability on the fact she shocked the shit out of me when she stripped down to her sports bra and that tiny scrap of pink lace. It's a move I'd expect from Natalie or one of the other girls who hang around me, but from Maeve Stevens? Entirely unexpected. Based on everything I've heard and observed, I was half-expecting her to enter the water fully dressed.

But I can't blame everything on that. Because I invited her to this field long before she took any clothes off. And I still can't believe I did.

There are a dozen soccer fields in Fayetteville, and I gave her the address to the only one I have any sentimental attachment to.

Before my family moved to Alleghany, we'd come visit my dad's brother for a week each summer at the same lakeside cabin I brought Maeve to last night. Every minute I wasn't at the lake, I'd spend with my dad at this park, playing football. Back then, it was the one week he fully detached from his work, and it's one of the few fond childhood memories I have with him, back when we had a functioning relationship. Even though we live only twenty minutes away from it now, we've never been back to this field together.

I always come alone.

Except for today.

I watch Maeve Stevens walk across the field toward me, clutching a water bottle in one hand with a soccer ball tucked under her other arm. She's wearing navy shorts with a matching tank top, and her blonde hair is up in a high ponytail that swishes as she strides along.

She stops a couple feet away from me, dropping the black and white patterned ball.

"Hey," she greets, studying me. A light flush works its way across her freckled cheeks, which I don't think is due to the warm summer air. She was quick to shut down any intimate moments last night, but if the number of glances she gave my body were any indication, it wasn't because she isn't interested. I'm assuming it's because she knows she shouldn't be. Something I should be thinking about too but can't seem to care about whenever she's around.

"Hi, Maeve," I reply, surveying her back.

Her green eyes are almost the exact shade of the lush grass we're standing on, and I quickly get lost in their bottomless depths.

"Are you—um, are you ready to play?" Maeve asks, and I realize we're still just standing and staring at each other. She's definitely blushing now.

"I've been ready to play with you for a long time, Stevens," I reply.

"I hope you know what you're in for, Cole," she flirts back, smirking. She drops her water bottle on the sideline and dribbles toward the center of the field.

I jog after her. "First to ten?" I suggest as we stop on either side of the white line drawn across the very center of the field. It's a fitting metaphor for our relationship. Or lack thereof.

"It's going to be a short game," Maeve predicts confidently.

She dribbles forward, and I match her pace as I move backward, giving her enough space to move but staying close enough to make my presence felt. She maintains eye contact with me rather than looking down at the ball, but her steps don't falter as we reach the penalty arc.

I make my move as soon as we cross the line, pressing forward and attempting to swipe the ball away from her. She dodges my sad attempt at a steal easily and moves to sprint past me. I stay in front of her, but only barely.

Maeve grins, showcasing the dimple in her left cheek. The last time I played against a girl was in elementary school, and my eight-year-old self certainly wasn't thinking about any of the things I want to do with Maeve Stevens besides playing soccer during recess basketball games. Maeve spins, somehow taking the ball with her.

My distracted brain takes a second to catch up, and it's a second too long. She sends the soccer ball slamming against the white netting of the goal, and even if I was paying close attention, I doubt I could have stopped. it. It's a seamless, practiced move, one I'm quite certain she could have demonstrated as soon as we started playing.

Maeve starts jogging backward. "Your ball, Cole!" She winks.

I retrieve the ball, and this time I'm the one who starts dribbling forward. Maeve doesn't give me a chance to move more than a few feet before she snags the ball and starts sprinting toward the goal I'm supposed to be defending.

I run after her, but to no avail. She doubles her lead.

It turns out Maeve was right. It doesn't take long for her to reach ten goals, and I only manage two in the same stretch of time. But we keep playing, employing a lot more physical contact than I think the rules of soccer allow for.

Not that I'm complaining.

Eventually, we come to a mutual agreement to call it. I dribble the ball over to the spot where Maeve left her water bottle, and she follows. We flop down on the grass side by side, both panting.

"This is a nice park," Maeve remarks, glancing around after she takes a long pull from her water bottle. "I've never been here before."

"I used to come here with my dad," I admit. "When we'd visit my uncle and his family at the cabin in the summer. The two of us would play football for hours."

"It's nice that you have those memories," Maeve says softly.

"Don't you? Coach Stevens totally seems like the type of dad who would start training his kids to catch the football as toddlers."

"Yeah, he was," Maeve replies. "With Liam."

I wish I could shove my question back in my mouth. "Maeve —shit, I'm sorry, I'm the last person who should be making assumptions—"

"It's fine, Wes," she assures me as she picks at blades of grass and drops them on her long, tan legs. "Don't worry about it. That's just always how it's been with us. In some ways, I feel worse for Liam. The pressure on him is relentless."

"Doesn't your dad support you with soccer? I mean, Maeve, you're good. Really good."

She smiles at my compliment. "He comes to my games when he can, but he spends most of the time talking to the other parents there about his season. Every sport except football is basically just a hobby to him." She shrugs, as though it doesn't bother her, but I'm getting better at reading her. I can tell it does. And it should.

"Did you used to be closer to him?" I ask.

"Not really," Maeve replies. "He was gone a lot when I was little, and—I mean, you've met him. He's hardly the warm and fuzzy type."

I snort, recalling some of the shouts coming from Glenmont's bench at our last clash. "True." After a brief pause, I ask another question. "Is it because of the drinking?"

Maeve's eyes flash from her knees to meet my gaze, and I wonder if she forgot she told me about her father's alcoholism freshman year.

"I think that's part of it," she finally says. "I don't remember much of it, honestly. Like I said, he wasn't home a lot back then. He was coaching at Arlington. But my parents would fight a lot when he did come back. Once, I think I was eight or nine, he came home when I was down in the kitchen getting a drink of water. He was stumbling around, slamming into everything. I got scared, thinking there was an intruder or something, so I hid under the kitchen table. My mom came downstairs, they started arguing, and that's when I realized it was actually my dad. I just remember thinking how if drinking could make my father act like that, I never wanted to."

"But he stopped?"

"Yeah, when Liam and I started fifth grade. I think my mom gave him an ultimatum. He quit his job at Arlington and moved back to Glenmont full-time. My friend Brooke's father owns an insurance company; he worked there for a little while, and then he started coaching at Glenmont when the position opened up. He took Liam to every practice and game, starting his very first season."

"Wow," I remark. "Liam's been watching high school games since middle school? I was sticking frogs in my teachers' desks at that age."

Maeve laughs, lightening the heavy moment. "I'm not surprised."

"I'm a big fan of a good prank," I inform her.

"Really?" Maeve replies, raising her eyebrows. "So the fact that someone dyed our pool blue—Alleghany blue—last fall…" She looks at me questioningly.

"Yeah, I came up with that," I admit.

"It was funny," she replies, smiling.

"Thank you." I grin back. Our mutual amusement fades slowly, and then I acknowledge the humorless revelations she just shared with me. "I'm sorry about your dad, Maeve. It's his loss, I promise."

"Thanks for listening," she replies. "I, uh—I've never told anyone any of that before."

"You can tell me anything, Maeve."

"Yeah, I kind of feel like I can," she whispers. Her phone vibrates on the grass between us, and she leaps up, dusting the errant blades of grass off her shorts. "Shit, I have to go get changed before work. I totally lost track of time."

"Work?"

"Yeah, I'm a waitress at *Mo's Diner*." She kicks the resting soccer ball airborne and catches it neatly before reaching down to grab her water bottle. "This was—uh, this was really nice, Wes. I'll... I mean, I guess I'll see you around sometime?"

"We could meet here again tomorrow?" I suggest. "You could decimate me at soccer again, or I'm supposed to be working on my throwing technique?"

I'm going for broke now.

We may have swapped some pretty personal secrets, but I'm asking Maeve *Stevens* if she wants to help me improve at football. Me. The guy standing between her father and brother, and a state championship. There's a very high chance she's going to tell me to go screw myself. And I wouldn't blame her if she did.

But I would care.

I would care a lot.

More than anything I've confided in her about, this is also my way of letting her know I trust her. Not just with some unpleasant truths, but with my football technique.

With my strategy.

With information Liam Stevens could use to beat me.

"I could—I could catch a football," Maeve finally says. I let out a long exhale I hadn't realized I was holding.

The release of air is followed by a rush of euphoria.

"Okay then," I reply, fairly certain my wide grin is betraying my casual words and letting her know exactly how much her agreeing means to me. "I'll text you and we can figure out a time to meet."

"Okay then," she repeats, and turns to walk toward the parking lot. I watch her go.

Maeve Stevens is like quicksand. I'm not even trying to get out, and I'm still sinking deeper and deeper.

I remain sitting on the grass until my phone buzzes. It's Chris.

"What's up?" I answer.

"Where are you, Cole? You said you'd be at the lake half an hour ago."

"I'll be there soon," I promise, before hanging up.

I climb to my feet reluctantly, stretching my arms above my head before heading in the direction of the parking lot. My body's not used to doing this much running. I rely on the power of my left arm to ensure the football reaches the end zone, and I have a new respect for athletes who play sports that don't allow them to sit back on their heels.

Specifically, Maeve Stevens.

There's only one other car in the paved rectangle that comprises the parking lot. I climb inside my SUV and head back toward Alleghany.

It takes me twenty minutes to reach my driveway, and I'm relieved to see both of my parents' cars are missing. I go in through the front door, kicking off the sneakers I wore to the park in the immaculate entryway.

I head into my room, not bothering to change my sweaty t-shirt. I simply swap out my athletic shorts for a pair of swim trunks, and then grab a baseball cap before heading back downstairs. I'm in and out in a matter of minutes.

It's a short drive to Alleghany's public stretch of lakeshore from my house. I park along the side of the road, behind the long line of cars overflowing from the parking area. I stroll casually onto the sand that's made from a mixture of beige and light gray grains. The central congregation is all Alleghany High students, with some families and younger kids present on the periphery. A few girls, who look to be freshman or sophomores, giggle as I pass them.

My arrival causes its usual stir as I infiltrate the grouping that consists mostly of seniors. Chris breathes an exaggerated sigh of relief when I make my way over to his side.

"Where the hell have you been, Cole?" he asks from his seat in the sand.

"I told you I was training," I reply, grabbing a sports drink from the cooler sitting in the sand.

"Yeah, three hours ago! You've seriously been practicing this whole time?"

"Uh-huh," I respond, taking a long drink of the cold liquid. I should have known better than to not bring a drink to the field after running sprints with Maeve last night.

I cap the bottle and pull my still-damp t-shirt over my head. The move draws several admiring glances from the girls gathered around us, but none of the heated gazes I feel on me have a fraction of the effect Maeve's did last night.

"Jesus, Cole," Chris remarks. "You weren't getting enough attention already? Way to make the rest of us look bad."

I roll my eyes. He spends as much time at the gym as I do. "I'm going swimming," I inform him.

"Water's freezing," Chris warns.

"Those two children seem to be managing all right." I laugh as I nod to the couple of kids splashing in the shallows.

Chris flips me off, and I grin at him before I head toward the sparkling water. I dive in as soon as the water reaches my waist, and the sticky residue of sweat disappears once I submerge myself in the refreshing liquid. I swim out a few hundred feet to the floating dock that's marooned offshore, but I don't pull myself up onto the weathered surface. I turn around and head back toward the shore instead.

When I emerge from the water, I make a point to send some errant drops of water Chris's way. He flips me off as I settle in the sand beside him. Charlie has appeared, but there's no sign of Adam.

"Hey, Wes," Charlie greets. "Chris said you were training?"

"Yup," I reply, retrieving my drink and taking another long sip.

I expect Charlie to give me a hard time about showing up late too, but he looks pleased. "Good. Glenmont started their captain's practices today."

"Are you serious?" Chris replies. "Already?"

"Yup," Charlie confirms. "It was all over their social media."

"Shit," Chris says. "I mean, it's not surprising after last year's game. We all knew Stevens would be out for blood. This is his last chance."

"We'll be ready," Charlie predicts confidently. "I already told the boys to make sure Glenmont knows our quarterback practiced all morning. Nice work, Cole."

I tilt my head casually in acknowledgement of his compliment, but my mind is racing.

Because I didn't spend the morning training to lead him to victory. I spent it flirting with a girl who's so off-limits she should come with a custom warning label.

A girl who's making me reconsider why I should hate the residents of the town I'm currently staring at across the calm surface of the lake.

The town that is home to the football team everyone I know is relying upon me to eviscerate.

And if the two guys sitting next to me knew any of that, I'm not sure if they'd ever forgive me.

CHAPTER SIX

MAEVE

I 'm returning from my break when I see them. Him. Wes and
a group of his friends have just entered *Mo's* and are in the
midst of settling in the corner booth.

I suck in a sharp breath as I walk over to where Clare is standing, manning the front counter.

"Perfect timing," she tells me. "I was just about to head over
to take their order." She nods toward Wes's table. "Can you cover
the register?"

"I'll take the booth."

Clare looks at me with shock. "What?"

I'm equally surprised by my own words, but I don't back-
track. "I said I'll take the booth."

"But—it's *Alleghany*. They're Alleghany football players."
Clare's looking at me like I've lost my mind. Maybe I have.

"I know." I grab an order pad and start toward the booth. I
regret the rash decision the moment Chris Fields looks up and
sees me, but it's too late. I try to channel my boldest alter ego as I
take the final steps that will place me directly in front of their
booth.

Unfortunately, even she screams this is a terrible decision. If I had a choice, I might listen. But more of Wes's friends are glancing at me, mouths agape.

"What can I get you guys?" My voice sounds even and calm, and I've never been so grateful for anything.

One of the guys sitting at the end of the booth looks me over. "Aren't you Coach Stevens' other kid? Liam Stevens' sister?"

"My name is Maeve," I reply evenly, surprised a random Alleghany football player knows my identity at first glance.

"I'll take that as a yes. We don't need a Stallion spy anywhere near us."

"Not sure what I would be spying on," I reply sweetly. "Didn't you boys end last season with three straight losses?"

I also spent four hours on Sunday catching their quarterback's passes, which I'm certain was more telling of their team strategy than their lunch orders will be.

I'm hit with a dozen glares at once in response to my snarky comment.

"Double BLT," Wes says. I finally let myself look at him, but he's staring down at his phone, typing something.

The guy at the end of the booth looks to Wes. "What are you doing? Didn't you hear what she just said?"

"She's a waitress. We're ordering food. What's the issue?" Wes looks up from his phone, but not at me. He looks directly at the guy who spoke to me.

"But—she's from Glenmont. A Stallion. A Stevens," the guy sputters.

"Who wouldn't be serving us if someone hadn't fucked all the waitresses at Burger Barn," Wes drawls. "Actions have consequences, Baylor." The other Alleghany players all laugh.

Baylor groans. "Fine. I'll take a burger. Medium rare."

The rest of the guys all call out their orders, and I scribble them down as quickly as I can. I walk away from their table rapidly and then stick the sheet of paper in the order queue.

Clare is looking at me with both eyebrows raised. I pretend not to see. Even though *Mo's* is in Fayetteville, we rarely get any Alleghany students in here. On the few occasions we have, I've always let Clare serve them, as the local.

I busy myself with all the mundane tasks I typically try to avoid to keep myself from looking over at Wes's booth. I refill all the salt and pepper shakers, take out the trash, wipe down the extra menus, and am in the midst of folding napkins when their large order comes up. I see Clare glance at me once before picking up the tray and carrying their food over.

Shortly after she delivers their order, the bell above the door clangs and a group of girls wearing Alleghany cheerleading outfits enter. Maggie's not with them, but I recognize a few from the party I went to. They all strut over to Wes's booth immediately.

I force my gaze back to the napkins.

About twenty minutes later, Clare comes over to me. I've moved on to sorting the silverware. I'm grateful there's only a half hour left on my shift because I'm rapidly running out of busy work.

"I'm taking my break, okay? Can you cover the register?" Clare asks.

"Yup, I've got it."

I walk to the register, entertaining myself with sorting the receipts as a new way to tune out the loud laughter I can hear coming from the corner booth.

"You haven't run out of shit to do yet?"

I startle at the sound of the unexpected, familiar voice, and look up to see Wes's grinning face. I glance over at his booth for the first time since I left it, surprised he's talking to me in public.

None of his friends are watching us, but a couple of cheerleaders are.

"I'm working." I roll my eyes.

"I can see that." He smirks, and my attention is drawn to his mouth.

I've kissed those lips. It's a bizarre thought to have when we're standing in public, in front of his friends, while we're so obviously Weston Cole from Alleghany and Maeve Stevens from Glenmont. Enemies.

"So, what's the damage?"

"Damage?" I'm still thinking about kissing him.

"The bill?" Wes holds up the wad of cash he's carrying.

"Oh, right." I pull up his table. "It's $86.43."

Wes holds the money out. "Keep the change."

I reach out and grab the offered money. He holds it between his fingers for a moment, then lets me tug the thick stack of bills away.

He starts to turn away, but then glances back at me. I can feel more eyes on us. "You should probably count it."

I raise my eyebrows. He smirks slightly before continuing back to his table.

I stare at the stack of money for a couple of minutes before I fan the bills out. There's a flash of white amongst the green. I pull out a ripped piece of napkin. It's unused, the cheap material void and vacant. I flip it over. Also unmarked. Wes gave me a *blank* piece of paper, and it's a struggle to keep my expression empty and not glance over at his table. I slip the ripped shred of napkin into the pocket of my jean shorts, and resume sorting the receipts.

Clare returns from her break just as I've moved on to wiping the counter, signaling the end of my shift. After saying goodbye to her, I literally flee from *Mo's*.

It's a relief to not have to keep myself from looking over at him.

To not have to wonder if he's looking at me.

Maggie and I made plans to go to the lake, and I make a quick stop at home to change before heading straight there.

The lake is crowded, which is hardly a surprise given how warm it is out. Liam and a bunch of other football players are playing volleyball, and several of them wave at me as I stroll down the beach. I wave back, and then am stopped by a few of my soccer teammates, followed by some friends from student council.

Maggie's easy to spot; she's the only solitary person on the entire beach.

"Sure you're willing to sit with a pariah?" she asks caustically as soon as I sit down.

I sigh. "I'm sorry, Mags. You know how stupid I think this whole rivalry is."

"You do?" Maggie asks, sounding surprised.

"Well, yeah. Don't you?"

"Now that I've lost most of my friends for no reason, yeah. But it's never taken anything from you. You're Maeve *Stevens*. I mean, the rivalry is in your blood, right?"

"I guess," I reply. But she's wrong. The rivalry with Alleghany has taken plenty from me. But it's never bothered me before, and I know exactly why it's bothering me now. "How is cheer going?" I ask.

"It's all right. A lot more intense than I'm used to." I grin at that, and Maggie rolls her eyes. "Yeah, yeah. I actually got invited to the lake last Saturday with the rest of the cheer team. And Weston Cole was there, so Natalie was actually bearable."

"Oh, really?" He must have gone after our soccer game. "Did you talk to him?"

My bold, brash best friend lets out a disbelieving laugh. "Yeah, right. I would have had to fight my way through twenty people to even get near him."

"Huh," is my only comment.

Aside from the brief glimpse of him in the kitchen at the party and just now in the diner, I've never seen Wes around his friends and classmates before. I know he's popular, obviously, but Maggie's words make me wonder about meaningless things. Impossible things. Like what it would have been like to be able to visit Alleghany's side of the lake this past weekend.

If I had been there, would I have had to fight my way through a crowd to talk to him?

"Maeve? Maeve!"

I look over at Maggie. "What?"

She rolls her eyes. "You totally zoned out."

"Sorry," I respond. "I'm pretty tired."

"I'm not surprised. You're doing your usual insane training schedule, working at Mo's, and doing that college prep class, right?"

"Yeah."

"You know, summer's supposed to be about having some fun," Maggie informs me.

"I'm having fun right now."

She smiles. "Good answer." Her phone dings, and she pulls it out of her bag. "How thoughtful." "The team went out to eat without me and posted photos, but I'm invited for the 'optional' practice." She tosses her phone back in her bag with a derisive snort. "They went to Mo's, weren't you just there?"

"Yeah," I shift uncomfortably. "I didn't want to say anything…"

"It's fine, Maeve." Maggie leans her head back against the

chair and lets out a long sigh. "Bit of a disappointing summer, no?"

I make a noncommittal noise in response, settling back in my own chair and letting the sun warm my face. It's an affirmative sound, but I don't agree with her rhetorical question.

Thrilling, exciting, tempting? Yes.

Disappointing? Not at all.

CHAPTER SEVEN

WESTON

"Your footwork was definitely more balanced that time," Maeve compliments, tossing the football back to me. "The spiral was perfect."

I'm quickly learning Maeve Stevens doesn't do anything half-assed. Meaning ever since the second time we met at this park a few weeks ago, when she stood and caught throw after throw for four hours while reciting vocabulary from the college prep class she's taking and spewing stories from the true crime podcasts she listens to, she's switched to sharing feedback on my throwing technique. And it's obvious she knows what she's talking about.

I told her she doesn't have to, and she simply shrugged and told me it's nothing my coach wouldn't tell me. I suppose that's true, but I've certainly never spent countless hours tossing the pigskin back and forth with Coach Blake.

"I've got to go," Maeve tells me after a few more throws. "I told my mom I'd be home by seven."

"Big plans tonight?" I ask as we gather up our belongings.

"Not really. You?"

"Nah, just going mini-golfing with some friends. I'd invite you, but…"

"That probably wouldn't end very well for either of us," Maeve finishes.

I laugh, even though I've come to view the Alleghany rivalry with Glenmont as anything but amusing. Mostly due to the blonde standing in front of me. "Probably not," I agree.

"Okay, well, I'll see you, Wes," Maeve gives me a small smile before she walks toward her sedan.

"Aren't we meeting tomorrow?" I call after her. We've met every Saturday for the past few weeks, since it seems to be the only day we're both always free.

Maeve spins around, biting her lip in what I recognize as one of her nervous tells. "Uh, no. I'm actually leaving for my grand-parents' early tomorrow morning. We always spend a week there before school starts."

I'm startled by how much the knowledge I won't see her for the next week bothers me. I've come to rely on hanging out with her more than I realized.

"Where do your grandparents live?"

"It's a small beach town. In South Carolina."

"Sounds nice."

"Yeah, it is. But my mom's real estate office has a branch there, so she'll end up working the whole time. And my dad will be preparing for the season and training with Liam. Plus, Liam convinced our parents to let him bring Matt along as a 'training buddy.' Maggie has cheer, and my other best friends are gone for the summer, so I'll mostly be playing card games with my grand-mother." She laughs. "Thrilling times."

"Matt Crawford is going on vacation with your family?" I hope my voice sounds nonchalant because I'm feeling anything but.

"Yup," Maeve confirms. "See you later, Cole."

"Bye, Stevens," I manage.

Maeve climbs into her car and pulls away, leaving me standing here. I've been so focused on all the reasons why she and I can't work, I never stopped to consider that she and someone else could.

It's an unsettling thought, but not as disconcerting as the realization of how much it would bother me. Seeing her with another guy.

I know I am attracted to Maeve, but this possessiveness?

It's new.

It's concerning.

I drive home, opting to slip in through the back door when I arrive. I can hear my parents arguing in the kitchen, and I have no interest in getting involved in their latest spat. I head up the main staircase, dropping my football bag on the dark wooden floor of my bedroom. I shower, and dress in my standard summer uniform of shorts and a t-shirt.

I head back out into the hallway as soon as I've finished getting ready and encounter my mother as soon as I hit the stairs.

"Weston!" she exclaims. "I didn't realize you were home."

"Not surprised you didn't hear me pull in," I reply. "Sounded like you and Dad were having another lively conversation."

She sighs. "Weston, don't start, please."

"Fine. I'm going out."

"Where?"

"I'm meeting some of the guys." I start down the stairs.

"Okay, don't be out too late!" my mother calls after me.

I don't respond. My father's car is already missing when I reach the driveway. I climb back into my car, and peel out of the driveway, headed toward the one pizza place in town.

Since it's a Friday night, the restaurant is packed when I

arrive. It takes me a while to navigate through the hordes of people wanting to talk to me, but finally, I plop down in the booth next to Chris.

"Sure you don't have a few more adoring fans to greet?" he asks, grinning.

I roll my eyes. "Jealous of my popularity?"

Chris scoffs. "Hardly. It looks exhausting."

I laugh. "It is. You guys order yet?" I glance across the table at Charlie and Adam. They both shake their heads.

"Damn. I'm starving."

"Where the hell have you been all day?" Chris asks. "I texted you earlier saying we were headed to Baylor's pool, and you never replied."

"I know. I was training."

"All day again?"

"Most of it."

"Should make my job easier in September," Adam remarks, shrugging. Charlie and Chris eye me dubiously.

"Yes, that's the reason I'm training so hard," I respond, rolling my eyes. "To simplify things for you, Powers."

After we devour several pizzas, we head to the mini golf course. Most of Alleghany High seems to be there already. Unless someone's throwing a party, evening entertainment is scarce. Natalie spots me and heads over with a group of fellow cheer-leaders in tow.

"Now I remember why we're friends, Cole," Charlie comments as the girls stroll toward us. "You're a total hot chick magnet."

"Haven't seen much of you this summer, Weston." Natalie gives me a sultry smile, and for once, it doesn't have any effect on me. Instead, I mentally add her dimple-less expression to the ever-growing list of things that make me think of Maeve Stevens, right after cola and pink lace.

"I've been around," I respond.

"He's been training," Chris pipes in.

"Good. You're going to make my job easy this season, right Weston?"

Adam rolls his eyes as she copies his line, and I choke back a laugh.

"I sure hope so." I step away from her to grab my ball and club from the window.

Natalie and a couple of other cheerleaders join our game, which means it proceeds at a snail's pace. Natalie brushes against me every time it's her turn, and I get a mixture of amused and envious looks from the guys every time she does.

We finally reach the final hole, and it takes me three attempts to sink the ball into the tiny opening. I step aside to let Adam go next.

I lean against the fake stone tunnel we just emerged from, and pull my phone from my pocket, scanning the notifications on the screen. Nothing from her. I tuck the phone away, only to pull it out again a few seconds later. After another minute of hesitation, I text Maeve. *What's your best mini golf score?*

Minus two of whatever you managed, she responds immediately. I feel a wide grin stretch across my face.

Why two? I reply.

One allows for a margin of error and I thought you'd think I was too overconfident if I said three Maeve sends back.

Margin of error? Are you doing your prep class right now? I ask.

Maybe is her first response. A minute later, *Yes.*

I send *Nerd* back, and she doesn't reply.

We've never had an elongated conversation over text before,

and I didn't realize just how much I rely upon seeing her expressive eyes to know what she's thinking. *I'm almost done here*, I finally add. *We could meet up after, if you want?*

Three dots appear and then disappear twice.

I've got a lot of packing to do, is how Maeve finally responds. I'm about to slip the phone back into my pocket when the indication she's typing appears again. *And I don't need any pity invites.*

I snort, annoyed. I send *If that's how you want to define me wanting to spend time with you* back. I wait, but she doesn't reply. I'm not really surprised. I half-regret the hasty words, but they're true.

I've never pitied Maeve Stevens. Sure, I relate to the strained relationship she has with her father. I think it's unfair no one pays attention to her athletic prowess and heaps attention on her brother. Which I get is hypocritical, coming from me.

But the past few weeks of playing soccer, going for runs, talking, and throwing the football to her had nothing to do with any of that.

The girl I can't stop thinking about thinks I spend time with her out of pity and is about to spend a week hundreds of miles away with a guy she could actually date.

And Charlie thinks I'm a chick magnet. If he only knew.

CHAPTER EIGHT

MAEVE

As someone who routinely gets up at six AM, I'm surprised by how unwilling my body is to climb out of bed this morning. Of course, it's likely due to the fact that I spent most of the night tossing and turning.

I hold up my phone to turn off the alarm that's blaring, and the sight of my face unlocks the screen, revealing the words I fell asleep reading over and over again.

If that's how you want to define me wanting to spend time with you.

I'm annoyed with myself for getting defensive and insecure, and I'm annoyed with Wes for having the perfect response. Most of all, I'm frustrated I'll be stuck with the lingering awkwardness of his last message for an entire week.

A loud banging sounds on my door. "Maeve, you up?" my mother calls.

"Yeah," I croak back.

"Okay, we're leaving in twenty minutes."

"Okay," I call back, rolling out of bed and almost landing in a heap on the floor when my ankle gets caught in the sheets. I manage to regain my balance before I fully topple, hopping on one leg until I twist myself free.

I rush around my room in a whirlwind, doing everything I should have taken care of last night instead of over-analyzing fourteen words.

Finally, I finish packing and change out of my pajamas into a pair of athletic shorts. After a minute of hesitation, I pull the latest addition to my wardrobe on over the tank top I slept in.

Wes offered me his sweatshirt in the park on an unseasonably chilly night a couple of weeks ago, and I've conveniently forgotten to return it to him ever since. As soon as the soft material settles around my torso, I'm surrounded by the musky scent of cedar and bergamot.

I grab my bulging duffle bag and head downstairs. Liam's best friend, Matt Crawford, is standing on our front lawn when I emerge outside. His own duffle bag is laying by his feet as he types something on his phone.

"Hey, Maeve," he greets when he spots me.

"Hi, Matt." I yawn as I toss my bag in the back of my father's SUV.

"You have everything, Maeve?" my father asks, rounding the side of the car.

"Yes, Dad."

"Good." He nods. "Liam! Susan! We're two minutes behind schedule!"

I open the passenger side door and slide the chair forward so I can climb in the way back. I have no interest in spending the next thirteen hours squished between two burly football players. I buckle my seatbelt and stretch my legs out along the full length of the leather seat, hoping to catch up on some of the sleep that evaded me last night.

Doors slam as my parents, Liam, and Matt all settle in the car as well.

"You packed everything I told you to, right Liam?" my father questions. "We can't afford to lose any training time this week."

"I have it all, Dad."

The car begins to move. I plug in my headphones and try to fall asleep.

I must doze off eventually, because the next time I open my eyes, we're at a rest stop halfway through Virginia. Everyone disembarks to use the restroom and grab snacks. I'm the third one back to the car; Matt and Liam are already standing next to it when I return. I lean against the glossy paint and scroll through my phone as they talk.

"Oh, I forgot to tell you," Matt says, "after you left practice yesterday, a bunch of the cheerleaders were looking at some of Alleghany's social media, and the weird thing? Cole wasn't in *any* of them."

I stiffen but keep my eyes on my phone.

"So?" Liam asks.

"One of the guys asked where he was in the video, and Fields said he was off training."

Liam scoffs. "Probably knew we'd hear about it and they're trying to psych us out. Cole always spends the summer partying and getting laid."

"I know, but he wasn't even *there*," Matt stresses.

"Who cares?" Liam replies. "You're overthinking it."

"Overthinking what?" my father asks as he and my mother reappear.

"Just a rumor about Weston Cole, Coach," Matt replies. "Someone said he's training hard this summer."

"We'll be training harder," my father responds, unlocking the car.

We all pile back inside to continue our trek south. I resume staring at Wes's latest text, hating how conflicted I feel.

We pull into my grandparents' driveway just before eight. As soon as Liam and Matt evacuate the middle row, I slide the chair forward so I can climb out and stretch my cramped muscles. Salty air fills my lungs and coats my hair. I can feel the ordinarily straight strands turning wavy as soon as I leave the confines of the car.

My grandparents sold the Glenmont house they'd resided in for decades several years ago to move to the beach house I'm staring at now on a permanent basis. I've always been partial to lakes over the ocean, but I can't deny the view overlooking the whitecaps is stunning.

"You're here!" My grandmother appears from the side of the house to welcome us. She greets my father first, and then makes her way through the rest of us, including Matt.

"Look at you, Maeve," she says when she reaches me. "You look so grown up!"

"You look so young," I reply, grinning. It's been our standard greeting to each other ever since I started going through puberty.

My grandmother laughs, and I'm enveloped by the scent of gardenia and lemon as she squeezes me tight.

"Come eat!" she urges. "You must all be famished."

We follow her through the sprawling gardens. My grandmother's favorite hobby is gardening, and my childhood years are littered with memories of digging in the dirt next to her. Thanks to South Carolina's more temperate climate, her yard here is even more vibrant than the grounds surrounding their old home in Glenmont were.

We approach the stone patio that juts off the back deck, and my grandfather comes into view. He's standing at the grill, flipping sizzling chunks of meat. The resemblance between him and my father is uncanny. Same proud chin, strong jaw, and sloped brow. Their similarities aren't just physical. They have the same steadfast, no-nonsense personality Liam also inherited. I guess I did too, to a certain extent.

My grandfather gives us all hugs as well, but they lack the exuberance my grandmother is bubbling with.

We all pile our plates and settle down at the patio table to eat. My grandmother asks my parents some questions about the drive down, and then my grandfather chimes in with a gruff question. "How's the season looking, John?"

They may look alike, and act alike, but the common thread between my grandfather and father will always be football.

"Can't we have one family meal without discussing sports?" my grandmother requests.

"I'm simply asking about my grandson's team, Greta," my grandfather responds. My grandmother clucks her tongue but doesn't say anything else.

"The team is looking good this year. We've got a lot more depth on defense, and I've had Liam running weight trainings to start getting the guys in shape this summer."

"Weston Cole still causing problems for you?"

I watch a muscle jump in Liam's jaw from his seat across from me.

"I won't have any official stats until their season starts. But he played well last year," my father replies. There's an unspoken *obviously* at the end of his sentence.

My grandmother jumps in, peppering Liam, Matt, and me with questions about our upcoming senior year for the remainder of dinner.

Once we all finish eating, she shoos the three of us off to the local ice cream shop down the road.

"You two seriously come here every summer?" Matt asks as

we walk along the quaint main street. "I'm so jealous. My grand-parents live in a condo next to a strip mall in the middle of Florida."

"Yeah, but I'm guessing *your* grandfather doesn't ask about Weston fucking Cole at dinner," Liam replies sullenly.

"Come on, dude. It'll be that much sweeter when we destroy Cole in November," Matt responds.

I don't say anything as I stick my hands in the front pocket of Weston Cole's sweatshirt. Have I always been surrounded by so many reminders of him? Or am I just hyper-aware of any mention now?

We arrive at the ice cream store to discover it's crowded and busy.

"Get me a peach cone," I instruct Liam. "I'll go grab a table before they're all taken."

I head over to one of the few open picnic tables. They're all painted various shades of pastel, and I settle on a light yellow one.

"Good strategy," a voice says to my left. I glance over to a see a guy with blond hair and a friendly smile. He nods toward the line. "Make your boyfriend and his friend order and snag a table."

"Uh, thanks," I respond. "He's not my boyfriend, though. That's my brother and his best friend."

I regret the correction when I see interest flare in the guy's eyes. He holds out a hand between our two tables. "I'm Eli."

"Maeve," I reply, shaking his hand.

"Do you live around here?" Eli asks.

"Nope, I'm just visiting for the week."

"Me, too," Eli smiles. "Would you want to meet up at the pier one day?"

"I'm flattered, Eli, but I'm actually kind of with someone," I respond. "Not my brother's friend; someone else."

My brother's enemy. Who I daydream about kissing and push away in real life.

"I'm not surprised," Eli replies. "He's a lucky guy."

"Uh, thanks," I respond as he turns back to his own table, still trying to figure out why I told him I'm taken.

A fling with a cute, random guy who's never heard of Glenmont or Alleghany is exactly what I should be pursuing. But all I could think about when he was talking to me was that his eyes were hazel instead of blue, and that his hair was blond instead of light brown.

"Was that guy bothering you?" Matt asks quietly as he takes a seat next to me and hands me my cone.

"No, he was actually really nice," I respond honestly.

"If you say so," Matt replies. "So, I was thinking—"

"They're out of cookie dough," Liam announces, taking a seat across from us. "Who runs out of cookie dough?"

"Evidently this place does," I inform him. Liam rolls his eyes. "What were you saying, Matt?"

"Nothing," he replies, taking a bite of ice cream.

The next few days pass almost exactly how I predicted they would to Wes. My mother works. My father, Liam, and Matt all talk, train, and obsess about football. And I spend most of my time playing card games with my grandmother. Her favorite is Spite and Malice, and I can never remember the complex rules, so she usually wins.

Our final afternoon in South Carolina, I emerge onto the front porch to find Matt sitting on the swing.

"Oh, hey," he says, looking over at me.

"Hey."

"You going for a run?"

"Yup. Needed a break from the card games. Plus, my training schedule has gotten a little out of whack this week."

"Want some company?" Matt offers.

"Uh, sure," I respond, surprised.

Matt has been one of Liam's closest friends since elementary school, but I could probably count on one hand the number of times we've ever hung out together, just the two of us.

"Let me just grab my sneakers." He stands and heads inside.

I take a seat on the front steps to wait for him.

He reappears a couple minutes later, and we start jogging down the street.

"I probably should have asked you this before, but how far do you usually run?" Matt asks.

I laugh. "It varies. Usually a few miles, but we can just go to the pier and back."

"How far is the pier?"

"No idea," I admit.

Matt chuckles. "Okay, I'm game."

It takes us about a half hour to reach the pier. Matt keeps up with me, but I'm guessing he's probably regretting joining me on this trip by the time we reach it. He sprawls across the sand as soon as we reach the beach, wheezing. I stop next to him and grin down as he pants.

"Come on, I'll buy you a hot dog," I offer. "And a drink."

Matt hauls himself to his feet. "Lead the way." We walk over to the hot dog stand, and I order two hot dogs and two waters. But when I go to pay, Matt brushes my hand aside and hands over the money instead.

"This was supposed to be my treat," I say.

"I've got it, Maeve."

"Okay," I acquiesce. "Thanks."

We walk back toward my grandparents' once we have our food. Matt's much chattier on the way back, but I'm not.

I've always looked forward to what's become an annual trip to South Carolina. But as nice as this trip has been—the beach, the time with my grandparents, and the escape from routine—there's someplace I'd rather be right now.

On a field of grass—actually anywhere—with Weston Cole.

CHAPTER NINE

WESTON

"Cheers to our dear, dear Weston," Chris shouts. "It's been such a joy watching you transform over these past three years. We never thought you'd amount to anything." He pretends to wipe a tear off his cheek, and I snort. "LET'S PARTY, EAGLES!" he bellows before shotgunning a beer and cannon-balling into the deep end of the pool.

As soon as he hits the water, loud music begins pumping through the backyard speakers again. I'm officially an adult, and Chris has taken the opportunity to throw the biggest, and final, bash of the summer.

"Happy Birthday, Weston," a couple of girls say as they pass me.

"Thanks, ladies," I reply, giving them a flirty smile.

I feel my phone vibrate and pull it out of the pocket of my swim trunks. *Are you free tonight?*

Eight days of radio silence, and that's all she sends me. With anyone else, I'd be pissed. I waver on whether or not to reply right away. Annoyed with my uncharacteristic indecision, I send *Not until nine* back to her.

Okay, I'll meet you at the cabin then is her reply. Nothing else.

Chris's party started at noon, and it's still in full swing by the time I beg off at six for dinner with my parents. Charlie tells me he had "something epic planned", which honestly makes me glad I have an excuse to leave.

Past plans have gone awry.

I head home, shower, change, and then follow my parents to Alleghany's fanciest restaurant. My mother wanted to go some-place in the city, but I told her I had plans with friends later and wanted to stay in town. At the time, it was an excuse to avoid spending additional time with my parents. It ended up being true if I were to characterize Maeve Stevens as a friend. I have no idea what to consider her. But it also gave me an excuse to take my own car, so there's that.

My parents are waiting in the restaurant lobby when I enter the building, and the hostess immediately shows us to a private table. Or at least she tries to.

Progress is slow as my father fraternizes with every diner we pass whom he knows. Which is almost everyone. Inevitably, I get pulled in as a result of some football comment, and my mother is forced to chime in as well. It probably takes us a good fifteen minutes to travel the fifty feet to our table.

My father begins talking as soon as we settle in our seats, no doubt eager to keep the happy family charade going now that he's alerted almost everyone in the restaurant to our presence.

"You know, I was talking to Joseph Andrews yesterday after a conference call," my father says. "He's still quite involved at Lincoln and thinks you'll be a shoo-in for sure."

"That's great, Dad," I mutter.

My father's been talking about me attending his alma mater, Lincoln University, for as long as I can remember. He continues prattling on about it while we order and eat.

Once he's exhausted that topic, he moves on to filling us in on all the business associates he's met with this week. I barely bother to pay attention to him as I pick at my steak.

Finally, the check arrives.

"Thanks for dinner, Mom. Dad," I add reluctantly, "I told people I'd be free at nine though, so…"

My mother nods toward the door. "Have fun with your friends. But be careful, and don't be out too late, okay?"

"Okay," I respond, kissing her on the cheek on my way out the door.

I speed toward the cabin. I'm late. I've always hated the pit that forms in my stomach whenever I'm not on time, but it's more than that right now.

Excitement churns in my gut at the thought of seeing her.

When I pull into the cabin's driveway, she's already here. Waiting. I park and climb out of my car.

"Nice sweatshirt," I state as I walk over to her. She's wearing the one I gave her weeks ago with jean shorts, and I feel ridiculously overdressed in my polo shirt and khaki shorts.

She smiles. "Happy Birthday, Wes."

"You remembered," I state the obvious.

"Yeah, thank God for social media reminders, right?"

"We're not friends on social media."

Maeve lets out a small laugh. "No. We're not." It's hard to tell in the dim light, but I think she's blushing.

I start toward the woods.

"Where are you going?" she calls out after me.

"What do you mean?" I turn back around. The handful of times we've met here, we've always walked down to the lakeshore.

"We're not staying here. I just wanted to take one car so I could surprise you."

"Really?" I arch an eyebrow.

Maeve nods.

"Okay." I walk back over to her. She opens the trunk of her car and pulls out a duffle bag. It's close to bursting, the seams straining against the contents. I eye it curiously. "If we're not staying here, how come you're unloading?" I ask.

Maeve bites her bottom lip. "Your car is better suited for my plans."

"What, are we off-roading or something?"

"Or something," she replies cryptically.

I head back over to my car, opening the trunk for her. She places the bag in the back and holds out her hand expectantly. "Keys, please."

I smirk. "You think I'm going to let you drive my car?"

Maeve doesn't waver. "Yes."

Twenty minutes later, I glance over at her from the unfamiliar vantage point of my passenger seat. "Are you planning to stop before we hit New York?" I ask.

Maeve scoffs. "Patience is a virtue, Cole."

"I don't have many of those," I tease.

She mutters something under her breath.

It's probably another ten minutes before Maeve begins to slow the car and takes an exit off the highway. Other cars keep whizzing past us as we roll down the exit ramp toward the dark, empty road it intersects with.

Despite the entirely empty street, Maeve still sits at the stop sign for a whole three seconds and flicks the blinker on before turning to the right. I smile to myself. She's a rule follower.

Which makes the fact she's currently driving my car all the more ludicrous.

We continue along the seemingly abandoned road until flashing lights suddenly appear to the right. Maeve pulls the car under the marquee display that reads *Olneyville Drive-In*.

"We're going to the movies?" I ask.

"I figured the Glenmont Cinema was out."

She hands the attendant some money, and the gate opens, letting us into the already crowded cement lot in front of the massive screen displayed before us. Maeve backs in the next available spot, so that we're facing away from the screen.

"Come on, Cole." She climbs out of the driver's seat and heads toward the rear of the car. I follow her, watching as she lifts the back door of my SUV and unzips her bag. She pulls out a fluffy blanket and a couple of pillows, followed by an assortment of candy and popcorn. I'm truly amazed she fit it all inside the duffel. She takes a seat on the tailgate, pulling off her sneakers and setting them to the side before spreading out the blanket and the pillows.

I climb in after her, pulling off my own shoes and lying down. We have a perfect vantage point toward the screen. Maeve lies down beside me, and she doesn't leave a lot of space between us.

My body immediately reacts to her proximity. To her now familiar scent, like citrus and sunshine. To the sight of her in my sweatshirt.

The opening credits flash across the massive screen, and I glance over at her, shocked. She shrugs, a small smile playing across her lips.

"You said it was your favorite movie."

"Yeah, it is," I reply softly. I hope my expression conveys how much this means to me, because I can't muster the right words right now.

We settle against the soft pillows as the movie starts, passing the snacks back and forth between us. She falls asleep halfway through the movie, and I give up on watching the familiar film as soon as she does, opting to study her instead. The pert tip of her nose, the eleven freckles that decorate her cheeks, the elegant curve of her jaw.

Someone slams a door shut in the car next to us, and she startles, groaning as she rolls over. We're already close, so she ends up half on top of me. Surprised green eyes suddenly meet mine when she realizes I'm hard.

I give Maeve a sheepish grin I hope appears more charming than lustful. "What? It's chemistry."

She laughs. "I think you mean biology."

"Okay, I'll blame that field of science too," I smirk.

She scoots up slightly, creating more delicious friction between our bodies and invoking even more of a response from mine. Our faces are only inches apart, maybe millimeters.

"Why did you kiss me back at that party, Maeve?" I whisper.

She bites her bottom lip, and we're close enough I can see the enticing pink retreat from the indentations her teeth are making.

Instead of answering, she tosses a question back at me. "Why haven't you kissed me since?"

I let out a long exhale. "I wasn't sure if you wanted me to. You know it's a bad idea. We're a bad idea. This is risky enough. Getting more involved will—"

"Yeah, you're right," Maeve interrupts. She tries to roll away, but I tighten my grip, holding her in place. Irritation flashes across her pretty features. "It would have been nice if you'd thought of that before the cheerleader party, Wes."

"The cheerleader party?"

"Yes. The party we were at together."

"That applies to more than one party, Maeve." She hasn't tried to pull away again, so I rest my hands on her waist. My thumb grazes the strip of skin between her shorts and sweatshirt. Her eyes flash again, this time with heat, not anger.

"Fine, the one where you kissed me, then. Or are we still pretending that didn't happen?"

"Do you want to pretend it didn't happen?" I counter.

"That's what I've spent all summer doing, Wes. You're the one who brought it up."

"Yeah, I did," I admit. "Because this feels…this feels like something more than being workout buddies."

"Because we're not working out?"

I smirk. "That, and this is the most thoughtful thing anyone has ever done for me."

Maeve breaks eye contact. "I felt badly. About how we left things."

"You don't need to," I reassure her. "But just to be clear, I've never asked you to do anything out of pity. The only reason I texted you that night was because I wanted to hang out with you. You were the only person I wanted to be around, actually."

"Saying shit like that doesn't make pretending any easier, Wes."

"Pretending what?"

"That I don't want you to kiss me."

"You want me to kiss you?"

"Wow, you're terrible at reading body language," she informs me.

I laugh. "Never been told that one before. My receivers say the opposite." I shift so our faces are even closer together.

Maeve stiffens. "What are you doing?"

"Well, I was going to act on the verb we've been discussing for what feels like the past ten minutes," I respond. "Is this your idea of foreplay?"

Maeve scoffs. "One, let me remind you again that *you* brought it up. And two, you literally just said it was a bad idea."

"I did," I confirm. "And I was relying on you to be the voice of reason. Which you failed spectacularly at, by the way. Because I spend a lot of time thinking about that bad idea. And badder ideas."

Maeve smirks. "Badder ideas? I'm not sure your idol, Shakespeare, would approve of that grammar."

"Maeve, you're literally lying on top of me right now. I'm not exactly thinking about proper grammar. Plus, the man was an innovator. Haven't you heard of iambic pentameter?"

"Who's the nerd now?"

I laugh, but then sober. "Maeve, I need you to tell me if you don't want this to happen. I'm losing willpower fast here."

"Lose it faster," she whispers, and I'm done.

I think I knew this was inevitable from the moment I stepped on the Glenmont running track. I've certainly hoped it would be, despite the many, many reasons why it shouldn't.

She kisses me first this time, and it's just as eerily incredible as it was in Josh's backyard.

It's not awkward or sloppy or hurried.

It's slow and languid and thrilling.

And exhilarating. Maeve Stevens exhilarates me.

I ease her back against the blanket she brought, angling my head as I slip my tongue inside her mouth. She whimpers as I tug on her bottom lip with my teeth, and she slides her hands into my hair. I groan as she drags her fingers against my scalp.

I ghost my fingers across the muscles of her abdomen and feel them ripple underneath my touch. We keep kissing, growing increasingly heated as we venture closer and closer to some of the "badder" things I've imagined.

87

The sound of the engine next to us revving finally breaks the spell. We pull apart, both breathing heavily.

"Because I'd thought about it for the past two years," Maeve says softly.

"What?" I was hoping for a *wow* or a *damn*.

"You asked me why I kissed you back last time. Because I'd thought about it ever since we talked at the end of freshman year. For the past two years."

"That's a lot of anticipation."

"I wouldn't say it posed any problem for you," Maeve admits, blushing slightly.

"That's good to know," I respond, grinning.

And then I kiss her again.

CHAPTER TEN

MAEVE

The first day of senior year is anticlimactic. Typical. Exactly what I've come to expect from the halls of Glenmont High.

With one exception.

One I'm daydreaming about during lunch until I realize Sam Jackson is talking to me.

"Huh?" I employ Wes's standard response.

"I heard you and Crawford had a nice little honeymoon last week, Maeve," Sam teases.

"Yup, it was super romantic triple dating with my parents and grandparents," I respond. "Oh, and with Liam as the seventh wheel."

"I'm sure you managed to sneak away from the fam for some alone time." Sam winks.

I laugh. "For hot dogs on the pier? I hope you have better things to do with your time than speculate about my dating life, Sam."

"I really don't," he replies, giving me a cheeky grin. "The

whole school's wondering if you're finally going to give a Glen-mont guy a chance."

He glances down the table to Matt, who flips him off. "Can it, Jackson."

I roll my eyes at his exaggeration, although I'm used to the comments about how the only guys I've shown the slightest bit of interest in have been from Fayetteville. With one glaring, secret exception. If people really do think Matt and I are a thing, I'm not surprised there's gossip. He's one of the most popular guys in school.

"I'm too busy to date anyone," I reply.

Brooke snorts from her spot across from me. "Maggie said your summer schedule was insane. That she barely saw you."

An awkward silence descends on the table in response to Maggie's name.

"What? We're going to pretend she doesn't exist anymore?" Brooke asks, glancing down the table at the football team.

"No one's pretending she doesn't exist. But she does live in Alleghany now. She's literally *cheering* for their team," Sam replies.

"Just to meet new people," I defend. "And they aren't being very welcoming, so she could use some support from us."

"You've been hanging out with Alleghany cheerleaders?" Sam asks in surprise.

I groan inwardly. "'Hanging out' is a generous term. I basically just stood there while they gossiped with Maggie."

"Anything good?" Brooke asks.

"One of them was trying to decide whether to stay on the East Coast or move to the West Coast for college," I reply. "That's about all I got."

"Where was this? At Maggie's new place?"

"No. She dragged me to one of their parties," I admit. That revelation earns me the attention of the entire table.

"You went to a party in *Alleghany* this summer?" Matt asks. Shock saturates his voice, along with a hint of betrayal.

"Sort of," I reply. "Maggie didn't tell me where we were going, and then basically dragged me inside. We didn't stay very long, just talked with some of the cheerleaders."

"What was it like?" Brooke asks.

"Fine. Same as ours are, pretty much."

"Was their team there?" Sam questions, but I'm saved from answering when Sarah appears and plops down next to me.

"First day, and I already have extra assignments," she groans.

"No, you *volunteered* to help Mr. Branner with the extra credit assignment for the freshmen," Brooke corrects. "There's a difference, Sarah."

"No one else offered!" Sarah glances around the table, most of whom are still looking at me. "What did I miss?"

"Maeve was just filling us in on the Alleghany party she attended," Brooke supplies.

"Oh yeah, Maggie mentioned that she dragged you to one at the start of the summer," Sarah says, and I'm thankful for her affirmation regarding my lack of enthusiasm. "She didn't say much about it aside from talking my ear off about Weston Cole. How was it?"

Any gratefulness disappears as soon as she says his name.

"Wait, *Weston fucking Cole* was there?" Brooke exclaims.

"Yup." It's not like I can deny it now.

"How did he look?" Brooke presses. "I've never seen him up close."

"Seriously, Brooke?" Sam groans. "We're sitting right here."

"No one said you have to eavesdrop on our conversation,

Sam," Brooke snaps. Of course, that makes everyone at the table pay even closer attention to it. "Well?" she prompts, looking at me.

"He, um, he's attractive," I finally say. I can feel my cheeks burning.

Brooke rolls her brown eyes at me. "He's attractive? I know that much. Come on, Maeve, give me some concrete details."

"What do you want to know? His height? Weight?"

Brooke laughs. "No, I know all that. It's on the team site."

"Still sitting right here and not thrilled to know you cyber-stalk Alleghany's football team," Sam chimes in. He looks genuinely miffed, and I wonder if it's because Brooke's the one bringing this up. I've always suspected he has a thing for her.

Brooke ignores him and keeps looking at me expectantly.

"They have photos of all the players on their team site as well," I say. "So I'm not sure what you're asking about."

"*You've* looked at their team site?" Matt asks me incredulously.

"I saw it when my dad was checking stats one morning," I reply, which seems to mollify the football players at the table. Checking out the competition is something they understand, but I was definitely doing so in the more literal sense.

"So, you've seen Weston's photo?" Brooke asks, still undeterred.

"Yes," I sigh.

"And? Is he just as hot in person?"

I blame Brooke's persistence and the fact I spent two hours making out with him last night in the backseat of his car on the next words that come out. "No. He's hotter."

Brooke squeals, and all the guys groan with disgust.

"Seriously, Maeve?" Sam asks.

"Better not mention you're lusting after Cole to Liam," Matt states, sounding annoyed.

"I'm not lusting after him," I lie. "I was just stating a fact."

"Whatever. Alleghany leaked his numbers from their preseason scrimmage, and Liam's even more peeved than usual. Some girl was looking at posts from Cole's birthday party in English earlier, and I swear I saw steam coming out of Liam's ears," Matt comments.

"Speaking of, did you see those? I get why Liam's freaked. Cole doubled his passing yards. In a scrimmage!" Sam exclaims.

"Yeah, I saw them," Matt says grimly. "I told Liam about the training rumors, but he didn't believe me. Our practices are already insane, anyway. I don't think there's anything else we could be doing."

"What training rumors?" Sarah asks.

"That Cole was training all summer instead of his usual partying and hooking up."

Brooke laughs. "A guy after your own heart, Maeve."

I shift awkwardly. If she only knew.

"I'll be right back," I inform my friends. "I forgot my cleats this morning, so I've got to call my mom and ask her to bring them."

"Why don't you just text her?" Sarah asks.

"She's usually driving between showings," I reply. "It's easier to call." It's true, but she always responds to texts quickly. Glenmont doesn't take long to drive around.

But I'm not calling my mother. I already texted her.

I stride over to the far wall of the cafeteria. It's composed mostly of glass, allowing for an expansive view of the soccer and baseball fields spread out behind the building. I scuff the toe of my sneaker against a yellowed discoloration in the linoleum as I listen to the phone ring.

"Hey, Mom," Wes answers casually.

"Weird way to answer the phone."

"No, I can't. I have practice until six tonight," he adds loudly. Lowering his voice, he continues, "Hey, Stevens."

"Nice intro."

Wes chuckles. "I'm at lunch with the guys. My mom is the only person who calls me like it's still 1986." His voice is teasing. "Aren't you at lunch?"

"Yeah, why?"

"Well, who did you tell your friends you were calling?"

"My mom," I sigh.

I can practically feel his smugness through the phone. "Huh."

I laugh. "It's worse when you say it over the phone."

"Cole! Let's go!" I hear called through the background.

"I'll be right there," Wes shouts back. He lowers his voice again. "So, what's up? Everything okay?"

"Yeah, everything's fine. I just—"

"Hey, Weston." I hear a girl's flirty voice in the background. There's a pause on his end, and I can picture the sexy smirk he's probably giving her.

"COLE!" is hollered again in the background.

"I've got to go," Wes tells me. I think there's regret in his voice, but I can't tell for sure.

"Right. Of course. Bye." I hang up before he can, faced with another uncomfortable reality. I called Wes for an assurance. Of what, I'm not quite certain.

That we still mean something?

That it doesn't matter he's surrounded by people who hate me, and I'm surrounded by people who hate him?

That we didn't always have a set expiration date?

Our brief call didn't answer any of those questions. It complicated things further.

Ever since he moved there, Weston's been Alleghany's most popular resident. I've seen the girls holding signs at our games against Alleghany. I've heard the rumors about his hook-ups. I've listened to my friends gush about how gorgeous he is.

Ever since our conversation freshman year, I've paid a little closer attention any time his name comes up. Wondering if the troubled, sad boy lamenting his parents' fissured marriage was still in there, or if I'd just caught him on a bad night. Wondering if he'd ever listened for rumors about his dad's infidelity the way I listened for rumors about my dad's alcoholism.

Talking and training with Wes all summer was a mistake. Spending every night since his birthday last week kissing him in the backseat of his car was a terrible idea. Both uncharacteristic, reckless actions. But allowable ones.

The feelings churning through me right now aren't inconsequential ones, though. The flashes of jealousy, envy, doubt, insecurity, and possessiveness indicate I've gotten a lot more attached to Wes than just appreciating his smirk. And that is not something I can afford.

I spend the rest of the day pushing Weston Cole as far from my mind as I can. Thankfully, the rest of lunch passes without any mention of him, and my afternoon classes pass quickly.

As soon as the final bell rings, I head to the office to pick up my cleats. Matt's leaning against the wall when I enter the room. I look between him and the empty desk where the elderly receptionist normally sits.

"Where's Mrs. Jones?"

Matt shrugs. "I just got here, and she was already missing."

"Huh," I reply, and curse internally, mentally adding *annoying vocabulary* to the long list of reasons why I should stay far away from Weston Cole.

"What did you forget?" Matt asks me, grinning.

You only come to the office for one of two things: a visit to our principal or to pick up something you forgot in the morning. I'm not surprised he assumes I'm here for the latter, since I've never entered this office for the former.

"My cleats," I respond. "You?"

"Football shorts," Matt admits. "My mom was unsuccessfully trying to get the grass stains out, and I forgot to grab them from the laundry room this morning."

"I've stopped buying any athletic clothes that aren't navy or black," I tell him. "Usually solves the problem."

Matt grins. "I'll keep that in mind."

We stand around for a few more minutes, with no sign of Mrs. Jones.

"Sorry about lunch," Matt finally says. "I know me and Sam were giving you kind of a hard time."

I shrug. "The rivalry with Alleghany is far from news to me. I get why me going to one of their parties bothered you guys. I appreciate you apologizing, but you don't need to."

"It feels even worse this year," Matt replies. "This is our last chance to finally beat Alleghany. To beat Cole. Liam's last chance. My last chance. Add in the fact Cole seems to be poised for one hell of a season, and—"

"What can I help you two with?" Mrs. Jones chooses this moment to join us in the office, and I send her an extra-wide smile in appreciation of her timing. "Oh, hello, Maeve," she greets when she sees my face. "How are you, dear?"

"I'm well. How are you?" I reply.

"Just wonderful; thanks for asking. Hard to believe you're a senior this year. It seems like just a few months ago you were in here collecting the paperwork to run for freshman student council."

I laugh. "It does."

"I've got your cleats right here. I heard you were selected as captain, which is just mighty impressive, dear. I don't know how you juggle everything."

"Thank you, Mrs. Jones." I smile as I take the plastic bag containing my soccer cleats from her.

"What can I help you with, young man?" Mrs. Jones turns her attention toward Matt, who's giving me a bemused look.

"I'm Matt Crawford, ma'am," he replies. "There should have been some shorts left for me?"

"Oh, yes," Mrs. Jones replies, handing Matt a heap of folded white fabric.

"Thank you."

"Have a good afternoon, Mrs. Jones," I say as I follow Matt toward the door.

"You too, Maeve."

Matt holds the door open for me, and I raise my eyebrows as I walk out of the office.

"Since when are you a door holder?" I ask.

"I figured it was the least I could do for Mrs. Jones' favorite student. An in with the school secretary is an important one to have."

I scoff. "Whatever you say."

"I'm serious. I went there at least once a month last year, and she didn't even remember my name!"

"Guess I'm just more memorable than you are," I tease.

"Yeah, I guess you're pretty special," Matt replies. But his voice isn't teasing. It's serious.

I glance at him in surprise, but his gaze is fixed ahead on the crowded hallway we're walking through. I experience an uncomfortable twinge.

"Thanks, Crawford," I keep my tone light, studiously ignoring any underlying meaning in his words. "I've got to stop at my locker before practice, so I'll see you."

"Bye, Maeve," Matt calls as I head to the right, down the adjoining hallway lined with lockers, including mine. I try to shake off the lingering uneasiness Matt's words left me with.

The girls' locker room is loud and raucous when I enter it. I spent the summer playing with these girls, and there's no awkwardness or repeated queries of "How was your summer?" as I navigate through the boisterous crowd to my locker so I can change.

"Hey, Captain," Becca Collins greets as she takes a seat on the bench across from me.

"I thought I told you not to call me that," I inform her grinning face.

"I'll call you Maeve when I see you at Chase's party on Friday night," Becca assures me. "But Captain when you're making us run suicides."

"You'll thank me when we win state," I say as I change into my practice jersey and shorts.

Becca laughs. "I have no doubt we're going to win. It's the only reason I've gone on those crazy early runs with you since freshman year when you made varsity and I didn't."

"You asked what I'd done to prepare."

"I expected you to recommend a couple of drills or something," she replies. "Not to tell me to meet you the next morning at six AM. And have it last *three* years."

"No pain, no gain," I tell her with a grin.

"I seriously have no idea why the only team people here follow is football. You're the crazy talented Stevens twin, in my opinion." Her words remind me of Wes's.

"Is this your way of sucking up to me because you know I'm planning to include suicides next captain's practice?"

"Well, not originally. But maybe now." Becca sighs dramatically.

I laugh as I lace up my cleats. "You ready to head out?"

The locker room is rapidly emptying; thanks to my trip to the office, I'm running behind almost everyone else. Becca nods, and we head out onto the spread of green grass that comprises Glenmont High's main soccer field. Most of the team has already gathered around Coach Bloom.

"Welcome to the first official practice of the season, ladies!" Coach Bloom calls out as the circle around her fills in. She's been coaching Glenmont's team for the past decade and has been one of my biggest supporters with soccer ever since I tried out for Glenmont's team on a whim freshman year. "Based on your preseason performance and the drills Stevens has had you running, I have a lot of faith this is going to be our most successful season in the school's history. Warm-up today is the regular route. Aim for under fifteen minutes, please. Collins, you set the pace. Stevens, a word, please?"

Becca starts jogging toward the trail that surrounds the high school campus, with the rest of the varsity team following her.

"Hey, Coach," I greet as I step forward.

"Good first day, Stevens?" Coach Bloom asks.

"Yeah, it was."

"Good. I've been blown away by your work this summer. Not only individually, but with the entire team as well. You're the most dedicated player I've ever coached, hands down. Selecting you as captain was a no-brainer."

"Wow, thank you."

Coach Bloom is never stingy with praise, but only when she feels it's been sufficiently earned. And I've never heard her compliment another player the way she just praised me.

"With your grades and work ethic, you're going to have some impressive options for next year. If you want them."

"You mean, you think I should play in college?"

"I think you'll have scouts fighting over you, Stevens."

"Uh, wow. I mean, I've considered it, obviously, but I wasn't sure if it was realistic or not."

"It is," Coach Bloom assures me. "We can discuss it more in the next few weeks, but I wanted to mention it to you now. I know you said Arlington is your first choice, so I'll make sure they're at a game."

"Okay. Thank you," I reply.

I've wanted to go to Arlington University ever since I first visited its ivy-covered campus with my mom and Liam during my father's coaching days. But their athletic programs are extremely competitive. I wasn't sure if I'd be able to play soccer there.

"Of course. Now get those girls moving."

"Yes, Coach," I reply, smiling before I set off toward the entrance of the trail. I took her parting words as a joke, but I haven't run more than a few hundred feet onto the trail when I come across the soccer team standing around.

"Let's go, ladies!" I call out. "What's the—" I stop talking when I reach the group and spot the attraction that's caught the entire team's attention. "Seriously?" I ask. "Drool after practice, let's go!"

My authoritative tone is enough to get the team moving past the bird's-eye view of the Glenmont football field, which is featuring a scrimmage of skins versus shirts.

"You got an ironclad libido, Stevens?" Becca asks me, grinning as she falls into pace beside me in the front of the pack.

"Nope. Just seen better," I retort.

"In this town? That's hard to believe. Looks and football talent seem to go hand in hand."

"Who said I was talking about Glenmont?"

Becca raises her eyebrows. "Can't think of anyone all that good-looking in Fayetteville, either. Only that guy you brought to prom last year."

I don't correct her assumption.

I wasn't talking about Fayetteville, either.

CHAPTER ELEVEN

WESTON

A final slash of red marks the last player on the roster as present.

"Hey Cole, any chance I can sneak out of here a bit early?" I turn to look at Josh, surprised. He's one of the more dedicated players on the team.

"How come?" I can't help but ask.

"It's the girls' soccer game against Glenmont. I told Caroline I'd try to make it for the second half."

"They're playing Glenmont today?" I repeat.

"Yup."

I let out a loud wolf whistle that captures the attention of every guy on the team. I beckon them in, and they jog off the track hesitantly. Probably concerned I've come up with a worse drill. Coach Blake is out sick today, so I'm running an optional captain's practice.

Which every player on the team showed up for. Wisely.

"We're done for the day," I inform them. "After we go to the girls' soccer game."

I receive a lot of questioning looks.

Chris laughs. "What?"

"They're playing Glenmont," I offer. That's enough to cut off most of the grumbling. These guys would attend a chess match if it meant cheering against Glenmont. We make our way over to the soccer fields as a large, huddled mass, and Chris falls into step beside me.

"Why are we doing this? I thought you hate soccer."

I shrug. "Josh wanted to see Caroline play."

"Guess that means they're on again," Chris remarks. Caroline and Josh's relationship status varies from day to day. "Surprised you're indulging him."

"Would you rather be running laps?" I shoot back.

"Dude, you're taking this captain thing *way* too seriously."

We approach the field, and I see Maeve's repeated complaints about the lackluster turnout at the girls' soccer games were warranted. There's maybe twenty people here, tops.

Which means we cause quite the stir when we take up the entirety of one of the empty bleachers.

I spot her immediately, but Maeve hasn't noticed us yet. Her back is turned toward the spectators as she talks intently with one of her teammates. Her hair is braided intricately, and the muscles in her calves flex as she shifts from side to side.

"Holy shit, Liam Stevens is here," Charlie suddenly says.

The statement draws the attention of everyone sitting in the top two rows. I glance over to the opposite set of bleachers, and sure enough, Liam Stevens is sitting with Coach Stevens and a blonde woman who must be Maeve's mother. They look a lot alike. She's watching the game closely, but just as Maeve said, her father is busy talking to the man seated behind him.

"No way," one junior breathes. "What the fuck is he doing here?"

"That's Maeve Stevens," Chris replies, looking out onto the field. "She plays for Glenmont's soccer team."

Most of the team follows his gaze to where Maeve is still standing with her back to us, proudly displaying the *STEVENS* emblazoned across the back of her white and maroon jersey.

Fresh anticipation thrums through my teammates in response to Chris's announcement. Cheering against Glenmont is one thing. Watching a Stevens play against Alleghany? Raises the stakes significantly.

Maeve finally turns around, and Adam lets out a low whistle. My hands clench into fists automatically. I hear a few other appreciative sounds from the guys seated around me and suddenly question the wisdom of dragging my teammates here.

It's too late to do anything but sit here silently, though, which is confirmed when a stutter in Maeve's jog out onto the field confirms she's seen the additions to the audience. Her other teammates are glancing toward us as well.

We're also attracting attention from Alleghany's soccer team now.

Josh stands. "Call me, Fourteen!" he yells to Caroline.

His obnoxious shout earns him a smattering of applause from our teammates and a few members of the soccer team. Caroline flips him off.

In an alternative reality, I imagine calling out encouragement to Maeve. But that fantasy is hard to imagine under the weight of the glares from her teammates. The Alleghany girls may be warming to our presence, but it's clear the Glenmont team has taken our presence as a personal affront. I wonder how Maeve feels.

We've barely talked since school started a few weeks ago.

Since the day she called me in the cafeteria. I texted her that night asking if she wanted to meet up, and she said she was too busy. It's been the same response the other three times I've tried to see her. I don't doubt she is, but it's feeling more and more like a brush-off.

I should be glad.

We had fun, and she didn't get clingy afterwards. Normally, that's all I want from to girls. When it comes to Maeve Stevens, I keep thinking of random shit I want to tell her. Keep fantasizing about the stretch of nights we spent in the backseat of my SUV for the brief period we moved past platonic before we swerved right back into the friend-zone. Not even the friend-zone. Barely acquaintances.

She uncomplicated the murky mess we were venturing into.

Why does that make me want to pull her back in?

Maeve takes her position on the upper half of the field and confers with her fellow striker and their goaltender. I observe her talking, gesturing with her hands as she instructs them on some strategy. They watch her raptly. Maeve stays put, the other two players return to their positions, and play resumes for the second half of the game.

I can't take my eyes off Maeve as she gains possession of the ball and streaks down toward Alleghany's half of the field. She's good. Even better than I thought.

Not even five minutes pass before she scores, giving Glenmont a 3-1 lead over Alleghany.

"Shit," Charlie states as the players around me deflate. Most of us know nothing about soccer, but you don't need to be an expert to tell Glenmont's the superior team. They're faster, more united, and more skilled. It's impossible not to realize why, as I watch Maeve weave along the length of the field, shouting suggestions and advice to her teammates.

"Did you see Matt Crawford just showed up?" Chris's question temporarily distracts my attention from Maeve.

I glance over, and sure enough, he's climbing the bleachers to sit with the Stevens family.

"What the hell is he doing here?" Adam adds.

"Rumor is he and Maeve Stevens have a thing," Charlie contributes.

My gaze snaps to him. "Where'd you hear that?" I ask in what I hope is a conversational tone. I'd guess it's more confrontational, though.

"He posted a photo of them, I think?"

I watch as Crawford chats with Maeve's mother, feeling a fresh surge of dislike toward him. Finally, I tear my eyes away before he catches me staring. That's the last thing I need.

There are only ten minutes left in the game, and Alleghany is starting to falter. I gain a fresh appreciation for football as I watch them continue to sprint up and down the long field. Both teams are clearly tired, but Glenmont's still pressing forward. They're the better conditioned team, and once again, I imagine Maeve Stevens deserves most of the credit. I had my own motivations for working extra hard when we would practice together, but watching her teammates look to her each play, it's clear she's the type of athlete that draws a better performance out of everyone she trains with.

Maeve sends a pass to one of her teammates, and Glenmont goes up by three. Most of the guys have stopped watching by now, but they all remain seated, not willing to leave until I do.

The game ends a few minutes later, and I watch as the Glenmont players all crowd around Maeve, hugging and cheering. For the first time since she saw my team arrive, she looks over at me. Green eyes meet mine, and we stare at each other for a protracted minute. Until Maeve's coach approaches and draws her attention away from me. The Glenmont coach is clearly praising Maeve, and I watch as she smiles in response.

Both teams line up for the traditional handshake. I've never witnessed one between Alleghany and Glenmont without participating in it myself. I watch closely as Maeve works her way down the line, shaking each girl's hand. She pauses to say something to Caroline and then keeps going.

"Okay, boys, you're free to go," I call out.

Most of the team rapidly disembarks from the metal bleachers, elated to be heading home an hour earlier than usual. Josh, Chris, Charlie, and Adam all remain in the stands beside me.

"Letting everyone leave early?" Charlie asks. "You're going soft, Cole."

I shrug. "Coach told me I could give you guys the day off, so technically, I already made everyone stay late."

Chris laughs. "The truth comes out. I was wondering why you called it 'optional' in your text."

The two soccer teams pack up, and Caroline heads across the field over toward us.

"I told you that you didn't need to come," she tells Josh. "And you brought the whole football team?"

"It was Cole's idea," Josh informs her.

Caroline looks at me, and I shrug. "You said no one cares about girls' soccer. Figured you guys could use some additional support."

"That's sweet, I guess," Caroline responds. "But your time probably would have been better spent preparing to beat Glenmont yourselves. Obviously, we weren't up to the task. Again."

Just past the border of Alleghany is the imaginary line that bisects the state into its eastern and western sports conferences. Meaning we only play Glenmont once during the season. Both teams can't advance.

This was Caroline's last chance to beat Glenmont, the same

way our game against them in seven weeks will be Liam Stevens' last chance to beat me.

I glance over to the bleachers where Maeve's family was seated and experience another rush of irritation as I watch Matt Crawford give Maeve a hug before she greets her family. Both Liam and her mother hug her as well, but I watch as her father simply says something to her and then heads toward the parking lot. Anger toward him briefly overshadows my jealousy as I watch Maeve's shoulders slump.

"Cole, you coming?" Charlie pulls my attention back to my friends. "We're going to grab some pizza."

"Yeah, I'm coming," I reply, following after them.

For once, Alleghany's solitary pizza parlor is almost empty when we enter it. Most of the high school is still at after-school activities, and it's too early for any families. We settle in the large corner booth and order four extra-large pies.

"Cheer up, C," Josh says as he takes a long drink of the soda he ordered. "Your season's barely started."

"Barely started. Basically over. Same thing," Caroline replies, sipping at her water. "We don't have any chance of making it to playoffs now."

"I thought you won both your first games?" Josh replies.

"We did, but those were against two of the worst teams in the league. We had to beat Glenmont today."

"You were right. Stevens is crazy good," Chris contributes. "That goal she scored? Insane."

"Yup," Caroline replies morosely, and Josh shoots Chris a glare.

"Sorry. Not helpful," Chris says, catching on fast.

"No, it's fine," Caroline tells him. "She raised it to a whole other level, and we weren't ready. And she even congratulated me after the game."

"She did?" I enter the conversation for the first time.

"Uh-huh." Caroline confirms as the waiter sets down the steaming pizzas in front of us. The discussion changes from sports to other topics as we all devour the greasy food.

My mother's the only one home when I walk through my front door a couple hours later. I drop my heavy backpack in the entryway and head into the kitchen to find her chopping carrots.

"Hey, sweetie," she greets. "How was practice?"

"It was fine," I reply. "Coach was out sick today, so I made the boys run a few drills, and then we stopped by the girls' soccer game."

"That sounds fun."

"I don't think anyone else thought so. They lost. To Glenmont."

"Oh." My mother doesn't follow a single sport, but it's impossible to spend more than a day in Alleghany and remain oblivious to the town's hatred of the one across the lake. "Well, I'm making dinner. It should be ready in about twenty minutes."

"I got pizza with the guys after the game," I inform her. "But I'll probably be hungry again in an hour or two if you want to set some aside."

"All right."

"Where's Dad?" I finally ask.

My mother's shoulders tense slightly. Our relationship is much more peaceful when we both pretend my father doesn't exist.

"He had a late work meeting."

"Huh," I reply. I have a feeling that's not the case, and the tightness in my mother's face suggests she doesn't think so either. "I'm going to do some homework," I tell her instead of voicing my suspicions, and I watch her slight frame visibly relax.

"Okay, sweetheart."

I hate how my father's philandering has sullied my relationship with my mother, but I also can't understand how she continues to turn a blind eye to it.

I head upstairs after retrieving my backpack from the front hall. I shower, even though I barely exerted myself at practice, and settle at my desk to start on my assignments due tomorrow. But rather than the math equations I'm supposed to be solving, my mind keeps drifting to Maeve.

I pull my phone out of my pocket, disregarding the messages and social media notifications displayed on the screen. I scroll through my contacts until I come to the three letters I saved Maeve's number as. *Huh.* I grin when I see them.

Rather than hit the message icon, or even the phone one, I tap the video symbol. I plug in my headphones, and the sound of ringing fills my ears.

Each second that passes feels eons long as I wait impatiently for her to answer. As I hope she doesn't.

Suddenly, the phone connects, and there she is. Sitting cross-legged on a navy comforter, wearing my light gray sweatshirt and a look of complete shock. The girl I can't get out of my head, and don't seem to want to.

"Good game earlier," I say in greeting.

There's utter silence from her end of the line.

"Uh, thanks," Maeve finally replies. Her green eyes are wide, and I grin to myself as I watch her fiddle with the messy bun that's barely containing her blonde locks, trying to wind some of the stray hairs back into place. "I was surprised to see you there. Do you attend many Alleghany girls' soccer games?"

"That was my first one," I admit.

"You wanted to see them beat us?" she asks. A current of challenge runs through her voice.

"No, I wanted to see you play, Maeve." Emotion flashes across her face in response to my honesty, but it disappears before I discern which one. "Why have you been avoiding me since school started?"

Maeve bites her bottom lip. "I—It seemed like it was for the best. It was one thing over the summer, but now…" She lets her voice trail off.

"I was the Alleghany quarterback this summer too, Maeve," I reply. "That didn't suddenly happen three weeks ago at the start of senior year."

"I know that, Wes." There's some exasperation leaking into her voice. "But it feels different now. It felt different when all the guys were complaining about your stats at lunch after I'd spent the night before kissing you in your car."

I can't help but grin, and she rolls her eyes, obviously realizing what I'm thinking. My smile fades as the implication of her words sinks in. "So, that's it?" I say quietly. I'm tempted to bring up what Charlie mentioned about her and Matt Crawford, but I refrain.

"It's not just the rivalry, Wes. We only just started our season, and Coach Bloom thinks I could play in college, so I've got a bunch of trips planned for that now, too."

"Where are you looking?" I ask, even though it's none of my business. She's a girl from Glenmont. Not to mention the fact she basically just broke up with me.

Maeve rattles off a long list of colleges. "Uh, Arlington has shown some interest too." I can tell from the way she says the last school's name that's where she really wants to go. I know it's where Coach Stevens both went and coached.

"Any of them would be lucky to have you. You kicked some serious ass earlier, Stevens."

"Thanks, Wes," she replies, almost shyly, and then silence falls between us. I let it stretch for a little while.

"Well, I don't think 'See you around' is the right parting phrase in this situation, but I can't come up with anything else," I finally say.

Humor flashes in Maeve's eyes. "I was going to go with, 'It was nice kissing you.'"

I laugh. "That works. Bye, Maeve."

I think I see regret in her eyes, but I'm not sure if it's real or I'm projecting what I want to see.

"Bye, Wes," she says, and I hang up.

Ending things between us is smart.

But I can't help but feel like it was stupid not to fight for us harder.

CHAPTER TWELVE

MAEVE

I've lost it. Officially. It wasn't when I spilled secrets to Weston Cole. It wasn't when I let him kiss me. It wasn't when I begged him to kiss me again. It's right now.

It's the only explanation for why I'm still in Alleghany.

After soccer practice ended earlier, I headed to Maggie's house. I've barely seen her since senior year started, the first time we've been in separate schools since kindergarten.

She pumped me for information about everyone in Glenmont and then embarked on a long rant about Alleghany High. I tried not to visibly wince every time she said the name Weston Cole. And she said it a lot.

After making plans to see each other this weekend, I left, telling her I needed to head home for dinner. Which I do. I just somehow ended up at Wes's house instead. At least I think it's his house. We shared our locations with each other over the summer, and I'm banking on the fact he's home right now.

If this is actually some random Alleghany girl's house, I could be setting myself up for a *very* awkward encounter.

It's been a week since Wes showed up at my soccer game with

the entire Alleghany football team. All of my teammates were pissed that they came. The Glenmont football team has never shown us that kind of support at a home game.

I didn't know what to think about their unexpected presence. Until Wes told me he came to see me play. With so much sincerity, it was impossible not to believe him. With so much sincerity, I had to get out. Because I was already in deep with Weston Cole. Deeper than I could believe I'd let myself sink.

So, I panicked, and I pushed him away. I went back to being the reliable, responsible Maeve Stevens.

Unfortunately, it turns out telling someone something doesn't make you believe it.

Do I think about Wes any less? No. Have I magically come up with a solution for the fact that the two of us together is a terrible, forbidden idea? Also no. But I've realized that it's a terrible, forbidden idea I want more than I want to be steadfast and loyal. That I can't banish Weston Cole from my mind.

I bypass the house and park on the street a few doors down. Thankfully, Liam was out when I left, so I convinced my mom to let me borrow her car. No *Glenmont Football* bumper stickers. I lock the car and start along the sidewalk.

It's a beautiful neighborhood—not that I'm surprised. The wide, pristine sidewalk is void of any scuffs or cracks, and the grass lining it is carefully mowed and adorned with flowerbeds every dozen feet. I stop in front of the house where Wes is showing up.

His Range Rover is parked in the driveway, along with two shiny Mercedes. The front yard is sprawling and immaculately maintained, and two massive oaks sit on either side of the brick walkway. All the lights are on downstairs, which is just starting to become necessary as dusk falls.

Two lights gleam upstairs, and I study the house, weighing my options. Should I ring the door? Text Wes? Leave?

A slight, dark-haired woman comes into view through the downstairs windows. Her face is twisted in anger, and I watch as a man follows her, also looking incensed. I dart forward, worried Wes's parents are going to glance out on the lawn and see me standing here.

I end up at the periphery of their front flowerbeds, looking in the window. There's a formal dining room on this side of the house, and a massive family portrait hangs over the fireplace. I let out a sigh of relief. At least I have the right house. And Wes's car is here, meaning he's home.

My interest in encountering either of Wes's parents disappeared as soon as I saw them arguing. Which strikes ringing the doorbell like a normal person. I study the roof that overhangs their front porch. I'd estimate it's about fifteen feet off the ground, and the railing diminishes about half the distance.

I creep through the mulch and hoist myself onto the edge of the porch. I grab the corner beam and pull myself up on top of the railing. The worn sole of my sneaker slips on the smooth wood, and I curse. There's no way I'd be able to explain breaking my leg in Weston Cole's flowerbeds.

Despite the anxiety and adrenaline racing through me, I persist. At this point, it would be just as perilous to turn back. I'm halfway there. I grasp the metal gutter and pull myself up until my elbow connects with the rough asphalt of the Coles' roof. I swing one leg up and use the momentum to roll my entire body upward. I lie there for a minute, shocked. I can't believe I came up with the idea to do this and am even more amazed I did so successfully. I just hope none of the neighbors are looking outside.

I crawl along the roof. I reach the first window and carefully raise my head to peer inside. It's a white-tiled bathroom. The shapes of the sink and toilet are barely visible in the light cast from the hallway. I drop back down on my hands and knees to continue my slow progression across the asphalt. I stub my finger against the edge of one of the hard shingles, which sends a stabbing pain up my arm. I move forward tentatively, only to feel the shingle slide with me. I sigh and grab it before I continue creeping along to the next window. I slowly sit up and glance inside.

Bingo.

Wes is sitting at a wooden desk, scribbling something in a notebook. I take a minute to study him until I realize I'm sitting on his roof and this is not the best time to do so.

I tap gently against the glass. Wes spins around and looks understandably shocked to see me.

He stands and walks over to the closed window, sliding it open when he reaches it. Rather than asking what the hell I'm doing on his roof, he grabs my forearms to help pull me over the sill and into his room. I half climb, half tumble onto a gleaming wooden floor.

Wes's arms are the only reason I stay upright. He must have just showered because I can see droplets of water in his brown hair. The cedar and bergamot scent that's begun to fade from his sweatshirt surrounds me as he shuts the window behind me.

I huff as I straighten. "Your roof needs some work," I inform Wes, handing him the stray shingle I picked up.

"I'll let my dad know. He might have some questions, though. Namely about what I was doing on the roof." He gives me a questioning look as he tosses the shingle in the trash. "What are you doing here, Maeve?"

I take a deep breath. "I want to talk to you. I—"

There's a knock on the door. "Wes?" A woman's voice calls.

I panic.

Wes is mouthing words at me, but they seem to spell out total gibberish. I wave my arms at him, trying to wordlessly convey I have no idea what he's telling me.

Finally, with an exasperated sigh, he grabs my arm and drags me over to the doorway. My eyes widen as he gently shoves me against the wall to the left of the door and then opens it, effectively shielding me behind.

"We're headed to the dinner," Wes's mother states.

"Yeah, I heard you and Dad discussing it."

"Weston, please don't start. I've had my fill of arguing for the night. You're staying here?"

"I'm staying here."

"Okay." Footsteps sound as Wes's mother moves away from his doorway, and Wes shuts the door.

"Your parents are leaving?" I whisper to Wes.

"Yeah," he replies. "Is that a problem?"

"No, my timing just sucks. I saw them in the living room, which is why I climbed onto the roof. If I'd waited ten minutes, I wouldn't have had to risk my life, or at least my soccer career, to talk to you."

Wes snorts. "The porch is only ten feet high. I'm not sure how much damage you could have actually done." I was slightly off with my estimate, apparently.

"Feel free to climb it one day. You'll see it's not as easy as it looks."

"I think I'll probably keep using the front door," Wes replies, smiling slightly. "So, what made you risk your life and soccer career to talk to me?"

I gulp. I was hoping to blurt it out to him as soon as I came through the window, so if he told me to get lost, I could just climb right back out.

"Maeve?" Wes prompts.

"I didn't mean it," I tell him. "I mean, I did mean it; everything I said last week was true. But I don't want this—us—to end. There are a lot of reasons why this is a really bad idea, but I can't stop thinking about you, and I—"

Wes kisses me, and I stop talking. He wraps his arms around my waist to tug me closer to him, and I let my fingers wander into his damp hair.

He guides me over to the large bed, and a thrill of anticipation joins the adrenaline already pumping through me. But Wes doesn't press things any further than we've already taken them. He hovers over me and just keeps kissing me. And kissing me. And kissing me.

I rapidly lose track of time, the same way I do whenever I'm around Weston Cole. Especially when I'm kissing him. It could have been minutes, or an hour could have passed by the time we pull apart.

"I'm going to take that as an affirmative response," I inform him.

Wes grins. "I'm good with that."

"Okay," I reply, smiling back. "I did mean what I said about being busy, though. I have soccer, and school, and student council, and—"

Wes cuts me off. "I don't exactly sit around all day, Maeve. I'll manage to entertain myself."

"I know; I didn't mean it like that," I assure him. "You just said I'd been avoiding you, which was kind of true, but it was mostly that I have a lot going on."

"I know you do. It was just the avoiding part I had a problem with," Wes tells me. "We'll see each other when we can, okay?"

"Okay."

We catch up on each other's weeks until I happen to catch a glimpse of the alarm clock on Wes's bedside table.

"Oh my god, it's already nine?" I've been at Wes's for almost three hours.

Wes looks just as surprised. "I guess so." He lets out a disbelieving laugh.

"I've got to go. I told my mom I'd be home hours ago."

Wes nods. "Okay. I've got a paper to write, anyway."

I slide off his bed, straightening my clothes. "This time I will see you around."

He grins. "It was still nice kissing you."

I feel myself blush. "As fun as the roof was, I'm going to use the front door this time," I say as I head over to his bedroom door.

"Good thinking," Wes replies. He climbs off his bed and grabs a sweatshirt hanging on the back of his desk chair. "Hang on, I'll walk you out."

"You don't have to do that," I assure him. "Start your paper."

"I want to," he insists. "Plus, I know how many of those true crime podcasts you listen to. I don't want you to survive climbing my roof, only to be snatched by a serial killer."

"You were actually listening when I was talking about those?" I ask, surprised.

I spouted a lot of random knowledge during our football sessions, but I didn't think Wes was paying attention, much less would remember what I was saying.

"Was I listening to you while you were talking to me? Uh, yes," Wes replies.

"Huh," I respond, and he grins.

"Your house is really nice," I compliment as I follow him down the grand staircase.

"I can't take any credit for it," Wes replies. "My mom likes to redecorate when she's upset or stressed. Which means she tends to redo things as soon as they're finished."

"It looked like they were arguing. When I saw them in the living room."

"They were," Wes confirms. "My mom found out the woman he had an affair with in the city was at a dinner he went to last night."

"That's awful."

"Yeah," Wes sighs. "I feel bad for her, but I don't know what else to say. It's her choice to stay, you know? I've told her I'm fine with them getting divorced."

He opens the front door, and I follow him outside into the quiet night. It's cooler than usual, the first traces of fall evident in the breezy air.

"I'm sorry, Wes. You know I have plenty of issues with my own dad, but I can't imagine going through what you are. I wish I could fix it for you."

"You help, Maeve. I've never talked to anyone about this stuff before. Talking to you helps."

"I'm glad." The trip back to my mother's car passes much more quickly with Wes by my side. "This is me," I say as we stop next to her silver SUV.

"New car?"

"No, it's my mom's. Liam needed the sedan. The team had an extra-long practice, or something."

Wes doesn't say anything in response, but he gives me another soft kiss before shoving his hands in his sweatshirt pockets and backing away.

"Night, Cole."

"Good night, Stevens," he replies. "I'm glad you came."

I smile. "Me, too."

I climb in my car and drive back toward Glenmont. There's a

goofy grin on my lips I can't seem to shake, even in the fifteen minutes it takes me to pull into my driveway. I'm surprised to see about a dozen cars parked on the street, most of them directly in front of my house. I climb out of the car, grab my practice gear, and hope my parents haven't called out a search party for me as I open the front door.

Our front hallway opens into the living room, and as I shut the door behind me, I'm greeted by the faces of every senior on the Glenmont football team. When I appear, they all look away from the diagram my father's drawing out on a whiteboard he must have brought home from school. At me.

"Uh, hey guys," I greet, self-conscious. I haven't glanced at my appearance since I left Wes's, and I really hope there's no obvious evidence I just spent a few hours making out with Alleghany's quarterback.

A few greetings sound from around the room, and Matt and Sam give me smiles.

"Where have you been, Maeve?" Liam asks. "Mom said you were supposed to be home hours ago."

"Yeah, I was at Maggie's," I reply, grateful for the first time they've all iced her out following her move to Alleghany. "I forgot to let Mom know I was staying so late."

"You forgot to let her know?" Liam echoes, sounding surprised. It's unlike me, and we both know it.

I shift uncomfortably. "I'll let you guys get back to learning plays."

My mother is at the kitchen table when I enter, squinting at the computer screen.

"Hi, Mom," I greet, strolling over to the fridge to pour myself a glass of water.

"Maeve!" she exclaims. "Where have you been? I expected you home hours ago! And you didn't answer any of my texts."

"I know, I'm sorry," I reply. "I was at Maggie's, and I lost track of time."

This lie is a slightly bigger gamble. My mother is friends with Maggie's. But I can't change my story from what I already told Liam. I can only hope it will never come up, and that if it does, enough time will have passed that no one remembers the discrepancy in the three hours it took me to make a twenty-minute drive.

"All right, just let me know next time," my mother tells me. I nod. "There's dinner in the fridge if you're hungry."

"Okay."

Matt enters the kitchen as I'm watching my meatloaf spin inside the microwave. "Hey, Mrs. Stevens."

"Hi, Matt," she replies, smiling warmly.

"What's for dinner?" Matt asks me as he grabs a sports drink from the fridge.

"Reheated meatloaf," I respond.

"That's what happens when you stay out gossiping until nine," Matt teases me. "Maggie doing okay?"

I'm tempted to encourage him to ask her himself. But for selfish reasons, that's the last thing I want right now. "Yeah, she is."

"She have a lot to say about Alleghany?"

I eye him apprehensively. "I'm not some sort of spy, Matt. And I don't think a rundown of who is hooking up with who in Alleghany is going to help you beat their football team, anyway."

The microwave beeps, and I pull my steaming dinner out.

Matt raises his hands in a placating gesture. "I was just making conversation, Maeve. No one's doubting your loyalty to Glenmont."

"I've got a lot of homework to do," I say. "So I'm going to head upstairs. I'll see you tomorrow?"

"Okay," Matt agrees. "See you tomorrow."

I give him a small smile before heading toward the staircase and up into my room.

As I eat my late dinner and complete the assignments I have due tomorrow, I contemplate the words that came to mind in response to Matt's hasty assurance he knows where my loyalties lie.

No one's doubting your loyalty to Glenmont, he said.

My first thought?

Maybe you should.

CHAPTER THIRTEEN

WESTON

Secret relationships are tricky. They're complicated, complex, and confusing. Especially mine, if for no other reason than I don't even know if we're *in* a relationship.

Partly because I've never been in one, and mostly because whatever Maeve and I have defies the norms of what any rational person would consider to be one.

We don't go out on dates. We don't spend time with each other's friends or family. If we ever saw each other in public, we wouldn't acknowledge each other.

We meet up someplace empty and deserted whenever we have a free, overlapping hour, usually either the park in Fayetteville or my uncle's cabin, and we talk and kiss. We don't label anything or talk about our feelings. We just...be.

But just because we haven't talked about our feelings doesn't mean I don't have them. I expected this year to be filled with football, and expectations, and meaningless flings.

I didn't expect to spend every spare second I have with a girl from Glenmont. And to have those stretches of time be the high-light of my week.

I text her as I leave practice, heading toward my car.

"Hey, Wes." I glance up from my phone to see Natalie is leaning against one of the tall trees that line the parking lot.

"Hey," I respond. "What are you doing out here?"

Natalie shrugs. "My mom was supposed to pick me up. My car's in the shop."

"Do you need a ride?" I offer. "It's not like it's out of my way." Natalie's house is a few doors down from mine.

"Yeah, that would be great, actually," she responds. "Let me just let her know I'm all set."

She types something in her phone, and then straightens, walking over to me. She's still in her cheerleading outfit, and I get a few envious glances from my teammates as she follows me over to my car and climbs in the passenger seat. My phone buzzes, and I pull it out to see a response from Maeve. *I'm free after eight.*

I shake my head in amusement. She wasn't kidding about her schedule. I'm busy, but I seriously don't know how Maeve juggles everything that she does.

EIGHT? I send back, along with a shocked emoji.

Past your bedtime, Cole? she immediately replies.

I feel myself grin as I let her know I'll meet her then. I shut off my phone and look up to see Natalie studying me. I set my phone in the center console and turn on the car.

"Sorry about that," I say. "Any musical requests?"

"I'm good with anything," Natalie replies.

"So…forcing the squad to do its competition routine to the song you selected since freshman year is just a rumor?" I tease.

Natalie laughs. "Okay, I'll choose something."

She fiddles with the controls of the stereo. Some pop song starts playing, and I half-regret saying anything. I only did because I was worried she might ask who I was texting.

"So, how have things been lately?" I ask, keeping my question vague, although I'm pretty sure I already know since she's riding in my car.

Sure enough, she sighs. "It's been worse lately."

Everyone at Alleghany High assumes Natalie and I started hooking up because we're each other's natural counterpart. Football captain and head cheerleader. Prom king and queen. Voted Most Popular.

While that was probably part of it, we first connected thanks to our less than idyllic home lives. A few months after my family moved to Alleghany, Natalie appeared when I was playing basketball in our driveway. She admitted to me her mother spends weekdays sloshed, and her father is hardly ever home. She was mostly raised by their housekeeper. I've never shared the specifics of my own family's drama, but enough to let her know I get what it's like to have a fractured family.

"I'm sorry, Natalie," I reply. "If there's ever anything I can do…"

She shakes her head. "It's fine. I'll be out of there soon. Maybe that will finally be enough to make my father face the fact his wife is an alcoholic. Are things okay with you?"

"Yeah, they are," I reply honestly. "I'm barely home these days, so that helps."

Natalie laughs. "Yeah, that definitely does. I feel like you've hardly been around, though. Did you even show up at Josh's last weekend?"

"I was there for a bit," I reply. "But I headed out early. We've got our game against Glenmont soon, and things are intense."

Natalie nods. "I get it. If you ever need some stress relief…" She lets her voice trail off suggestively. We haven't hooked up since the start of the summer, and I'm surprised it's taken her this long to bring it up.

I debate how honest I should be as I drive along the familiar roads. "I'm not sure that would be the best idea."

"Did you find a new hookup?" Natalie asks.

"Not exactly," I hedge. "I'm just not into having sex for the sake of having sex anymore."

"And that's all it would be to you?"

"Yes," I admit. Natalie's hinted before she would be open to a relationship, and I've always danced around the topic. Maeve Stevens has made my answer clear.

"Okay." She's good at hiding her emotions, so I can't help but confirm.

"You're sure? I didn't mean to—"

"It's fine, Wes," Natalie says. "Really. I appreciate the honesty. It's more than most guys can manage."

There's no trace of hurt in her voice, but I feel like she's being more cavalier than she feels. I certainly don't want to draw the topic out, though, so I let it drop.

"Want to stop for ice cream?" I suggest.

"What are we, five?" Natalie asks. But she's smiling as she says it.

"I didn't realize there was an age limit on enjoying ice cream," I inform her as I pull into the parking lot. She rolls her eyes but hops out of my car eagerly.

We attract a lot of stares as we make our way over to the order window. Boastful as it sounds, we're probably Alleghany High's two best-known attendees.

"Ladies first," I instruct Natalie as we reach the window. She scoffs and then leans forward to place her order. I'd guess the boy working the register is a freshman or sophomore based on the way he stutters and stammers as he takes her order. I give her an amused smile as she steps away, and she rolls her eyes. I order a milkshake, and then follow Natalie over to the green picnic table she selects.

We sit in companionable silence, eating the frozen dessert.

"Are you worried about the Glenmont game?" Natalie eventually asks me.

"About losing? No."

"What else would you be worried about?"

Maeve Stevens hating me.

"There's going to be a lot of scouts there," I say instead, which is true.

"Isn't Lincoln pretty much a sure thing at this point? I know you've still got your official visit this week, but that's what Chris and Adam were indicating, at least."

"Yeah, it is," I affirm. "I'm just not sure if I want it to be a sure thing."

"Oh," Natalie replies. "Do you want to talk about it?"

"There's not really anything to discuss," I tell her honestly. "I'll see what my options end up being, and then I'll have to make a decision."

She nods.

"What about you?" I ask. "Any idea where you want to end up?"

"No idea," Natalie replies. "Probably someplace far, far away from here. I'm over this town."

"Small towns are exhausting. I definitely miss living in the city," I respond. "For example, if we were there, I don't think every person would be staring at us."

Natalie laughs. I'm not exaggerating.

We finish eating, and I drop Natalie off at her house before continuing down the street to my own. When I pull into the drive-way, I'm surprised to see both Charlie and Chris's cars already parked. I enter my house to find them both sprawled out on the couch in the living room.

"Funny running into you two here," I inform them. "In my house."

Chris laughs. "We thought you might want to play some pickup, since today was a film day."

"Adam had to get home," Charlie adds. "But we told him we'd fill him in on whether you and Natalie are back on."

"So that's why you two are here," I realize. "Seriously? You weren't even in the parking lot when we left."

"Oh, how sweet and innocent you are," Charlie teases. "I'm sure the whole school knows you drove her home. What took you so long, anyway? We've been here for like twenty minutes, and we left after you did."

"We stopped for ice cream," I admit, knowing they'll hear about it anyway.

"How wholesome," Chris remarks. "Do you think you'll manage to move on to holding her hand sometime this month?"

"It's none of your business, but nothing is going on with me and Natalie," I inform them. "We're just friends."

"You're just friends," Chris states disbelievingly. "With the hottest, most popular girl in school, who's had a thing for you since you moved here?"

I shift uncomfortably. We barely talk in public. I hadn't realized Natalie's feelings were evident to anyone else.

"We're just friends," I repeat.

"Well, that's seriously disappointing," Charlie remarks, sighing. "But I guess we can play some football anyway."

We head out into my sprawling backyard. Colorful autumn foliage surrounds us as fallen leaves crunch underfoot. We've just started tossing the ball around when my father's flashy car pulls in the driveway. I groan as he parks at the end of the row of cars already filling our driveway and steps out.

Charlie and Chris send me questioning looks that indicate the sound wasn't very quiet. I've never hidden how I feel about my father in front of them, but I've also never told them why I treat him with such disregard. Considering he acts like Father of the Year in front of them, I know our tense relationship confuses them.

I could probably count on one hand the number of times I've seen my father not wearing a suit, and this is not one of them. He strides up the driveway, looking every inch the uppity businessman.

"Good afternoon, boys," he greets. "Didn't get your fill at practice?"

"It was a film day, Mr. Cole," Charlie answers when it becomes clear I'm not going to.

"Ah, I see. Well, I'll catch you boys later. Looking forward to the game this Friday." He heads inside the house.

"Looks like you and your father are closer than ever," Chris observes.

"Yup," I respond, sending the ball spiraling through the air again.

Chris and Charlie exchange a glance, but don't say anything else.

CHAPTER FOURTEEN

MAEVE

"Spill it, Maggie," Sarah instructs as we all take seats out on her patio to enjoy the warm sunshine before the cold weather fully descends. That's fall in Connecticut for you. Summer one day, winter the next.

"Spill what?" Maggie replies coyly, taking a sip of her lemonade.

"You're our Alleghany spy! Give us all the gossip!" Sarah tells Maggie, bouncing in her seat.

I roll my eyes and take a sip of cola.

"Honestly, there's not much new from last week, when you complained you didn't know anyone I was talking about." Maggie rolls her eyes to emphasize how offended she still is we cut off her speculation about a couple we've never seen or met after thirty minutes. "Alleghany High is not that different from Glenmont, to be honest. Same drama, just different people."

"What about Weston Cole?" Brooke chimes in with. "There's always good gossip about him. Don't you see him around school?"

I play it completely cool. Meaning I half-swallow, half-spit the soda and then begin coughing violently.

"Shit, Maeve. Are you okay?" Sarah asks.

"Fine," I croak, taking another sip of carbonated liquid to soothe my burning throat. "Wrong pipe."

I should have expected the topic of Wes might come up, but I didn't.

Satisfied I'm not choking, Brooke turns back to Maggie. "Well?"

"Not really. We don't have any classes together, so I hardly see him at school. The only Alleghany party I saw him at was the one I dragged Maeve to at the start of the summer. He's at practice and games, obviously, but that's basically it. I've never even talked to him."

Brooke sighs loudly. "Well, that's seriously disappointing. You having the chance to hook up with Weston Cole was the only part of you moving to Alleghany I was excited about. There are some cute guys in Glenmont, but he is in a league all of his own."

"You're preaching to the choir, sister." Maggie sighs. "There was a rumor he and Natalie were a thing again, but I haven't seen them together."

An uncomfortable weight settles in my stomach. Brooke begins questioning Maggie about the Alleghany cheer team but I'm barely listening, lost in my own thoughts. I've seen even less of Wes lately than usual, and I assumed it was because of his upcoming college visit and the game against Glenmont. But I never considered he might be seeing other girls. We've never discussed being exclusive over the last few weeks of sneaking around; I just assumed that we were.

We head inside when the sun starts to go down, and I excuse myself to go to the bathroom. I walk into Sarah's kitchen and lean against the counter. I pull my phone out of my pocket and find

Wes in my texts. His name in my phone is still *good at one thing*, and I can't help but smile when I see it, despite the confusion I'm grappling with.

Can you meet now? I send him.

Immediately, three dots appear at the bottom of the screen. *Yes.* Then, *Everything okay? Thought you were busy until eight tonight.*

Yup. Plans changed. I'm leaving now, I reply.

"I thought you were going to the bathroom?" Maggie asks, walking into the kitchen. I'm so startled I drop my phone on the counter.

"Uh—yeah, I am. Going to," I stutter, grabbing my phone and making sure the screen is off and unshattered.

"Are you okay, Maeve?" Maggie asks. "You've been acting weird all afternoon."

"I'm fine," I assure her. "I'm just—actually, my stomach is kind of bothering me, so I think I'm just going to head home."

"Sarah was just saying we should sleep over!" Maggie says. "Are you sure you don't want to stay?"

This new information solidifies my resolve. I don't want to wait until tomorrow to see Wes.

"Yeah, I'm feeling worse," I tell her. "Can you let Brooke and Sarah know? Tell them I'll see them at school tomorrow."

"Okay..." Maggie replies, still looking at me suspiciously. Whatever she's thinking, I'm certain it's nothing close to the truth.

I pull my car off the main road into the cabin's driveway fifteen minutes later, and Wes's car is already there. He's leaning against the side of his SUV, typing something on his phone. I climb out of the driver's seat and close the door behind me.

Night has almost completely fallen, and I shiver at the rapidly falling temperature as I walk over to Wes in the dusky light.

He looks up and smiles, and I'm a goner.

This boy.

I walk right up to him. "Hey—" he starts, but I don't give him a chance to finish.

I kiss him urgently, eagerly, grasping generous handfuls of his soft shirt and using them to tether myself to him. It's the furthest thing from a quick peck. I immediately seek entrance to his mouth, and he gives it to me, letting me slip my tongue inside. The hard ridges of his abs are outlined underneath the cotton material I'm pulling taut. I tug his bottom lip between my teeth. Wes groans in response, and I feel the vibration reverberate against my tongue.

I angle my head to deepen our kiss, and he winds his arms around me to pull me flush against his body. I can't stop kissing him, driven by some urgent need to mark my claim. To prove to myself I can.

Wes's lips leave mine to plant open-mouthed kisses along my neck, and I moan at the sensation of his tongue against the sensitive skin. I let go of his shirt and shove my hands in his hair so that I can pull his lips back to mine. He thrusts his talented tongue back inside my mouth. I let one hand trail down along his shoulder and the muscled planes of his chest until I reach the waistband of his joggers.

Wes pulls back abruptly. We stare at each other, chests heaving from our hot and heavy make-out session.

"Are you hooking up with other girls?" I blurt.

"What? No!" Some of the pressure leaves my chest following his immediate, adamant response. He studies my face. "Did someone say something to you? Why do you think I'd cheat on you?"

"It wouldn't be cheating, Wes. I just wanted to know."

"What do you mean, 'it wouldn't be cheating'? Are you hooking up with other guys?"

"No, of course not! I just—I mean, we've never—some of the girls were talking about the rumors about you, and since we don't —I thought maybe—it would have been fine…" I trail off when I see Wes's confused expression.

"I didn't follow any of that," he admits. "You text me hours before we're supposed to meet, attack me like we're acting in a porno, and then ask if I'm hooking up with other girls? I don't get it."

I sigh. "I was at my friend Sarah's house. Maggie was there— the one who moved to Alleghany over the summer—and some of my other friends started asking her about things there. And then you came up. And she didn't say much, except that you haven't been around a lot, but she mentioned a rumor about you and Natalie, and I realized that there could be other girls. That we never talked about it. About what this is. Or is not." I'm studiously avoiding eye contact and fairly certain I'm blushing. "Especially since we're not having sex."

I glance up to see Wes grinning broadly.

I shove his shoulder. "It's not funny, Wes!"

He laughs once and then turns serious. "You're right. It's not. Listen to me, Maeve Stevens. I have not—and will not— touch another girl when I have the option to touch you instead. Okay?"

"Okay," I mumble.

"I'm flattered you were gossiping about me, though."

I roll my eyes. "It actually sucked. Listening to my best friends going on about how hot they think you are."

Wes's cocky smirk grows. "Unfortunately for them, I can't seem to stop thinking about this one girl."

The heat I extinguished with my blunt question rapidly flares to life.

"Really?" I ask, stepping closer to him again. "What's she like?"

Wes laughs. "Are you fishing for compliments, Stevens?"

"Yes."

His expression softens. "Well, she's a wicked climber, and she's feisty, and thoughtful, and she throws a mean spiral."

"Not sure anyone else would call me feisty," I inform him. "Probably more like easy-going."

"Lucky me, then."

"I can't tell if you're being sarcastic right now."

He laughs. "I'm not. I love how stubborn you can be."

"I feel like I don't have to be perfect around you," I admit.

"Uh, thanks?"

"It's a good thing," I assure him. And it is. Wes makes me feel bolder. Braver.

Like I'm my own person, not the collection of assumptions people make about me by extension of my family.

"Anything you'd like to tell me in return?" Wes asks, grinning shamelessly.

"Uh, you're hot?" I respond, smirking.

"Wow. I'm touched," Wes replies. "But I'm glad you think so." His voice deepens. "Especially since you know I can't keep my fucking hands off you." He ghosts his lips across my cheek, and I pull in a shaky breath.

"I wouldn't mind a reminder," I whisper.

Wes chuckles.

I kiss him with just as much fervor as before, and he stumbles back, opening the back door of his car and sliding me across the leather seat in what's become a familiar maneuver.

I slip my hands along his abdomen and back down to his waist again.

"Maeve. We don't have to do anything," Wes whispers to me.

Despite some very heated make-out sessions, he's never pushed for anything more, and I've been too nervous to initiate it myself. I'm assuming his hesitation is because he's correctly surmised he's much more experienced than I am.

"I know. I want to." I tell him.

It's true. After the conversation we just had, I'm not worried Wes is going to look elsewhere if we don't escalate our physical relationship. But I want to take advantage of the fact I'm the one able to touch him this way. The one he wants to touch him this way.

He lets me slide my hand down and inside the loose material, and sucks in a sharp breath when I stroke the long length I encounter. He's already hard.

"Tell me what to do," I whisper in his ear as I pull his sweatpants down.

Wes groans. "Harder." I increase the pressure of my hand as I glide along his shaft. "Fuck, Maeve," Wes kisses along my neck again, and it's my turn to groan as I stroke him faster and faster.

He flexes in my hold, and I feel powerful. Desired. I would never admit this to anyone, but I've spent a lot of time fantasizing about this very moment. What it would feel like to have Weston Cole at my mercy. Throbbing pulses of heat fill my own body as the sound of Wes finding his release fills the car.

He cleans himself up and then rolls so he's on top of me. "You're so fucking sexy, Maeve." His voice is rough and husky, and it sends shivers along my skin.

Wes dips his hands underneath the hem of my sweatshirt and

lets them drift upwards, taking the soft material with them as he kisses along the exposed skin. Goosebumps trail in their wake. He tugs my jeans down.

I'm wearing the same pink thong as the night we went swimming a few hundred feet from where we are now, and I can tell Wes remembers by the way his eyes flare with additional heat.

His hand slides down my abdomen and inside my lacy underwear. Every nerve ending in my body comes to life as he moves his fingers in my most intimate place, and it doesn't take long for pleasure to erupt through every last one, blanketing my entire body in warmth despite the chilly temperature.

Wes leans down and kisses me again. It's not as frenzied as before. It's soft and intimate. Filled with shared secrets and singular moments.

We're quiet after that, soaking up each other's company. I feel closer to him than I ever have before. Not because I just shared more with him physically than I have with anyone else, but because it's accompanied with an emotional intimacy I've never shared with anyone else, either. With an emotion I'm scared to name.

"Do you want to go inside?" Wes asks. "It's getting cold."

"Inside?" I ask.

"Yeah. I have a key to the cabin."

"What? You do?"

"My uncle only comes for a couple weeks in the summer now. He likes to have me look in on the place during the rest of the year."

"Your uncle gave you keys to a cabin he never uses? That's convenient."

Wes smirks. "I've never used it like that. I just stop in a couple times a month to make sure everything's working. I've been here more with you than in the past three years combined. I would have suggested it before, but I didn't want you to think I expected anything."

"You're not worried about that now?" I ask.

"Not really," Wes replies, still smirking. "You obviously have no issue escalating things when you want to."

I blush. "It's not that I haven't wanted to before," I admit. "But that—that was the first time I'd done any of that."

Wes gives me a soft smile. "I'm not in a rush, Maeve. I'm good with whatever. I promise."

I study his features, ones that have been familiar ever since the Glenmont game against Alleghany our freshman year catapulted him to local fame. The county newspaper the following morning featured a full page spread, heralding him as Alleghany's saving grace after they'd resigned themselves to another four years of frustration.

I don't see Alleghany's quarterback when I look at him now, though. At the twinkling blue eyes and the ruffled light brown hair.

They're right there, those three words. On the tip of my tongue.

"Let's go inside," I say instead.

Being alone with Wes in the cabin suddenly seems less dangerous than staying in his car. We both get fully dressed, and then slide out of his car and head to the front door of the cabin. I study the structure closely for the first time.

I'm normally too eager to see Wes to take in the scenery, although I've spent dozens of hours sitting right in front of it over the past couple months.

The cabin is small. Welcoming. Rather than traditional logs, the exterior of it is constructed from vertical boards of wood. The planks are weathered from years of exposure to the elements. A small fire pit sits to the right of the front door, and directly behind it is the outside shell of a massive brick fireplace.

I follow Wes up the two front steps, shivering. Now that we've left the wind shelter of his car, the icy gale rips through the cotton material of my sweatshirt with no barrier to block it.

Wes unlocks the front door and flicks on the lights. I step on top of a striped, multi-colored rug, glancing around the living room curiously. An overstuffed, plush couch stretches almost the full length of the room, facing the massive fireplace that takes up most of the wall. A small coffee table sits between the couch and fireplace, the surface littered with old magazines and well-worn paperbacks. There's a dark green wood stove sitting in the corner.

The floor plan is open, so I can see past the couch into the kitchen, with a small eating nook off to one side. A sliding door leads to a screened porch that juts off from the wall of the cabin, overlooking the woods that separate it from the lake.

"I like it," I tell Wes, smiling.

He grins back. "Yeah, I loved coming here as a kid. I used to beg my parents for a bunk bed back in the city the same way I had here."

"How come your uncle doesn't come here anymore?" I ask.

Wes shrugs. "I'm pretty sure my mom told him about the affairs. Or he found out somehow. He and my dad never got along, but things have been especially tense the past couple of years. They've barely spent any time here since the summer after our freshman year."

"They?"

"My uncle, aunt, and cousin. He's the one who threw that party we first talked at."

"Oh, that's right," I recall. "Are you guys close?"

"We were when we were younger. Not so much anymore. He's a few years older, and we hardly see each other these days."

"Is this you?" I ask, picking up a framed photograph of a young boy holding up a small fish proudly. I know it is. The little kid has the same eyes and dimpled smile as the grown-up Wes standing in front of me.

"Yeah, it is."

"Who's this?" I ask, pointing to the older man just visible behind him.

"My grandfather. He had this place built when my mom was little."

"So she grew up coming here, too?"

"Yeah, she always wanted to move to Fayetteville, actually, but my dad said it was too important for his business to stay in the city. Guess her catching him with his secretary finally made him open to the idea." Wes lets out a derisive snort, but I hear the underlying pain in his words.

I give him a sympathetic smile. "How come you moved to Alleghany, then?"

"She found a house she liked better there," Wes replies.

"Huh."

My use of Wes's casual catchphrase doesn't accurately convey how I'm feeling. I'm imagining how different—how much easier —my life would be if Weston Cole had moved to Fayetteville instead of Alleghany.

Wes follows my train of thought. "Yeah." He sighs.

We rarely discuss the rivalry anymore. Not because it's become any less a part of our relationship—the exact opposite. Every piece of myself I give to Wes is a part I lose elsewhere.

It was one thing to talk to Wes, to confide in him. A mistake, but a minor one. A forgivable one.

Kissing him? I know everyone in Glenmont would consider it a betrayal. Treason. Even Brooke and Sarah, despite their repeated comments about Wes's attractiveness.

Having feelings—serious, fathomless—feelings toward him? Inexplicable.

And can only end badly.

"There a bathroom in this place?" I need a minute. Away from his knowing blue eyes.

"Yeah, through the kitchen to the left."

"Okay, I'll be right back."

I head toward the kitchen, barely registering the decor through the rest of the cabin. The building extends back further than I estimated. I pass two bedrooms before I come to the bathroom; I realize why when I enter the bathroom. I look out the window into a grove of pines. It gives the impression of being inside a treehouse, which I realize was probably the architect's intent.

I go to the bathroom, and then study my reflection in the mirror above the sink as I wash my hands. I look the same as always. Blonde hair, green eyes, smattering of freckles. My straight hair's a little more mussed than usual, which I blame on the wind I can hear howling outside. Wes's hands also probably deserve some blame.

I don't look any different. But I feel different.

Something changed between Wes and me in the car earlier. Aside from the obvious. I didn't realize how much I trust Wes. How the original attraction and fascination between us has hardened, deepened into emotions I've never felt.

Maybe my brazen actions started as a way to prove something to myself—as a way to mark my claim. But I wouldn't have followed through unless I trusted Wes. Fully. Not just believed he was a good person—believed he would keep what I told him in confidence—but really trusted him.

I'm in deep with Weston Cole. I've known it for months, and I think I knew there was the potential for this when we first talked in the woods almost two and a half years ago.

Before he told me about his dad.

Before I told him about mine.

I don't believe in love at first sight. You can't love someone, really love them, just based on how they look. You love someone based on their dreams, their character, their hopes, how they make you feel. But I do believe you can spot potential at first sight. Because I had an inkling Weston Cole had the potential to implode my cautious, predictable world from that moment in the woods, long before I had any real reason to suspect he might.

He's chipped away at one of the things I thought was set in stone for months, and with one bout of jealousy, I just forever altered it.

I'm from Glenmont. I'm obligated to hate anyone from Alleghany.

And I don't hate Weston Cole. I love him.

Most girls would probably be thrilled about this realization. And a part of me is. But it also poses a serious problem with no easy answer.

I'm screwed either way now.

I'm stuck between a rock and a hard place, between Glenmont and Alleghany.

Between love for Wes and my allegiance to my hometown. To my father and brother.

When I re-emerge into the living room, it's to find Wes has started a fire in the wood stove. It fills the room with a cozy crackling sound and welcome heat. He's also sprawled across the massive couch, looking completely at ease. His expression doesn't change when he looks at me, and I'm relieved. I was half-worried he'd be able to read my amorous feelings for him on my face.

"I was going to start a fire in the fireplace instead, but I wasn't

143

sure how long you wanted to stay for," he explains. "The wood stove can just die down on its own."

"I'm good to stay for a bit," I tell him. "My parents think I'm at Sarah's still and won't be expecting me back for a while."

I take a seat on the opposite end of the couch. It's a testament to its length we're both able to fit. Wes is easily over six feet, and I'm five foot eight.

"You have your trip tomorrow, right?"

"Yeah," Wes replies. "It was supposed to be right before Thanksgiving break, but I was nominated for this award, and Coach Blake said I needed to attend."

"An award?" I ask.

Wes is confident, but I wouldn't describe him as cocky. At least around me. So I'm not surprised he looks a little sheepish when he replies. I'm guessing it's also because the sport he plays is a sensitive subject between us.

"Yeah, it's for the senior who contributed the most to the school's athletic program. They don't give it out every year, so it's kind of a big deal, I guess."

"Sounds like a big deal to me."

Wes shrugs a silent affirmation.

His reluctance emboldens me. "Do you think you'll win? Against Glenmont?" I ask, despite the epiphany I just had in the bathroom.

Maybe because of it.

We're rapidly approaching the peak of the Alleghany and Glenmont rivalry. The moment everyone's been anticipating ever since Weston Cole and Liam Stevens first collided as freshman. The finale.

Everyone but me.

Everyone else has already chosen their side.

Everyone will think they know which side I'm on.

But I don't.

Wes had been staring at the fireplace, but his eyes leap to mine as soon as the words leave my mouth.

"Do I think we'll win?" he repeats.

It's my turn to nod. I keep my face blank, not wanting to sway his response one way or the other. I know how badly Liam wants this, but I know Wes does too. And I don't think Wes will lie to me.

"Yeah, I do," he tells me seriously, and I feel a rush of elation and unease.

Elation, because I want him to succeed. Unease, because him succeeding means other people I care about won't. Not just my father and Liam, but Matt, Sam, all the Glenmont players who I've watched prepare for the final battle against Alleghany with single-minded determination.

"Okay," is all I say in response.

"Okay?" Wes echoes, searching my face.

"I was just wondering," I tell him. "There wasn't a right answer. Or a wrong one."

Wes's probing gaze makes me worried he's going to push for a more telling explanation, so I lean forward and grab a deck of playing cards off the coffee table.

"Do you know how to play Spite and Malice?" I ask him.

"Should I take the name personally?" Wes replies, sitting up.

"I didn't come up with the name," I promise him, smiling slightly. "It's my grandmother's favorite card game, and how I spent most of the week in South Carolina."

"I've never played it."

"Want to?" I ask, starting to shuffle the deck.

"I told you I'm good with whatever you want to do."

"I thought you were talking about sex, not card games," I reply, as I deal the cards.

Wes smirks. "I was, but it applies here, too."

I can't help but smirk back at him as I explain the rules of the card game. And contemplate what a dangerous offer that is.

Because when it comes to Weston Cole...I'm rapidly learning there's not much I *don't* want to do with him.

CHAPTER FIFTEEN

WESTON

The start of the trip to Lincoln University is expected. My parents smile in public and argue in private. I was surprised my mother decided to come with us. There's not much we do as a family these days. I tend to avoid being around my father as much as possible, which he doesn't seem to have any problem with unless he needs me for some reason.

Of course, that's the whole point of this trip. For my father to relive his glory days, and to show me off. Interestingly, my father never played football. People always assume that he did, and I can tell it irks him. He played baseball in high school, and never pursued any sports in college.

He plays it off when people ask, saying he was too busy with academics to worry about a game, or that he chose to get involved with other activities on campus. He's never discouraged or encouraged my playing, but I know the accolades I receive from football are a source of pride to him.

Maybe the only source where I'm concerned.

They're also the centerpiece of this visit.

Lincoln's campus is stunning. Perfectly maintained, imposing, and impressive. Brick buildings line the smooth path that cuts through the very heart of campus.

I've let my father's urging negatively color my impression of the school, but walking along the tree-lined pavement, coming here doesn't seem like such a hardship. The feeling is amplified when the football stadium comes into view.

Alleghany's football stadium is larger and nicer than most high school facilities. But it pales in comparison to Lincoln's. I catch my first glimpse of the massive structure looming ahead long before we reach it.

A gray-haired, stoic man is waiting for us outside the main gates. Even before he introduces himself, I can tell he's the head coach. He has the same no-nonsense, I-have-the-power-to-make-you-run-until-you-puke air about him Coach Blake always exudes.

Sure enough, he gives my hand a firm shake and introduces himself as Coach Alberts. I follow him through the main gates and down a long, cement-paved walkway. And then we're inside the stadium.

"Wow," I breathe.

Coach Alberts seems to appreciate my reaction. "Yup, it gets me every time, too," he admits. "Even after fifteen years."

The thrill of running out onto Alleghany's football field in front of a screaming crowd always electrifies me, but Lincoln's stadium has an undeniable presence all of its own. Even empty.

Thousands and thousands of seats gleam under the late fall sunshine, curving upwards to allow every occupant the best possible view. I can only imagine what it would feel like to play in front of such a massive audience. Like you're on a stage? Under a spotlight?

Coach Alberts leads me and my parents through a side door I

hadn't noticed, into the team locker room. Once again, it's nicer than Alleghany's excessive facilities—almost ostentatious.

Every surface shines, and each locker is made of a dark brown, almost black wood, with a gold nameplate above each one inscribed with a player's jersey number and last name. Past the lockers, I see a laundry room, kitchen, and an array of training and physical therapy equipment. A giant mural is painted on the wall displaying the university's mascot, with the words *No Excuses, No Egotism* prominently painted over it.

"I like the tagline," I say, nodding to it.

"One of my former players came up with it. Bit ironic, since he had an ego roughly the same size as his home state of Nebraska. The team voted to have it painted when he won us a national championship a few years ago."

I grin as I study the elaborately drawn letters.

"Come on, I'll show you folks the rest of the facility."

I follow Coach Alberts deeper into the locker room, with my parents close behind. The plush surroundings continue until we finally reach the end of the long hall. He leads us out another doorway, down a hallway, and we're back outside the stadium in the same spot we started.

"Well, there you have it. If you'd like to grab lunch on campus, you should have received meal tickets for the dining hall from the Admissions Office," Coach Alberts tells us.

My father replies before I have a chance to. "We did, but I wanted to show Weston around Lincoln's downtown and eat there as well. I haven't had one of Joe's burgers in years."

My mother and I both look at him in shock.

"They are the best," Coach Alberts agrees. "You're in for a treat, Cole."

"I'm looking forward to it," I respond.

"All right, then. We'll be in touch with your coach and you

directly, Cole," he tells me. "I'm not authorized to tell you anything official, but between us, I think there's an excellent chance you'll be invited to suit up in Lincoln green next fall."

"Thank you, Coach Alberts," I reply. "I appreciate it, and you taking the time to show us around today."

"My pleasure, Cole. Every player who receives an official offer has an opportunity to come back to campus and practice with the team. I hope to see you then."

Coach Alberts shakes my hand, and my parents', and then heads back inside the looming stadium.

"That went well," my father remarks as we head in the direction of the parking lot where we left our rental car.

"I thought so, too," my mother contributes. "Seems like you'll definitely have Lincoln as an option, Weston."

"Option?" my father scoffs.

"It's his decision, Richard," my mother replies. Her response is unexpected. I thought she would back my father up on this.

To my surprise, my father nods. Not surprising? "He'd be a fool not to, though. And I know I didn't raise a fool."

We reach the sedan rented from the airport and head back toward the small downtown area we drove through on our way to campus. My father parks the car in front of a small bookstore.

"Come on," he urges my mother and me as he exits the car.

We both climb out and follow my father along the cement sidewalk. It's a cute town, probably twice the size of Alleghany, but still retaining the charm and individualism absent from most cities. The storefronts are all displaying handmade decorations of turkeys and fall leaves in anticipation of the upcoming holiday. Pedestrians milling around us stop to say hello to each other.

As we walk along, my father slings his arm around my shoulders while he points out the coffee shops, bars, and restaurants he used to frequent during his college days. It's strange. There's no one around to see us—no one that we know, at least. And yet my father is acting like the present, loving figure I recall from my early childhood. The one who would sneak me extra s'mores around the campfire after my mother had cut me off. The dad who would spend hours attempting to catch the throws that would often reach the grass long before him, back when my forearm was shorter than the football I was tossing.

It's a foreign feeling, the heavy weight over my shoulders. Not only because I'm taller than my father for the first time since he's done this. I thought I hated my father. That any chance at a functioning, normal relationship died with his fidelity. It's both reassuring and alarming to realize that might not be the case.

Knowing my father, it won't take long for him to set fire to this olive branch, though. So I don't shrug his arm off. I let it rest there.

I pretend like I'm a normal guy, with normal problems and normal parents.

I pretend the Alleghany rivalry with Glenmont doesn't exist and my father didn't destroy our family.

We reach the end of the downtown area, and my father turns to the right. Set back from the street is a small building with neon lights proclaiming it to be *Joe's Burgers*, and my father heads toward the front door.

It's one of the last places I can picture my pretentious father stepping a loafer-clad foot inside, and my mother looks equally startled by our destination.

"Come on," my father urges. "I'm starving."

My mother and I trail after him reluctantly. The small restaurant is bustling with activity that swirls around the grease laden air we emerge into. My father flags down a waitress, who directs us to a small booth that contains some of the last available seats.

I drop on the cracked vinyl, and my mother sinks down next

to my father rather reluctantly. The last time the three of us went out to eat together was for my birthday, and the mix of boisterous chatter and loud eighties music surrounding us is a stark contrast to the upscale steakhouse where that strained meal took place.

Another waitress comes over as soon as we've sat down, depositing glasses of water and menus on the metal tabletop. She looks to be close to my age, and she eyes me with an interest that seems a bit excessive, considering the fact I'm obviously here with my middle-aged parents.

"Afternoon, y'all!" she chirps, snapping her gum. "Any drinks besides water? Gathering you're not locals, so I'm guessing you'll need a minute on the menu."

"I went to Lincoln," my father informs her. "So I already know what I'll be ordering." He gives her a charming smile, and I have to resist the urge to roll my eyes. "But these two will probably need a few more minutes." He gestures to my mother and me.

"No problem," the waitress says. "I'll be back in a bit." She sashays away, and I drop my eyes to the laminated menu.

"What are you getting, Dad?" I ask.

"Their original burger," he responds. "You should try it, son. Best burger I've ever had."

I'm surprised by his response. Not only because he called me 'son', but because he's talking as though he's genuinely nostalgic. I always thought he was pushing Lincoln on me for the satisfaction of telling his business partners and clients I would be attending one of the most competitive schools in the country. For the continuation of his legacy. Looking at him leaning back against the cheaply upholstered booth, I wonder if that's actually the case.

"You shouldn't order a burger, Richard," my mother comments. "You're supposed to be watching your cholesterol."

"Catherine, I have been. I even ate that broccoli casserole you made last week. One burger is not going to kill me."

"Famous last words," my mother retorts.

"What if I get a side salad?"

I view my parents through fresh eyes as I watch them argue over the health of my father's heart. I've always wondered how the facade of a perfect family could be so important to my mother she'd be willing to endure my father's infidelity.

But listening to her listing off the studies she's read about reducing cholesterol, I wonder if that's really the reason she's chosen to stay with him. I figured love fled their marriage the same time my father's eye started wandering, but watching them together now, I wonder if that's truly the case.

If my feelings for Maeve have taught me anything, it's that sometimes you love the people you shouldn't. Because I do. Love her. Even though there are a lot of reasons why I probably shouldn't.

Those reasons have never made sense, though, and they've become sillier and sillier the more time I've spent with Maeve. I have no reason to hate anyone from Glenmont, really. I don't want to beat their team any less, but the rivalry with the neighboring town is meaningless. Pointless.

But I don't know what to do about it. Don't know how Maeve feels about it now. She's more invested in it. She's grown up with it. Her family's invested in it.

I'm also worried. Worried she won't pick me if she has to choose a side.

So I keep putting off bringing the subject up. I figure it will be an easier conversation to have once the football season has ended.

The same waitress comes back over a few minutes later to take our lunch orders. My mother orders a turkey sandwich, and I end up selecting the burger my father suggested to me. He smiles at me when I do.

But my father doesn't order it.

My father orders a salad with grilled chicken instead of the burger he was praising, and for the first time since I discovered he was unfaithful to my mom, I wonder if he still loves her, too.

CHAPTER SIXTEEN

MAEVE

"Happy Birthday, Maeve!" My mother calls the greeting out as I appear downstairs, making her way over from the kitchen table to kiss me on the side of my head.

"Thanks, Mom," I respond, heading over to the fridge and pouring some orange juice.

"Any big plans for the day?" she asks as I help myself to a bowl of cereal and take a seat at the kitchen island.

"Not really. I have practice after school, and then I was thinking of sleeping over at Sarah's tonight." I wait, but my mother doesn't bat an eyelash.

I'm grateful the real estate market has been booming. She hasn't been to her book club in months, which is the only way I've been getting away with the number of times I've supposedly been at one of my friend's houses lately.

"Sounds good, honey," is all she says. "We'll celebrate as a family on Saturday, all right?"

"Yup, that sounds good," I reply, shoveling cereal into my mouth. I glance at the clock. I'm running late. Rapidly finishing my breakfast, I put my dishes in the dishwasher. "I've got to get to school. Did Liam already leave?"

"Yes, he and your father headed in early for some film review, I believe. I'll be glad when this game against Alleghany is over. Those two are running themselves ragged."

"Yeah, I will be too," I reply. More than she knows. "I'll see you later, Mom."

"Bye, sweetie."

I'm late enough I have to park in the furthest lot from the school's main entrance. I'm glad I put on my down winter jacket on the way out the door. It feels especially chilly this morning. Any trace of summer is long gone, but the brisk gusts of wind making the dead leaves that litter the parking lot dance indicate winter is just around the corner.

I burst through the blasé front doors of Glenmont High just as the morning announcements are starting. I rush past the few students lingering in the hallway and hurry into my first period Chemistry class. I give my teacher an apologetic smile as I take my seat.

As soon as I settle in it, I'm reminded Glenmont High includes birthdays in the morning announcements. When every head swivels in my direction. Just like every other year since kindergarten, Liam and I's names are the only two announced.

Once the loudspeaker shuts off, Sam starts an off-key rendition of "Happy Birthday" that the entire class joins in on. It's both sweet and supremely embarrassing.

I'm flooded with well wishes from classmates all morning. On my way to third period, I see Liam for the first time. He gives me a hug.

"Happy birthday, little sis."

"Happy birthday, big bro by two minutes," I respond.

Liam grins at me before continuing down the locker-lined hallway.

When I enter the cafeteria, Brooke and Sarah both leap up and give me hugs.

Sarah pushes a small pink box toward me. "Happy Birthday, Maeve!" I open it to find a chocolate peanut butter cupcake from my favorite bakery in Glenmont.

"Awww, thank you guys," I tell them. "You didn't have to do this."

"Of course we did," Brooke replies. "You only turn eighteen once, Maeve. Speaking of, when are we celebrating? You only have practice until six tonight, right?"

I'm saved from having to answer when I'm suddenly lifted up and spun around. I turn to see Matt's smiling face. "Happy Birthday!"

I smile. "Thanks, Matt."

"A twirl, Crawford?" Sam asks as he takes a seat at our usual table. "You better up your game. I managed a thirty-person serenade, and I'm not even the one with a thing for Maeve."

The words are teasing, so I expect Matt to laugh or make a joke. Instead, he glares at Sam. An awkward silence descends upon the table, and I scramble to fill it.

"I can't do today, Brooke. But let's celebrate this weekend, okay?"

She's quick to follow my lead. "Perfect. I'll start planning!"

That worries me slightly. Birthday celebrations Brooke has planned in previous years have included prank calls and a visit from the Glenmont Fire Department. But I'm more preoccupied by what Sam just said, and how Matt reacted. Sam's always been a jokester, but something tells me he was stating the truth about Matt's feelings.

I add Matt's possible interest in me to the ever-growing list of things that could easily implode on me at any moment.

The rest of lunch is uneventful, and the twenty-five minutes that normally feel short seem to drag. Mostly because I keep checking my phone.

Sarah catches me obsessively tapping the screen. "You expecting a message, Maeve?" she teases.

"Ha, no," I lie. "Just eager for school to be over."

"Amen to that," Brooke chimes in with. "I've got a quiz next period."

I make a sound of sympathy as I check my phone again. Still nothing from Wes. The disappointment is silly. We're not friends on social media. He doesn't go to Glenmont, so he didn't hear the announcement. I mentioned the date to him once. Months ago. And we're already supposed to meet later tonight, so it's not like I won't see him. But stupidly, selfishly, I want him to remember.

When lunch ends, Matt lingers. We have English together next, but I usually walk with Brooke and Sarah, and he typically leaves with the football guys.

"You coming, Maeve?" he asks.

I watch Brooke and Sarah exchange a *look*. "Yeah, sure," I say casually.

I need to figure out a way to make my feelings clear to Matt, and I'm not sure how to do it. It's not like I can blurt out I'm dating Weston Cole. Despite my father and brother's indifference, no guy from Glenmont has ever shown a serious interest in me, and the fact that it's Matt makes it all that much worse. He's one of Liam's closest friends, and my parents practically consider him a second son. I don't want things to turn awkward between us, and I don't know how to keep them from becoming so.

Matt chats easily as we walk down the hallway about how awful the essay we got assigned last class is, but I'm barely listening. I'm weighing whether I should say anything to him. Before I can decide, Erin Waters approaches us.

"Maeve! I've been looking for you all day. Big news! The school committee approved all the prom plans."

"That's great, Erin," I respond. "Thanks for all the work you did on that. I know I haven't been pulling my weight on student council lately."

My vice president makes a *pffttt* sound. "Please, I know how hectic things are for you. I was happy to do it, and you came up with some great ideas. Just wanted to let you know. Happy birthday, by the way!"

"Thanks," I call out as she bounces down the hallway.

"I always forget you're our class president," Matt remarks as we continue along.

"I try to as well." Freshman year, I ran for the position, mostly because no one else wanted to, and one of my teachers suggested I should. I've always been a people pleaser. Not so shockingly, no one ran sophomore year either, and here I still am senior year. It's a fun group of people, but a thankless job.

Matt asks me some questions about what our meetings are like, and that carries our conversation until we reach English class. I'm torn, half grateful the topic of Sam's comment didn't come up, half mad at myself for chickening out and not setting him straight.

Practice feels like it lasts longer than usual, but the clock in the gym reads six exactly when we all finish the last set of sprints.

"Nice work, ladies!" Coach Bloom calls. "That's the hustle I want to see on Friday. And in the finals, since I have full confidence we'll be playing in that game, as well. Rest up. I'll see you all tomorrow."

Everyone begins to filter toward the locker rooms, including me, but I stop when Coach Bloom shouts my name.

I turn around and head back over to her. "Yes, Coach?"

"Just wanted to check in with you, Stevens. I know how much you've got going on. Everything okay?"

"Yes, I'm good."

"Okay. You still up for running morning practices the week of the championship?"

"Yes, I am," I confirm.

"All right, we can discuss details that week. We should also have another conversation about colleges now that you've started applying. I expect there will be a lot of scouts at the championship game, and if you keep playing the way you have been, you'll have no shortage of options."

I nod. "Okay. Thanks, Coach."

"Of course, Stevens. Happy birthday."

I smile. "Thank you."

I head into the locker room and gather my things to take a shower, which I don't normally do. I only live ten minutes from the high school, and it's usually easier just to shower at home.

Becca raises her eyebrows at me as I walk back into the main locker room with dripping hair. Everyone else has already left.

"Big birthday plans, Stevens?" she asks.

"Nope," I lie, keeping my tone light. "Just going out to dinner with the family. Wasn't sure if I'd have time to shower when I got home."

"All right." Becca buys my explanation readily enough, and I feel a twinge of guilt. How many times have I lied to my friends and family today? Dozens? Over the past few months? Hundreds? It's an unsettling realization. "Happy Birthday, Maeve."

"Thanks, Becca," I respond. "See you tomorrow."

She nods and leaves me alone in the empty locker room. I dry off and pull on the outfit I carefully selected for tonight before putting on my down jacket and shielding most of it. At least *I'll* know I look good.

I grab all my soccer gear and head out into the parking lot. Only a few cars remain, barely visible under the sporadically spaced lights. One is flickering, and I hurry along, eager to reach my car. Wes was right. I do freak myself out listening to those true crime podcasts. I reach the safety of my car and toss my bag in the backseat before turning the key in the ignition. The engine roars to life and I blast the heat in an attempt to dry my damp hair. I pull out of the parking lot, embarking on the now familiar route to Wes's uncle's cabin.

The black SUV is already waiting when I arrive at the cabin, and I eagerly jump out of my car as soon as I park. I round the back bumper and then freeze.

Wes is leaning against the trunk of his car, holding a bouquet of flowers.

"Happy birthday, Stevens." He flashes me the dimpled smile that gets me. Every. Single. Time.

I swallow the lump in my throat and force my feet to keep walking forward. "You remembered," I whisper as I reach him.

He hands me the colorful bunch of blossoms and gives me a quick kiss. "Of course I did," Wes replies. "Now come on, the pizza is getting cold." He heads toward the driver's seat of his car, and I climb in on the passenger side. Sure enough, his car is filled with the delicious aroma of hot pizza. "I was thinking we could go to the park," he tells me. "But it's colder than I was hoping."

"I'm willing to risk frostbite," I tell him. I'd sit on an iceberg if it meant I could be alone with him.

Wes chuckles. "All right, then."

We haven't been back to the park where we met over the summer in a while, and I'm surprised by how nostalgic I feel as Wes parks in the lot and we climb out. This was where I first fell in love with him, even if I didn't realize it at the time. Wes grabs a thick blanket, paper plates, a stack of napkins, two cans of cola, and a pizza box from the backseat, and I trail after him, impressed.

"Were you a Boy Scout or something?" I ask as he spreads the blanket and sets everything else down on top of it.

Wes grins. "No, I just copied what you brought for my birthday. Blanket and food."

I laugh at that as I settle down on the soft fleece. "So? How was Lincoln?" I ask as I grab a slice of the steaming pizza. I blow on it for a minute before taking a bite. The gooey cheese contrasts the crisp crust perfectly. I haven't seen Wes since he returned from his college trip, and all he sent me was *Good* when I texted him asking how it went.

"It was good," he replies.

I roll my eyes. "So you said in your text. That doesn't really tell me anything, Wes."

"I know," he admits, as he sits down and helps himself to his own slice of pizza. "The truth is, I don't know how to feel about it."

"What do you mean?"

"I liked it. I liked it a lot."

"Isn't that a good thing? A great thing?" I respond.

"I guess. You should've seen my father. He was thrilled. Showing us all around, bringing me to all these places. He was…"

"Acting like a dad," I supply. It means something different to us, and I know he'll understand my meaning.

"Yeah. Exactly," Wes replies. "I didn't want to go there just because he wanted me to. Now…I don't know if I *really* want to go there, or if it's because he wants me to. If the same reason I didn't want to go is the reason I might want to now. Does that make any sense?"

"It makes perfect sense."

"It's in Michigan," Wes adds. The words are innocuous enough, but his tone indicates he considers the location to be a downside.

"Do you have some sort of issue with wolverines I don't know about?" I joke.

Wes snorts. "It doesn't have anything to do with the state's nickname." He pauses. "It's not close to any of the schools you're considering."

I stare at him, stunned. Finally, I regain my voice. "I, uh, I actually applied to Lincoln," I admit to him.

"You did?" Wes is the one who looks shocked now.

"Yeah, I did."

"Are they recruiting you?"

"I'd have to try to walk on there. Coach Bloom said she thought I'd have a shot, so I applied."

"Wow. I didn't realize you were—I mean, you didn't mention Lincoln. Before."

I shrug. "Things change." It's as close as I'm willing to get to admitting he's the sole reason I added Lincoln to my list.

"Yeah, they do," is all Wes says.

We're both quiet as we eat the rest of the pizza and survey the stretch of grass before us.

It's a perfect moment—until it begins to pour.

We both scramble. Wes balls up the rapidly dampening blanket while I grab the remains of our dinner. The two of us race side-by-side back to Wes's car, eagerly clambering inside before we're entirely drenched. Our wet clothes squeak against the leather seats.

"That was not in the weather report," Wes grumbles as we stare at the heavy drops pummeling the earth.

I laugh at his disgruntled expression. "It was still my favorite birthday dinner," I inform him.

"Can't ask for more than that," Wes replies as he turns on the car.

Hot air flows out of the vents, warming the saturated fabric of our clothes. I pull off my winter coat, glad it deterred most of the water from reaching my outfit.

I lean back against the leather seat and watch the dark silhouettes of the trees flash by as Wes heads back in the direction of the cabin.

The song playing on the radio changes, and I smile when I recognize the introductory strains to "Shut Up and Dance."

"I love this song," I tell Wes.

He smirks over at me. "Keeping up with all the current hits, huh?"

I roll my eyes.

Wes suddenly pulls the car over onto the shoulder of the road.

"Is something wrong with the car?" I ask him, confused and slightly panicked. How the hell am I going to explain what I am doing in Weston Cole's car?

"The car's fine. Get out," Wes instructs.

"What?" I laugh. "It's raining."

"Listen to the song, Stevens." Wes grins at me and exits the driver's seat.

"That's the girl's part," I call out after him. I hear him laugh as I open my own door and climb out into the downpour.

I round the back of Wes's car to see he's opened the trunk, providing a slight respite from the precipitation and allowing the strains of *Walk the Moon*'s song to drift through the SUV and outside to us.

"Dance with me, Maeve."

I study him for a moment as the rain saturates my hair and begins dribbling down my face. I'm fucked. Completely and totally screwed.

Because Weston Cole is looking at me like he's in love with me, and I'm already in love with him.

Finally, I comply with his request and walk underneath the makeshift canopy so I'm standing in front of him. He wraps his arms around me and spins me so my back is to his front. I lean back against him, letting him support most of my weight. We sway together, much more slowly that the beat suggests.

I watch the sheets of rain fall as I lean against the sturdy support of Wes's body. I've always loved the rain. There's something soothing about it. Refreshing. The way it rinses and cleanses everything. The way it leaves everything looking better than before it fell. The way it provides a fresh start.

New opportunities.

Endless possibilities.

The song ends, but neither of us moves away. Wes doesn't say anything. I'd think I was leaning against a wall, if not for the heat his body is exuding and the thud of his heartbeat against my back. It's not until a car whizzes by, sending a spray of water that misses us by inches, that we both move.

I dash back toward the passenger side door. Only one thought crosses my mind as I make the short journey through the rapidly falling drops of water.

That I hope the possibilities between Wes and me always feel this limitless.

CHAPTER SEVENTEEN

WESTON

Maeve leans over and kisses me as soon as I park the car outside my uncle's cabin.

It's not a quick, cursory, goodbye kiss. She climbs across the middle console to straddle me, and I groan as I slip my hands underneath the soft sweater she's wearing. She shivers as my hands meet her smooth, warm skin, and begins to gyrate her body against mine in a way that makes thinking clearly extremely difficult.

Which is why I pull away before I can't think at all.

The only sound is the tapping of rain against the roof of my car and our heavy breathing.

"Why did you stop?" Maeve whispers.

"Did you not want me to?" I ask, smirking at her.

Maeve huffs out a laugh. "Of course not. Especially on my birthday."

"I don't want you to think I'm only after one thing."

Her eyes soften. "I don't think that." Maeve pauses. "You said we could do whatever I wanted to."

"I also said I was in no rush. It's a big deal, Maeve."

"How many girls have you slept with?" she counters.

I tense slightly at the question no guy wants to answer, and our bodies are still pressed together, so I'm sure she can tell.

"Sev—uh, eight," I admit.

I can tell by the way she stills it's more than she expected.

"I'm not going to apologize for my past, Maeve. But none of them meant anything to me. It sounds shitty to say, but it's true. I couldn't even tell you most of their names."

"I don't expect you to apologize, Wes," Maeve replies. "But that's—that's a lot of girls to be compared to."

"There's no comparison, Maeve. I've never had sex with a girl I have feelings for. I have feelings for you."

I'm tempted to tell her just how strong my feelings are, but immediately following a revelation of my sexual history doesn't feel like the perfect moment.

Maeve studies my face in the dim light cast by the dashboard for a long moment. "I told my parents I was spending the night at Sarah's," she confides.

My heartbeat quickens. "You did?" I say, like an idiot. Because she literally just said so. But she also just said a lot more than that.

She nods, biting her lip.

"You're sure?"

"I'm sure." There's no hint of hesitation in her voice.

"Okay, let's go inside."

Maeve climbs out of the car as soon as the words leave my mouth. Rather than heading toward the cabin like I expect, she darts over to her car and retrieves a bag before she heads for the porch. As soon as she does, I let out a deep breath and then grab my own gym bag from the backseat.

I run through the rain to the porch where Maeve is already waiting. I unlock the front door, and flip on the lights that illuminate the living room and the rain streaking down the glass windowpanes.

The cabin is just as chilly as the last time we were here, so I head over to the wood stove to get a fire going. I take my time piling the wood inside and lighting the match. I'm nervous. And I don't get nervous. Not around other girls, not before big games.

This moment feels weighted. Important. And I'm terrified I'm going to mess it up. The fire roars to life as soon as I drop the match, and I move the grate back into place with a loud scrape. It rattles into the perfectly shaped opening.

I can feel Maeve's eyes on me as I turn around. I pick up the bag I dropped and head toward the ladder tucked in the corner.

She follows.

"Ladies first," I tell her. Maeve raises her eyebrows at me but slings her bag over her shoulder and starts climbing the worn wooden rungs without comment. I follow her.

"Romantic," Maeve remarks as I reach the top.

I snort as I study the loft I used to stay in when I visited Fayetteville with my parents. "My grandparents and parents stayed in the rooms downstairs. It felt weird to take you into one of those."

"But bunk beds seemed like a good idea?" I look over at Maeve, and she's grinning.

"Shut up, Stevens."

She drops her bag and strolls over to me. The thudding of my heart quickens with every step. She doesn't stop until she's close. Close enough, it feels like we're touching, even though we're not.

I can see every fleck of green in her eyes. Olive. Sage. Mint. Moss. Pine. Each shade is there. Swirling with the heat and the admiring emotion in her gaze.

She kisses me first, breaking the anticipation that's been steadily building between us. We stumble our way over to the bottom bunk. It's twice the size of the upper twin bed, but it's still a tight fit. I'm not exactly short, and neither is Maeve.

We tumble onto the faded quilt, side by side. We kiss for a while before Maeve grows impatient. Once again, she makes the first move, sliding her hands underneath the hem of my crewneck sweatshirt and pulling the material up and over my head, taking my t-shirt with it.

Maeve's eyes turn molten as she drags her hands across the exposed planes of my chest. She tugs at my jeans next, and I oblige her, pulling the denim off. Maeve does the same with hers. I yank the sweater over her head, and then we're both down to our underwear.

I pause, letting my eyes trail along her body until they stop to rest on the green eyes that have come to rule my world. She's stunning, but it's the trust teeming in her gaze that guts me.

Maeve Stevens trusts me. And it feels more potent in this moment than any other we've shared. Trust is a two-way street, and for us it's one littered with potholes and landmines. One that should have been a dead-end road based on nothing but our addresses.

For some reason, I placed blind faith in those green eyes sitting in the woods two and a half years ago, and I'm thankful for whatever compelled me to do so. I don't think we would be here if I hadn't.

I'm still experiencing the foreign feeling of nerves. Every other time I've done this, it's been a series of fumbled touches in the dark. Not the purposeful way we discarded most of our clothing.

The lights I turned on when we arrived are far from a spotlight, but they cast enough of a glow I can see everything. Every speck of green in her eyes, every freckle, every line of muscle.

I'm also entirely sober, which is another departure from what I've come to expect from sex.

I roll away from Maeve and grasp the gym bag I brought inside, digging through the assortment of clothes, granola bars, and empty water bottles until I find my wallet. I grab the condom out of it, pull down my boxer briefs, and roll it on. I turn to find Maeve has shed her underwear as well. I walk back over to her and hover over her figure, gradually closing the distance between our bodies until we're skin to skin.

I stare at her, trying to memorize this moment. The feel of her warm body against mine. The emotion swirling in her eyes.

"You *have* done this before, right?" Maeve teases as I continue to hesitate. I catch a glimmer of self-consciousness in her words.

"Stevens, I'm trying to set a mood here, okay?"

"Well, my current mood is impatient. Do you need me to do something? I thought this part was all you." She grins, and I laugh.

"I can handle it," I assure her as I ease inside. The amusement disappears from her face, and her startled gaze meet mine. "Are you okay?" I ask softly.

She nods rapidly a couple of times. "Yeah, it feels good. Weird, but good."

"Good," I repeat, trying to focus on anything besides how perfectly tight she feels.

I try to retain everything about this moment because I can feel it's one of *those*. A snippet of time I'll look back on and want to relive. Over and over and over again. I'm not thinking about anything. My mind goes blank. I just feel and observe. Details imprint on my brain.

The way Maeve's hair looks like spun gold in the soft light.

The sound of the rain lashing angrily against the metal roof above us.

The pleasure unfurling across her freckled face as I touch her everywhere.

Afterwards, Maeve lays snuggled against me, tucked under my throwing arm like a football. Reality filters back in, and with it comes the chilly air. Not much of the heat from the wood stove has diffused upstairs yet. I feel Maeve shiver, so I sit up and lean over to grab the blue gym bag that I left on the floor. I haul it on the bed with us and start pulling clothes out.

"I think I have a sweatshirt in here."

"I'll just wear this."

I look over to see Maeve is pulling the silky material of my football jersey over her head. A sight I never thought I would see. Maeve Stevens wearing a blue Alleghany Football jersey.

She looks like a goddamn fantasy—my goddamn fantasy—as she gives me a coy smile in response to the lust I'm sure is prominently displayed on my face.

"Fuck," I breathe.

"You like?" Maeve asks, grinning deviously as she stands on the side of the bed, not constrained by the smaller one above to give me the full effect. The blue fabric falls to her mid-thigh, and she twists so I can see my name and number displayed on her back.

I grab Maeve's bare legs, forcing her to tumble down on top of me.

"I love," I correct. I pause, teetering on the edge of a declaration that will upend our relationship for the second time tonight. I tip. "I love you, Maeve."

She just stares at me for a protracted moment. Her face is blank with shock, giving me absolutely no indication of how she feels about my statement. I doubt it's been more than a few seconds, but it seems like hours. I'm starting to panic when she finally speaks.

"You know, you were supposed to tell me you love me before we had sex. Or during. So I could second guess everything and wonder if you only said it to get laid or in the throes of passion."

I laugh. Only Maeve would use the phrase "throes of passion."

"Well, it's the first time I've said it," I admit to her. "So, figures I would do it wrong. I'm only good at one thing, remember?"

I watch as some of the moisture that's collected in Maeve's eyes spills over.

"I love you, Weston Cole."

CHAPTER EIGHTEEN

MAEVE

A week after my birthday, I enter my room and drop my backpack and soccer bag on the ground. I turn, and Sarah's sitting in my bed.

I jump.

"Shit, Sarah, you scared me. What are you doing in here?"

"I stopped by to see you. Your mom let me in before she left for a showing. She seemed surprised to see me...since apparently you spent several hours at my house last night?"

Crap.

"I must have said your house instead of Brooke's by mistake," I lie, pulling off my jacket and draping it on my chair.

"I was at Brooke's last night working on our English project," Sarah says flatly. "And you weren't at her house either. What the hell is going on with you lately, Maeve? You're hardly ever around anymore, and you're acting strange when you are."

I sigh. "Nothing's going on. I'm good, I promise. Just busy."

"Then where were you last night? Hell, where have you been the past few months? And don't say school, or soccer, or student council. Because you've always juggled all that before and still hung out with us."

I drop the gaze of one of my best friends, trying to come up with an excuse. Any excuse. I can't summon one.

"There's a guy," I confess.

Sarah's expression immediately shifts from concerned to delighted. "Oh my god! Seriously?!"

I nod.

"Who? Is it Matt?"

"What? No! Why would you say that?"

"Maeve, he's had a thing for you forever. Didn't you hear what Sam said at lunch last week?"

"Yeah, I did," I admit.

"So? Who is it, then?!"

I take a seat on my bed next to her. "I don't want to tell you."

As expected, Sarah looks even more intrigued. "Maeve! Tell me!"

"You have to swear you won't say anything to anyone else. Not even Maggie and Brooke."

"Are you serious?"

"Sarah!"

"Okay, okay, I promise. Tell me!"

I pick at a stray thread on my navy comforter. "Weston Cole."

"Maeve, I promised, okay! Be serious. Who is it?"

I look her straight in the eyes. "I already told you."

Both Brooke and Maggie cheer, so Sarah is my only close friend who doesn't play a sport. Who's never faced Alleghany and the barrage of bad blood head on. She also tends to be amenable. Pragmatic. There's no trace of either trait right now.

Sarah looks absolutely floored. "Weston fucking Cole? WESTON FUCKING COLE, Maeve? Please tell me you're joking. WESTON COLE?"

"Stop yelling his name," I hiss. "My dad is home. Probably Liam, too."

"I seriously can't believe this is happening. Is this even happening?"

I roll my eyes. "You don't believe me?"

"You're just saying his name to make whoever you're really secretly seeing seem totally fine, right?"

"Why would I lie to you about this?"

"Maeve, I was certain you hate Weston Cole as much as every other person in this town. More than most people. After the last three years…everything that he represents. Not to mention your dad. Liam! And I could maybe, *maybe* see Brooke or Maggie telling me something like this. Especially Brooke! She always talks about him, and she never thinks things through. But you think things through. You're loyal. And you're telling me you've been—what? Seeing Weston Cole? That you like Weston fucking Cole?"

I gnaw on my bottom lip. "I more than like him."

Sarah gasps. "Oh my god! Have you kissed him?"

One of my favorite things about Sarah is how unassuming she is. I know Maggie or Brooke would be much more blunt. I embrace the boldness Wes seems to pull out of me and tease my reserved friend a bit. "Yes. And a lot more."

Sarah looks at me, wide-eyed. "This isn't happening. This isn't happening," she chants, leaning back against the wall my bed is pushed against.

"Calm down, Sarah. You're the one who begged me to tell you."

"Maeve, we've been best friends since kindergarten, and I seriously can't think of anything you could tell me that would surprise me more than you telling me you've hooked up with Alleghany's quarterback. Is this some sort of prank you, Brooke, and Maggie came up with? Are you filming this?"

I climb off the bed and grab my jacket, pulling my phone out of the pocket.

"What are you doing?" Sarah asks.

"Proving it to you."

I tap *good at one thing* and my phone begins ringing. The video connects after only a couple of seconds.

"Hey, Stevens." Wes sends me a dimpled smile. His hair is damp, and he's shirtless. My mouth goes dry at the sight.

"Can you put a shirt on, Wes?"

"You're asking me to put clothes *on*? This is a change."

My cheeks burn. "Sarah came over and my mom mentioned how I was at her house last night…" I let my voice trail off. Wes is well aware I didn't spend any time last night with Sarah.

"So you told her," Wes supplements.

"She didn't believe me." I roll my eyes.

"Is she still there?"

"Yes, this is my way of proving it to her."

"How will she know you didn't hire a body double to pre-record this fake call?"

Sarah's mouth is literally agape as she listens to our conversation.

"You're not helping, Wes."

Wes sets his phone down and I watch him pull on a white undershirt and ruffle a towel through his short hair.

"I'm decent." He winks at me.

Sarah's still sitting on my bed, so I walk over and hold out the screen so she can see Wes.

"Hi, Sarah," he greets.

"Um, hi—hi," she stutters. "Weston," she adds, sounding a little out of breath.

I laugh, and she shoots me a glare. I turn the phone back to myself. "Thanks for showing your face."

"No problem." His grin grows devilish. "It's actually nice to be asked to show something on here other than my—"

I know Wes well enough to know where he's going with this. Or at least threatening to go. "Bye, Wes!" I hang up on him up mid-sentence.

I look over at Sarah. She still looks shell-shocked.

"Believe me now?" I ask.

My phone buzzes, so I glance down at it. I unlock my phone again to see I have two new texts from Wes. *By the way, I love you*, the first one reads. *Wasn't sure if I should say it with an audience*, the second one adds.

I love you, too, I reply. *I'll see you tonight.*

"Yeah, I do," Sarah replies. The shock hasn't faded from her face.

We sit in silence on my bed.

"You guys seem…serious." Sarah finally says.

"Yeah, we are."

"And he's *Weston Cole*."

I sigh. "I'm well aware. He's a lot more than a guy who happens to live in Alleghany, though. At least to me."

"He doesn't just live there, Maeve. He's their quarterback. *The* Eagle. Any guy from Alleghany would be bad, but him?"

"I know all that too," I assure her.

"And no one knows?"

"Except for you, now."

"I said I wouldn't say anything, and I won't," Sarah says. "But Maeve, this isn't going to end well."

"Probably not."

The months since Wes and I first kissed haven't yielded any solution to our main issue; I simply concluded I wanted him more than I cared about the consequences. And I clung to a naïve hope the fascination with him would fizzle and I would never be worse off.

"It just...happened."

Sarah nods, although I can tell from her expression she doesn't understand how it could. Honestly, I'd probably be thinking the same thing if I were her. She and I aren't the type of people to just let things happen. We overthink and over-analyze and assess every outcome. But in this instance, any reasonable outcome wouldn't have included Wes.

"I should get going," Sarah says, sliding off my bed. She hesitates before speaking again, and I know they'll be cautionary words even before she utters them. "Be careful, Maeve. Just be careful."

I nod. I don't need the reminder.

As soon as Sarah leaves, I shower and change into a pair of jeans and the gray sweatshirt Wes gave me. I finally washed it, so it doesn't hold even the slightest hint of cedar and bergamot anymore. All I smell is the lavender scented laundry detergent my mother buys, but the oversized material is still comforting.

I grab my phone and head downstairs. "Liam?" I call out.

"Yeah?" he shouts back from the living room.

"I'm ready to go."

Liam pokes his head out of the doorway. "Go where?"

"*Mo's*! I told you last night I'm covering Clare's shift, and you said you need the car later, so that you would drop me off. Mom's at work."

All my explanation yields is a blank expression.

"I did?" Liam asks.

"Yes!" I exclaim impatiently. "Come on, I have to go now, or I'll be late."

"Fine," Liam grouses, grabbing a baseball cap from the front hall and heading out the front door. I roll my eyes as I grab the sedan's keys from the hook by the door and follow him. He's already realized his oversight when I emerge outside, having retraced his steps halfway back up the front stairs.

"You might need these." I toss the car keys to him.

"Thanks. I'm losing it these days. Dad's got my head so full of football plays I barely even remember the day of the week. I just have to get through tomorrow."

Something twists in my chest in response to the reminder Glenmont and Alleghany's annual clash will be taking place tomorrow night.

"You will," I reply.

Liam grunts as he pulls out of the driveway and heads in the direction of *Mo's*. He's never been one for small talk, and I'm grateful for that as we drive along. We haven't spent much time together, just the two of us, in months. We've both been exceptionally busy, but I know that's not all of it.

Liam and I have always gotten along. We're similar, but in a way that complements each other.

We look alike, but we're not identical.

We're both athletic, but we're very different athletes. Liam takes the role of a general heading into battle; I'm more of a cheerleader, constantly pulling my teammates along with me.

Liam's reserved and shy, and I can be, but I'm often friendlier, more social.

We rarely argue because we each stick to our own paths. We've never dated each other's friends, we're never in the same classes, and while our friends overlap, our closest ones are distinct from each other. He's closer with our dad; I'm closer with our mom.

We have an unwritten agreement I broke the very first time I talked to Weston Cole, and one I've made a mockery of since he kissed me. There's no real reason for Glenmont's rivalry with Alleghany. It's tradition. A nonsensical, sacred tradition.

It feels delinquent that I'm so blatantly disregarding it.

But it's nothing compared to the guilt swarming me when it comes to my brother. I can live with being disloyal to Glenmont.

Betraying Liam? That's a lot harder.

I have to tell Liam about Wes, and I don't know how to. It was one thing when I didn't know exactly what Weston Cole and I were. I wasn't willing to tell Liam about a fling. After my birthday? Well, fling doesn't really apply. If it ever did. I'm factoring him into my future. He told me he loves me. I handed him my virginity.

I've been dreading the game against Alleghany for months. If Alleghany wins tomorrow night, I know Liam is not going to take it well. Learning I love their quarterback and have been seeing him for months? I feel nauseous just imagining his reaction.

"Maeve? Maeve!" I'm so lost in my own thoughts I don't even realize we've stopped in front of *Mo's* until Liam calls my name.

"Thanks for the ride," I tell him, preparing to climb out.

"You good, Maeve?" Liam asks, looking at me with concern.

"Yeah, I am," I reply. "Just thinking about my own game."

We're playing in the state championship next Friday. Just eight days from now. It's my final chance to win it. We lost in the final last year, and it was the first time Glenmont ever made it that far. That's what I should be thinking about. Planning the drills for the morning practices I'll be running starting Saturday.

Wes is a distraction, but I can't bring myself to regret a single thing that's happened between us.

I head inside *Mo's*. I hardly ever work during the school year, but Clare couldn't find anyone else to cover her shift tonight. It's quiet and empty inside, the only customers an elderly couple already close to finishing their meal.

Steve, the cook, gives me a smile from the kitchen as I step behind the counter. "Hey, Maeve."

"Hi, Steve."

"Hope you brought some homework or something; looks like it'll be a slow night," he tells me.

"I see that."

I busy myself with scratching out soccer drills to run at morning practice on paper napkins for the next couple hours. The bell above the door tinkles a few minutes before my shift ends, and Matt strolls in.

My stomach sinks in response. I still haven't said anything to him, and it's one of the many things gnawing away at my conscience right now.

"Hey, Maeve," he greets me easily.

"Hi, Matt," I reply. "My shift's about to end, but if you know what you want, I can put your order in before I head out."

"Oh, I'm not here for food," Matt replies. "I'm here to pick you up."

"You're what?" I ask, sure I misheard him. My mom is supposed to get me on her way home from the office.

"Well, me and the guys. We were at your house. Your mom said you needed a ride, and we were headed out anyway." He gives me a mischievous grin that makes me feel like I'm missing something.

"Oh-kay." I draw out the word as I stuff the napkins I scribbled on in the front pocket of Wes's sweatshirt and grab my phone. "Goodnight, Steve!" I call out as I follow Matt toward the door.

"See ya, Maeve!" Steve replies.

Rather than the sedan I'm expecting to see, Sam's silver

Suburban is the car waiting in the parking lot. I climb into the car filled with every senior member of Glenmont's football team.

"What the hell is going on?" I ask Liam, who's sitting in the front passenger seat.

Sam is the one who answers. "We're just taking a quick trip. To Alleghany's football field." He gives me a wicked grin from the driver's seat.

This can't be good. "Why?" I ask cautiously.

"Just a little something I came up with," Sam replies as he pulls out of the parking lot, heading in the direction of Alleghany.

Unease continues to trickle through my veins. I pull my phone out of my pocket and send a quick text to Wes. *Running late. Be there as soon as I can.* I hope he doesn't check my location. I don't want to risk sending him a longer message, though. Not in a dark car filled with Glenmont football players.

We pull up to the football field, and the stadium is quiet and empty. But the lights are on, same as in Glenmont. Eternally shining.

Everyone piles out of the car, and I reluctantly follow. I look around, seeing Wes's school with fresh eyes. I haven't been here many times, and this will probably be the last. We alternate who hosts the Glenmont versus Alleghany game each year. They'll be traveling to us tomorrow night.

"Come on, Maeve." I turn back to see each football player is grabbing a plastic bag from the trunk of the SUV. The contents clank and clink.

I follow them out onto the pristine field and watch as Glenmont's football team begins distributing metal horseshoes across the green grass. It's kind of brilliant, and I'm relieved we're not vandalizing anything. As far as pranks go, this is pretty harmless. Hopefully Wes will think the same. And after the pool prank he admitted to, he doesn't have much of a leg to stand on with this.

Matt offers me a handful of his horseshoes, and I scatter them across the field. This feels like penance, in a way. I've been far from a loyal Stallion as of late.

Thanks to my help, Matt's bag depletes faster than everyone else's. Sam's the closest one to us, and he's a good fifty feet away. We stand, watching the spread of metal horseshoes glinting under the bright lights, and I take a deep breath.

"Matt, there's something I've been meaning to talk to you about."

Matt turns to me, his face friendly and open. "Oh, yeah? What is it?"

"It's about what Sam said. In the cafeteria last week."

Matt's face goes from affable to wary, and I know he realizes what I want to discuss. "Yeah," he says, scuffing his sneaker against the blades of grass we're standing on. "I thought you caught that. I've been meaning to bring it up, but I thought it would be better to wait until next week. Once your season had ended." He takes a deep breath. "I like you, Maeve. I really like you. I have for a while. I wasn't sure what to do, because of Liam, and I know you're crazy busy with soccer and everything right now. But I'd like to take you out sometime. On a real date."

"Matt…" I start, and then stop. I'm not sure what to say. This is harder than I thought. I glance down to collect my thoughts, which is a mistake. Because suddenly Matt's right there. He tilts my chin up and kisses me, and I freeze.

It's unfamiliar. He's several inches shorter than Wes, but my response is what feels most foreign. My body is bereft of the delicious shivers and pulsating heat Wes's touch always incites.

Matt's kiss feels wrong. Disloyal.

How my first kiss with Wes should have felt but didn't.

I break through the shock and push him back. "Matt! You

can't just kiss me! I didn't realize how serious you were, and I— I'm sorry, but I'm with someone else."

That pulls him up short. "What? Who? You said you were too busy to date anyone at the start of the year."

I sigh. "I know I did."

"Who is it?"

"You don't know him," I lie.

"Real convincing, Maeve. You don't have to make someone up to spare my feelings. I just wish you'd give me a chance."

"I'm not making him up," I insist. "I swear."

"Maeve! Matt! Let's go! We've got to get out of here," Sam calls. I look over to see he and everyone else have finished spreading the horseshoes over the field and are heading back toward the parking lot. I hope none of them saw Matt kiss me.

I turn back to Matt, but he's already jogging away.

This time, I claim the passenger seat from Liam. I don't want to risk having to sit next to Matt. Awkward tension crackles between us, and I hope everyone else in the packed car is oblivious to it.

"Check this out!" Sam leans over the center console and shows me a picture he took of the field. It's an impressive sight, I have to admit, looking at the metal half-moons scattered across the entire field.

Until I spot something in the corner of the photo that makes my stomach drop with a sickening slosh.

It's me and Matt. Kissing.

Panic claws at me. "Don't send that photo to anyone, okay?"

"Already did. Cole's going to lose his mind."

He's right, but not for the reason he thinks. Wes will care less about the stupid prank. Matt kissing me? I doubt he'll be so cavalier.

I look at the photo again. My back is to the camera, but the insignia on the back of the sweatshirt is clearly visible. On the back of *Wes's* sweatshirt.

"You need to drop me off first," my voice is panicked, and I don't bother to hide it. "Now."

Sam gives me a weird look but puts the car in gear. "What's the big rush?"

"I have a study thing," I improvise wildly.

"Now? It's almost ten."

"I told one of my teammates I'd help her out. This was the only time we could both meet." I'm barely cognizant of the words coming out of my own mouth, but Sam doesn't question me further, so they must have made some sense.

I jump out of the car as soon as we pull up outside my house. I dart inside only to grab the sedan keys and then climb in the car. There aren't any messages on my screen, and my unease grows. I text Wes *Leaving now,* and he doesn't respond. I check his location. He's at home.

The drive to Alleghany is an agonizing one. Did he check my location? Did he see the photo?

I park in front of his house. There are a couple of lights on, but I'm saved from the conundrum of how to enter his house when I hear the pound of a basketball against the pavement.

Wes is shooting hoops into the basket fixed above the garage door. His shoulders tense underneath the *Alleghany Football* shirt he's wearing as I approach, but he doesn't turn or greet me. I know he's already seen the photo before I see his face.

"You knew," his voice stutters, and it guts me. "You knew that was the one—the one fucking thing that I couldn't forgive."

"Wes—I didn't cheat on you. I know the photo looks bad. I do. And I'm sorry I didn't tell you where I was. But it was not because I was cheating on you. I made it clear to Matt I'm not interested. He caught me off guard, and I pushed him away. I didn't know Sam was taking a photo—it was just a split second, and I—"

"Leave." Wes finally turns to me, and it's with an expression I haven't seen since the second time I encountered him in that Alleghany kitchen. Glacial. Austere. Distant.

Light years away from how he normally looks at me.

"Wes. Please listen—"

"We're playing Glenmont tomorrow night. I can't even look at you, and I've got to go there tomorrow—Was that your plan all along? To get me to fall in love with you and cheat on me the day before we play the Stallions?"

I jerk back, stung by the accusation. "How the fuck can you ask me that?"

"Or is it that he's from Glenmont? And can cheer for you at soccer games and is friends with your brother? You got sick of slumming it in Alleghany? Thank God I didn't tell any of my friends about you. That none of them know the photo they sent me was you cheating on me with Matt fucking Crawford on my fucking field." Venom drips from every harsh word.

"Are you sure you're not just looking for an easy out now, Wes?" I fire back. "Shit got real between us and you can't handle it, so you're willing to look at one photo and forget about the past six months?"

I've never seen Wes look so angry. "You need to fucking leave, Maeve. Now."

So, I do.

Before either of us can do any more damage.

Before I say anything else I can't take back.

Before I let Weston Cole see me cry.

CHAPTER NINETEEN

MAEVE

I'm a zombie the next day. The only bright spot is I don't have to see him at school. It's also the worst part. I'll see him at the game tonight, but that's an annual event.

After tonight, there's every possibility I'll never see Weston Cole again. Less than twenty-four hours ago, I was trying to figure out how to tell Liam and my parents about him. It's a dizzying change. And no one knows.

It feels like the world has just fallen out from under my feet, but to everyone else, my life looks unchanged. I'm grateful to be spared from the stares and the gossip I've seen my classmates endure after break-ups, but this is almost worse.

It's like we never happened.

Never existed.

His name is a constant refrain in the halls throughout the day. I don't have to see his messy brown hair or knowing blue eyes, but I can't escape his presence.

Matt ignores me at lunch, but I'm too emotionally tapped out to care. I'm hurt, indignant, and incensed by the accusations Wes hurtled at me last night, but I also feel guilty and ashamed. I don't know how I'd react if I received a photo of him kissing another girl, because the possibility never even crossed my mind. I doubt it crossed his.

Practice is brutal, and it's a relief to focus on something besides the ache in my chest. But even pushing myself to the limits, I can't bleach Wes's disgusted expression from my mind. Forget his stinging words. Disregard the staccato of the basketball bouncing against the pavement, each ricochet pounding the pain deeper.

The whole team showers and changes in the locker room, and then we head over to the football stadium for Glenmont's game against Alleghany.

I take a seat on the cold metal of the bleachers, surrounded by my teammates. Everyone around me is laughing and cheering. I feel like I'm going to throw up.

The nausea gets worse when Alleghany players begin trickling out onto the field. I scan them, but Wes isn't one of the blue jerseys. Panic mixes with the stress. He wouldn't skip the game. Not because of me. Right?

"Weston Cole looks pissed," Becca says beside me. I don't reply as I follow her gaze to see Wes is entering from the opposite end of the field.

Chris Fields is walking along next to him, talking urgently. Wes's face looks like it's carved from stone. I know the effortless confidence he's known for on the field irks Liam, but the menace in his strides is intimidating, and I see him receive several double takes from the Glenmont football team. I wonder if that's why he chose to take the long route onto the field.

Both teams fall into huddles around their captains, and I bounce my gaze between the two clusters. One royal blue, the other maroon. The groups disperse, most heading to the sidelines. Twenty-two head out onto the field.

Then, the game begins.

It's brutal. And the bar was high after the last three years. It's not even because of my own personal investment. Everyone feels it, and I see Sarah flash me a few concerned looks from her seat three rows down.

Probably because the shift is largely because of Wes. He's always beaten Glenmont with an ease—an indifferent air.

Maybe it was because he moved here freshman year and didn't grow up coming to these clashes the way the rest of us did.

Maybe it was to separate himself from his parents and their focus on perception, the way I theorized to him when we went swimming in the lake.

There's no serene composure tonight. This game is personal. Because of me. It's terrifying, realizing that power. Watching Wes bark orders and take risks. Watching his rage bleed across the field. I don't want the responsibility.

And it's not just personal toward me. I watch Matt take sack after sack. I'm not the only one who notices.

"Jesus," Becca mutters. "Did I miss something at the start of the game? How did Matt manage to piss off Alleghany so much?"

I wince.

With two minutes left to go in the first quarter, Wes scores Alleghany's first touchdown, breaking the deadlock at zero. There's no sign of the showboating I've seen him perform at previous games, though. His expression barely changes as his teammates celebrate around him. He looks haughty, and I see him glance at Liam.

My brother stands like a statue as the scoreboard changes. He rarely lets emotion out; he gets quieter and stiller the more upset he gets. And this game was already progressing poorly, even before Wes's touchdown.

Alleghany is the better team.

Thunder rumbles in the distance, and it's a foreboding sound if I've ever heard one.

"Is it supposed to rain?" I ask Becca.

She shrugs. "No idea. I don't bother to check the weather. It's usually wrong."

My question is answered a few minutes later, as the second quarter is just about to start. The rumbling is no longer in the distance. Menacing black clouds encroach the sky overhead. Rain begins to pour. And a flash of lightning illuminates the entire world for a split second.

Both teams halt their progression onto the field, looking at their coaches. There's a cover over most of the bleachers, but the field is completely exposed to the elements. And the deluge of water is rapidly puddling on the field.

My father walks over to the referees, with the Alleghany coach close behind him. They huddle briefly, and then the loud-speaker comes to life. "Looks like that'll have to be it for the night, folks. We'll discuss with both teams and reschedule."

The whole audience sits in shock. Not a single other game I've attended has been halted due to the weather, and this is the game against Alleghany.

"Well, all right then," Becca states, standing. "You guys all coming to Sam's?"

Everyone confirms they are, and more people begin to stand, accepting the unexpected ending to the game. I finally do as well.

We join the rest of the crowd that's filing out of the stands. Each group pauses before leaving the coverage and then makes a mad dash through the rain. When it's our turn to make a break for it, I halt too. But not to locate the sedan, or to assess the buckets of water still falling from the sky.

I hesitate to watch the line of blue jerseys filing onto the coach bus with *Alleghany Athletics* printed across the side.

There's a solitary figure trailing behind the rest of the team. I don't need to look at the name or number on the back of the jersey to know who it is.

Wes doesn't look domineering or stoic now. He looks broken.

Head down.

Shoulders slumped.

He looks like he just lost. I watch him board the bus, and the leaden weight on my chest doubles in size.

"Maeve! Let's go!" Becca calls out, already bolting through the rain toward my car. I follow her, with a few more of our teammates close behind.

The mood at Sam's is exuberant. We were losing, and now Glenmont is going to have a clean slate. Also, I'm guessing most of the team is aware there's a good chance they won't be celebrating after the rescheduled game. This is a partial victory all of its own.

I don't see Liam, and I avoid Matt. I mostly stick to the living room, talking with my teammates. Brooke and Sarah show up about an hour after we arrive.

"I had to change out of my cheerleading outfit," Brooke explains when they walk into the living room. "We got totally soaked out there."

I'm talking to Becca about some drills I came up with for morning practices when I feel my phone buzz. My heart quickens. I pull it out, but it's not him. It's Maggie.

"Hey," I answer. "What's up?"

"Can you come get me? There's something wrong with my car, and my mom's in Vermont for some girl's weekend. I'd try to talk someone here into driving me, but they're all wasted."

"Sure," I respond. "Where are you?"

"Thank you! Thank you! Thank you!" Maggie replies. "I'll text you the address."

"Okay." I hang up and look over at Becca. "I'm going to head out. Maggie needs a ride, and then I'll probably just go home. Early practice, you know?"

Becca grins. "Yeah, my captain's a real hard-ass, too."

"Hilarious, Collins."

I head over to where Brooke and Sarah are standing. "I'm headed out, guys," I reply.

"What? Why?" Brooke asks, pouting.

"Maggie called. She needs a designated driver to pick her up. Plus, I'm exhausted. I'm running extra morning practices all week to prepare for the championship next week."

"Do you want me to come with you?" Sarah offers.

"No, no, it's fine," I'm quick to say. The last thing I want is to be trapped in a car with Sarah right now. The only person who knows about Wes. I'm sure she has questions after the spectacle earlier. "Have fun, guys."

I give them both hugs and head outside into the rain. Maggie's already sent me the address, and I plug it into my phone's GPS and start driving.

As soon as I pull up outside the stately house, she rushes off the front porch and toward my car. I don't look over as she opens the passenger door and climbs inside. I'm too busy staring at the house. It's *the* house. The location of the Alleghany party Maggie dragged me to at the start of the summer. And Wes's black Range Rover is parked in the driveway.

I turn off the car.

"Uh, what are you doing?" Maggie asks. Her voice is filled with confusion.

"I'll be right back."

The thunder has stopped, but the rain still hasn't. I'm drenched as soon as I step out of the car, but I don't care. I do waver for a minute, though. Based on our last conversation, this could be bad. But I need to see him.

I haven't tried to call or text Wes since last night. I'm worried he's blocked me. But mostly, it's because I know this is a conversation we need to have in person.

I can't watch another repeat of tonight, and if nothing changes between us before the next game, I know that's exactly what it will be. This is my best chance at talking to him in person. I can't show up at Alleghany High, and I don't want to risk going to his house again. The last Alleghany party I attended, no one but him gave me a second glance. I hope that'll be true tonight.

I march up the brick path and inside, on a mission now. I recoil slightly at the wall of noise and exuberance that greets me when I open the front door.

"Maeve!" Maggie calls behind me. Her shout attracts a few glances, but I forge ahead. He's not in the living room. I head into the kitchen. Not here either. I spot an Alleghany football player heading toward a door around the corner.

He opens it, revealing a set of stairs he heads down. I follow him.

The basement is better lit than the first floor. Bright enough for me to see Alleghany football player after Alleghany football player. But not the one I want to see.

There's no music playing down here, just a babble of voices, although the bass pounding overhead is audible. I reach the bottom of the stairs and am about to turn around to go back up, when I see him.

He's slouched against the wall in the corner, and there's a girl draped over him.

His gaze meets mine, and then he bends his head and kisses her.

I feel all the blood drain from my cheeks. It's a slap to the face. A blow so forceful I'm surprised I don't stumble.

I said it first. That I couldn't forgive cheating. And he's doing it in plain sight for everyone to see.

For me to see.

He might as well have just stabbed me. It feels like he did. And the wound bleeds out all the guilt, angst, and uncertainty I've felt ever since Matt kissed me.

All that's left behind? Fury. He pulls away from the girl to take a sip of beer, and his beautiful blue eyes meet mine defiantly.

I finally hate Weston Cole, but it's for all the wrong reasons. I don't hate him because I'm a girl from Glenmont and he's a boy from Alleghany. I hate him because I was stupid enough to think our hometowns didn't matter. Dumb enough to give the last person I should have the power to hurt me.

There are a lot of things I could say or do right now, but most of them would stoop me down to his level. And I refuse to do that. Because he's the one in the wrong here, not me. Regardless of what he thinks.

But I'm not going to let him think this is acceptable.

Let him assume he can treat me this way.

"You're a fucking coward, Weston Thomas Cole!" I don't raise my voice above a normal volume, but there's enough wrath in my tone the basement goes mostly silent. I'm staring at Wes too intently to register anyone else's reaction. I watch him flinch, and I know that my pointed words have found their mark.

I spin and start up the stairs, bypassing Maggie, who's standing there with her mouth agape. She scrambles to follow me as I push back through the teenagers partying in the living room and emerge outside.

I'm not sure if the water streaming down my face is rain or tears. Probably a combination of the two. I climb back into the car, and I'm glad I have a few seconds head start on Maggie. It gives me time to scroll through my phone. She climbs in the car, and I press play on the first song I see. The intro to "Dancing on my Own" by Robyn thrums out of the speakers. The lyrics are eerily fitting.

"I'm guessing you don't want to talk?" Maggie asks when she climbs inside. I can barely hear her over the loud music.

I look over, and burning questions fill her eyes.

I shake my head and turn up the music.

CHAPTER TWENTY

WESTON

I'm drunk. And furious. It's a lethal combination.

I'm mad that the game got canceled when we were going to win.

I'm mad that Coach Blake announced on the bus ride back the game was rescheduled for next Friday. Meaning I have to wait a whole week to get closure against Glenmont. Meaning my parents won't be there because my father has a business trip scheduled and my mother will go because she feels like she has to babysit him.

I'm mad that it's raining and I'm stuck in Josh's hot, stuffy basement.

And I'm so fucking pissed at Maeve Stevens I can hardly think straight. I hate that she came here. Hate that I care. Hate the confused stares I'm receiving after the vitriol she publicly spewed my way.

Most of all, I hate that it doesn't make sense. She should be consoling Matt Crawford right now. Instead, she came here and yelled at me. In front of half the football team.

Charlie makes his way over to me, and I hastily crack open

another beer and take a long sip. "Jesus, Cole, leave some for the rest of us."

I shrug and take another long pull from the can.

"You alright, dude?" Charlie asks. I've been in a shitty mood all day, and I know it hasn't escaped anyone's notice. I'm usually easy-going when it comes to football. Serious, but I don't let it become more than a game. That wasn't the case tonight. I was merciless.

I like to lead by example. Tonight, I shouted at anyone who stepped a toe out of line.

"I'm fine. Celebrating." The words sound flat to my own ears.

"Adam said Maeve Stevens was here. What the fuck?"

I clench my fists at the reminder, and the metal can contracts loudly in protest. I take another sip from the bowed shape.

"Cole, you're kind of freaking me out. What's going on?"

"Nothing," I grit out. "Maeve Stevens hates me. No surprise there."

"I'm not surprised about that. I'm surprised you're acting like you give a shit."

"I don't."

"Is it your parents?" Charlie knows my home life is far from idyllic, but I've never told him the full extent of it. Only her. And that only makes me angrier.

I told her I couldn't forgive cheating, but that was before I was in love with her.

I know my mother's decision to tag along on all my dad's business trips back to the city to "catch up with friends" is simply an excuse. She's going to try to curb my father's wandering eye. I don't feel that way about Maeve. The possibility she might cheat on me never crossed my mind until I saw that photo.

Is that because I love her more than my parents love each other? Or because I want to believe her? That she somehow ended up on Alleghany's football field with another guy's tongue down her throat by accident?

It doesn't make any sense, but neither does anything else. Despite the accusations I flung at her last night, I don't really believe Maeve went into our relationship with any nefarious intentions. It was too unexpected, too genuine. Too risky. She had as much on the line as I did. Maybe more.

"Yeah, I'm fine," I finally answer. My voice is hollow. I'm wavering, and I hate myself for it. But it's nothing compared to how loathsome I felt when I saw the look on Maeve's face after I kissed Natalie in front of her.

A junior linebacker stumbles over to us. "Sick throws tonight, Cole."

"Thanks," I mutter, taking another long drag of beer and hoping he'll take the hint.

"Who was that hot blonde yelling at you? I've never seen her before. Man, I would love to get a piece—"

I push away from the wall and stalk off. Before I can continue my series of stupid decisions. Like punch out my teammate for talking about my enemy.

The rest of the night is a blur of more beer and loud music, and when I wake up in one of Josh's guest rooms the following morning, it's to a blaring headache. It feels like a hammer is pounding against my temple.

Thankfully, I'm alone. I'm not sure how I feel about Maeve right now, but I know having sex with someone else would haunt me. It's bad enough I kissed Natalie.

I stumble out of the bedroom into the hallway. The house is a total wreck. Red plastic cups, empty beer bottles, and random articles of clothing dot the pathway to the kitchen. Josh is standing at the stove frying eggs when I walk inside. Caroline's perched on the island, drinking from a mug.

"You look like shit," she greets, appraising me over the rim of the ceramic.

"I feel like it," I say, slumping down on one of the island's stools. "There coffee?"

Caroline nods to the fridge, and I see a coffeemaker tucked in the corner. Thankfully, the glass pot is filled with dark brown liquid. I heave myself up and look through three cabinets before I finally locate the mugs. I pour myself some steaming coffee and sit back down.

"You were quite the party animal last night, Cole," Josh informs me as he flips the eggs.

I groan. After Maeve left, most of the evening is spotty. Mainly because her appearance sobered me up, and I overcompensated on the alcohol after she left as a result.

"How so?"

"Hmmm, where to begin?" Josh says, obviously enjoying this way too much.

"Don't fuck with me," I warn. "I'm not in the mood."

"Oh, I know. You were in quite the mood yesterday, too. Long before you started drinking. Want to explain on what that was about?"

"Just having a bad day," I reply, taking a sip of coffee. It does nothing to ease my headache, but the jolt of caffeine helps some. "So? What did I do last night?"

"Lots of drinking. Gave a five-minute speech about how much you hate the rain. Little bit of dancing."

"Any girls?"

"Not that I saw. Aside from the kiss with Natalie, but that was before you got really wasted, so I'm guessing you remember that."

Chris stumbles into the kitchen then, his dark hair looking like a bird spent the night in it. "Morning." He yawns.

"Perfect timing, Fields. Was just filling Cole in on his drunken shenanigans."

"Wouldn't miss this," Chris says as he fills his own mug of coffee. "You break the rain poem to him yet?"

"I'm calling bullshit on that," I interject.

"How come? You're a total English nerd. Remember when you won that essay award sophomore year?"

I roll my eyes. "That wasn't poetry."

"All right, fine. It wasn't a poem. If I wasn't so hungover myself, I could have come up with a better story. You don't usually drink until you have amnesia." Chris gives me a questioning look.

I shrug. "Bad day."

Chris takes a seat on the stool beside me. "So, you and Natalie are just friends?" He raises his eyebrows.

"I was drunk."

"Yes, we've been over that, Cole. Doesn't change the fact you adamantly said there was nothing to your adorable ice cream outing, and then made out with her last night in front of half the team, according to the rumors I heard. You didn't do that even when you guys *were* a thing."

"Sure would be nice if people could mind their own business," I mutter into my mug.

"Which brings me to the second bit of buzz I heard I missed while I was playing Flip Cup. Maeve Stevens came here and called you a, and I quote, 'fucking coward', and then stormed off?"

My grip tightens on the mug the second he says her name. "Yup."

"Why the hell would she do that?" Chris wonders.

I shrug again.

"Maybe it was a dare," Josh speculates.

I look up at him and see Caroline studying me closely. I shift under her shrewd gaze as I finish my coffee and stand.

"I've got to get going, guys. My mom's probably worried. Thanks for letting me crash, Josh."

"No problem, Cole," Josh replies.

"You're around later, right?" Chris asks as I head toward the door.

I pause. "Yeah, why?"

"I'm planning a team meeting. To brainstorm on how to get back at Glenmont for the horseshoes prank. It's perfect now that we have another week. But we've got to give them enough time to clean up whatever we do, since they're hosting Friday."

I chuckle. "Okay. Just let me know when; I'll be there."

It only takes me a couple of minutes to drive home from Josh's. My dad's car is missing from the driveway, but I spot my mom's in the garage. I head in the back door, and she's there. Waiting.

"You missed your curfew by ten hours," she informs me.

I sigh. "I know, I'm sorry. I crashed at Josh's after the party, and I forgot to text you."

"Weston…"

"I'm sorry, Mom. I mean it. It won't happen again."

She finally nods, then studies me a bit more closely. "Everything okay, Weston?"

"Yeah, I just had a bad night," I respond.

"Anything you want to talk about?"

I shake my head.

"Okay. This happens again, there will be consequences. Got it?"

"Got it," I affirm.

"Too bad about the storm last night, but you played well."

"Thanks," I reply as I head toward the stairs. "I'm going to take a shower."

The first thing I do when I get upstairs is pop a couple of painkillers, and then I step under the steaming hot spray. The vaporous mist helps soothe my pounding head.

Back in my room, I pull on sweatpants and a t-shirt, and then flop on my bed.

I stand only a few minutes later, restless. I grab a sweatshirt from the hook on the back of my door and head downstairs, tugging it over my head as I do. I can hear my mom washing dishes in the kitchen as I tie my sneakers and head out the front door.

The air outside is brisk, but the sunshine helps to temper the chill as I jog along the sidewalk. Usually I listen to music when I run, but there's something cathartic about hearing nothing except the pound of my sneakers against the smooth pavement.

I run for a long time.

Longer than I intended to.

Until my lungs are gasping for air and I'm drenched with enough sweat, I'll have to take another shower. I finally slow to a walk, resting my forearms across my head to open up my lungs.

I feel better. My problems are all still there—Maeve, football, my parents, college—but I feel like I put some distance between myself and them. They're not smothering me anymore.

I halt on the sidewalk when I reach Natalie's house, and then start up her paved walk. I ring the doorbell, and her mother answers.

"Oh, hello, Weston," she greets, giving me a smile. "It's lovely to see you. Such a disappointment about the game last night, but I have no doubt you'll beat them whenever the game is rescheduled."

"Thanks, Mrs. Jacobs," I reply. It's eerie, how happy and

normal she appears the few times I've been to their house. According to Natalie, it's because her father is home on the weekends. "Is Natalie here?"

"Yes, she is," she replies. "One moment." Mrs. Jacobs steps back from the open door, and I hear her call Natalie's name.

Natalie appears a couple of minutes later.

"Hey," she greets, studying me curiously.

"Hey," I respond. "Can we talk for a minute?"

"Sure." Natalie steps outside of her house, closing the door behind her. I follow her over to the porch swing and take a seat next to her.

"I'm sorry. About last night. Kissing you."

"Why?"

"Why am I apologizing?"

Natalie rolls her eyes. "Why did you kiss me, Weston? After making it very clear we were over."

"I was drunk, and I was having a bad day," I admit to her.

"I already knew both those things. You were crushing cans of beer like it was water, and the whole squad heard you barking orders on the field. There was something else going on. Is it your parents?"

It would be easy. So, so easy to blame this on them. But I can't. "No. I mean, they won't be there next week for the make-up, which sucks, but that's not why I kissed you." Natalie doesn't say anything, but she keeps looking at me expectantly. I cave. "I was trying to make another girl jealous. Or get revenge, maybe? I don't know. I was in a bad place. Still am, to be honest."

Natalie looks stunned. "You were trying to make another girl jealous? There's a girl you like? Have actual feelings for?" Her voice grows more incredulous with each question.

"Yup."

"Who is it?" Natalie asks.

"It doesn't matter. We're over. Whatever was between us—well, it's long gone." I think.

I can tell Natalie wants to ask more questions. Her eyes are brimming with them, but she doesn't.

"I've got to go. We've got a team meeting in a bit. I just wanted to clear the air. Make sure we're still good."

Natalie snorts. "I'm not pining over you, Weston. I mean, yeah, if you were interested, I wouldn't turn you down, but we're good. I won't be crying myself to sleep over your mystery girl."

I huff out a laugh and stand. "Okay. Bye, Natalie."

"See you, Weston."

I turn and head back down her walk. After my talk with Natalie, one problem is already close to catching back up to me.

I can't outrun Maeve Stevens forever.

Probably because I don't really want to.

CHAPTER TWENTY-ONE

MAEVE

A throat clears behind me as I'm setting up cones before Monday morning's captain practice. I stand up slowly, not sure what I want more.

For it to be him, or it not to be him.

I turn and let out a deep breath. "What are you doing here?" I don't let any emotion seep into my voice.

Wes shifts his weight awkwardly back and forth between his feet. He's wearing a black hoodie with his letterman jacket over it, and a pair of light gray joggers. There are dark circles underneath his blue eyes, and I hate how attractive he still is despite them.

"I'm having trouble figuring out how *you're* the one who's mad at *me*," he finally responds.

"Oh, really?" I retort. "Let's start with the girl you were kissing on Friday night."

"We were broken up."

"If you believed that you wouldn't be here, Wes," I reply sharply. "You made some assumptions, gave me no chance to explain, and then—"

"I made some *assumptions*? They sent me a fucking photo of you kissing another guy! What other *assumption* is there to make, Maeve?"

"I know it looked bad. I admitted it looked bad. That's no excuse for why you shouldn't have at least listened to me. My word should have meant more to you."

"So you're admitting it happened and you're mad I didn't let you stick around so you could give me the play-by-play?"

"God, you're infuriating!" I shout. "And I'm so sick of you acting like you're the only one taking any risks. You only moved here a few years ago! I've lived in Glenmont my *entire* life. Not only that, this is my family we're talking about! Do you have any idea how Liam would feel if he found out about us? That—"

"If you were so worried about people finding out about us and ruining your perfect reputation, then maybe you shouldn't have shown up at Josh's Friday night!" Wes yells back. "I had to spend the rest of the night listening to people gossip about you. I almost punched my own fucking teammate because he made a comment about how'd he like to—"

"I hope you let him know you already beat him to it," I snap.

Wes looks stricken. "No—Maeve, I would never—"

"Awful lot of rumors about your sex life for that to be true," I retort.

Anger returns to Wes's face again. "You don't believe me?"

"Well, you promised you didn't want to touch another girl, and that obviously changed, so…"

"I was fucking hurt, Maeve!"

"Oh, if you were hurt…well, that's okay then," I reply sarcastically.

"I didn't handle it well, okay? I know that."

"You didn't handle it well? Is that what your mom did?"

Wes's face darkens. "Don't you dare bring my parents into this, Maeve."

"Seems relevant to me. They're why you're acting like this, right?"

"No, I'm pretty sure Matt Crawford having his tongue down your throat would bother me even if I was from a perfect family like yours."

"My family isn't perfect, and you know that. But you're responsible for your own actions, and I thought you were better than cheating on me right in front of me."

"We were broken up!" Wes shouts.

"Then why are you here?" I yell back. "What are you doing here, Wes?"

The anger recedes, replaced with vulnerability. "I don't know."

"Well, go figure it out somewhere else. I have practice, and I don't want anyone to see you." I spin around, only to see most of my teammates are already assembled on the bleachers, staring at us. "Shit," I swear under my breath. I walk reluctantly over to the metal risers. "Morning!" I say in the most cheerful voice I can muster. "Usual warm-up, and then I'll explain the first drill."

My teammates scramble off the bleachers to head toward the running path. Either my voice was more commanding than chipper, or they're that eager to gossip about what they just witnessed. Probably both.

Becca lingers behind, just like I knew she would.

"That was Weston Cole," she states.

"Yes."

"Weston Cole was at Glenmont High, yelling at you."

"Yes."

"You were yelling back at him."

"Yes."

"So Weston Cole is the owner of the superior abs you were talking about?" Becca asks.

I'm caught off guard she makes the leap so quickly, so it takes me a moment to remember what she's referring to. "Uh, yeah. He is."

"I'm sorry, Maeve."

"It's fine. I was stupid to think we'd ever be anything more than enemies."

"Yeah, maybe. Or brave." Becca starts after the rest of the team before I have a chance to respond.

Throughout the day, I catch about a dozen random stares. I'm not surprised. We're far from the only team with early practices, and I doubt Wes managed to arrive and leave Glenmont High without being seen. Alleghany's quarterback doesn't pay social calls in Glenmont.

And I don't know what his visit means. He was still plenty angry, but he came. Because he has regrets? Because he needs closure? The only thing I know about his visit is it means I need to have a conversation with my brother. And it's one I'm dreading.

After my second soccer practice of the day ends, I head straight home. I shower first and then eat my dinner alone in the kitchen. Everyone else has already eaten, and my parents are out at a friend's. I eat each piece of fettuccine individually, trying to avoid the inevitable.

Finally, I drag my fuzzy sock-clad feet up the stairs.

"Hey." I knock on Liam's half-open door. "Can I come in?"

"Sure." He stops scrolling through his phone and sits up on his bed.

I take a seat backwards on his desk chair. "I know we haven't really talked since Friday. I'm sorry the game got postponed. Hopefully this week's goes better."

"Thanks, but I doubt it will." Liam heaves out a long sigh. "They're better than us. He's better than me. One thunderstorm isn't going to change that."

He flops back on his bed. "Eagles can't manage to string a decent team together for years. The four I'm eligible to play... Weston fucking Cole moves to town."

I clear my throat awkwardly.

"Sorry, I'll stop complaining. Who knows? Maybe we'll get lucky and Cole will still be in a shitty mood next Friday. He wasn't doing himself any favors terrorizing his receivers. Wish I knew what set him off so I could replicate it." Liam lets out a slight laugh.

I close my eyes. I've imagined having to say this a lot of times. The reality is worse.

"Maeve?"

"I have feelings for him," I blurt. "For Weston Cole."

Liam bursts out laughing. The hysterical sound fades slowly when he realizes I'm not sharing his amusement.

Eventually, even the grin slides off his face.

I wait for him to yell, but that's never been Liam's style. He's thoughtful, strategic, measured. The rare exception has usually been when it comes to Weston Cole, however.

"You're not kidding." Liam states. His statement drips with disbelief. It's not a question, but I shake my head anyway. "Weston fucking Cole, Maeve? Half the guys at school have crushes on you, and you decide to lust after Weston fucking Cole? The guy who's made me look like a fool for years? Who has ruined my high school football career? The *Alleghany quarterback*?"

I nod hesitantly, disregarding the "half the guys" comment. Liam stands up and starts to pace. "Liam, I never wante—"

He cuts me off. "Evan mentioned someone from Alleghany

posted you were at their party on Friday and called Cole a coward? I figured it was bullshit. Some other blonde girl he pissed off, but it wasn't, was it?"

I shake my head. Stupidly, I hadn't even considered people from Glenmont might hear I went to the Alleghany party on Friday. Freaking social media. I wonder how Alleghany and Glenmont students spied on each other back in my father's day. Intercepted telegrams? Landline taps?

"Why did you call him a coward?" Liam asks.

I sigh and look over at his bookshelf. "He was kissing another girl." The admission stings, like I'm reliving it just by saying the words. I can still see the vengeful glint in his blue eyes.

Liam snorts. "Typical. You dodged a bullet, Maeve. Which I should not have to tell you." He shakes his head. "He's shameless. What? Did he flirt with you and then kiss this other girl when he realized who you are?"

The insinuation stings. That I'm a fool who would fall for a few cheap lines and lose my cool over a failed fling.

"No, he thinks I cheated on him." I state emotionlessly. "With Matt. Matt kissed me at the field during the horseshoes prank, and it was in the photo Sam sent them."

"I know he did. Matt's been sulking about your rejection for days. You could have let the guy down a little easier, Maeve."

"A heads up from you would have been nice," I reply.

"I didn't want to get involved. I just told him I didn't have a problem with him asking you out." He pauses. "You said cheated? As in, you were actually in a relationship?"

"Yes," I confirm. We've already passed the point of no return.

"With Weston Cole?" I think it's the first time outside our mother's presence I've ever heard Liam say his full name without the profanity.

"Yes," I repeat.

Liam finally stops pacing and sits back down on his bed. "Wow. I never—I mean, he doesn't seem like the type to commit."

"Based on what? His football stats? You don't even know him!" I contend.

Liam's eyes are wide as he takes in my defensive tone. "And you do?"

"Yeah, I do." My words ring with conviction.

"How long were you two…uh, involved?"

I sigh, knowing Liam will see this as a further betrayal. "Since June," I admit.

"Six months! Are you kidding me, Maeve?"

"I know. I'm sorry, Liam. I didn't mean for things to get so… complicated. But it's over now. I just needed you to know the truth."

"It's over because Cole thinks you cheated on him with Matt?"

I nod.

"And that's why the whole Alleghany line was going after him on Friday?"

"Probably. I'm not exactly on speaking terms with their quarterback at the moment."

"Wait," my brother finally sheds the shock and begins to look excited. "At the moment? But you have been for the last six months?"

"Yes…" I reply cautiously, wary of his shift in tone.

"And Cole told you stuff? About his team? About their strategy?" I realize why my twin is suddenly so eager. He thinks I'm a woman scorned. He thinks I'll turn on Wes.

I stand. "*That*. That right there is why you don't know him. Because ever since I first talked to him freshman year, he's never once asked me the same questions about you."

Liam looks at me as though I'm naïve, idiotic. "Because he doesn't *have to*, Maeve. He's beaten us every year."

"But that's how you want to win? With intel I got when I was in the backseat of his car?"

Liam looks horrified. "Maeve, don't tell me shit like that."

I almost want to laugh. "I'm not telling you anything. You're both more important to me than the stupid sport you play."

I walk toward the door.

"So, what are you going to do now? If he realizes you didn't cheat? You're going to actually date him? An Eagle?"

"I don't think that's going to happen." *The one thing you knew I couldn't forgive.*

"Then why did you tell me, Maeve?"

"He came to my practice this morning, and people probably saw. I wanted you to hear it from me."

CHAPTER TWENTY-TWO

WESTON

"Heard you crashed a Glenmont girls' soccer practice," Chris says as he drops into the seat across from me in the Alleghany High library.

I flip a page in the book I'm pretending to read. "For two towns that claim not to talk to each other, information seems to pass back and forth between them pretty fucking quickly."

"You're hardly in a position to judge. From what I've heard, you've done a lot more than just talk to someone from Glenmont."

"So, everyone knows?"

"I wouldn't say everyone—there was one girl in my Stats class who had her headphones in and wasn't paying attention to what the rest of us were talking about...but aside from that I'd say there's a clear majority in the know now, yes."

"Shit." I close the book, no longer interested in looking busy.

"Pretty much. Maeve Stevens? Maeve fucking *Stevens*, Wes? What the hell were you thinking?"

"I wasn't," I reply. "It just...happened."

"*It just happened*? That's not going to fly with the team, man.

They're pissed. You don't *just happen* to hook up with a girl from Glenmont. You didn't get that memo the first day you moved to town?"

"She's not just a girl from Glenmont. I—I care about her. Okay?"

Chris stares at me as though I've just told him I'm quitting football. "You care. About Maeve Stevens."

"That's what I just said."

"Who are you and what the hell have you done with my best friend?"

"Chris, be serious."

"I am! I've never seen you do more than exchange small talk with a girl unless it's to hook up. And now you're telling me you've got feelings for Liam Stevens' sister? I figured you were just trying to get in her pants."

I don't answer, and Chris correctly interprets my silence. "You already did."

"I'm not discussing it with you." I think that surprises Chris more than anything else I've said so far.

"I can't believe you got Maeve Stevens to sleep with you. She—"

"I said I'm not discussing it!" I snap.

Chris raises his hands in a gesture of acceptance and leans back in the heavy wooden chair.

"I'm starting to think Maeve Stevens might have something to do with the horrific mood you've been in since—when? Thursday?" I don't answer. "Let's recap the last few days. You spend the game Friday acting like some sort of robotic general. Then you get wasted, kiss Natalie right after—"

"That's plenty of commentary, thanks," I interrupt. But it's too late. He's already put it together.

"That's why you kissed Natalie. Because Maeve Stevens showed up."

"Chris…"

"Well, that's one way to let a girl know you care. Kiss—"

"Chris!" I snap. "Shut up or leave."

"Fine," Chris retorts, standing. "But if we lose on Friday because you're letting Maeve Stevens mess with your head, I'm never going to forgive you. And neither is the rest of the team." He strides off to another section of the library.

Just when I thought things couldn't get much worse.

I leave study hall fifteen minutes early, but no one tries to stop me. I head straight to the locker room, changing and heading out onto the field. Right now, I feel like throwing the football as far and as fast as I can. But there's no one here to catch it. So instead, I jog around the track.

I knew there was a chance there would be rumors I went to Glenmont this morning. Maeve was griping last week about how early she'd have to get up for the morning practices the days before her championship game, and there's no way I was going to risk going to Liam Stevens' house. I needed to see her after Friday night. See how I felt. How she felt. Now, I'm more confused than ever.

I'm not concerned about Alleghany High gossiping about my sighting at Glenmont High. But I'm not willing to let my team think it's going to impair my judgement on Friday. We're not playing against Maeve. We're playing against Glenmont. There's a difference.

My teammates start to trickle onto the field, along with Coach Blake. They all give me questioning looks as I continue jogging around the track. Once the cluster around Coach Blake has grown to its usual size, I slow and walk over.

"I like the initiative, Cole," Coach Blake compliments as I join the group. "Now, boys—"

I step forward. "Could I say something to the team, Coach?" I ask.

He raises a grizzled brow. I've never interrupted him before. Neither has any other member of the team. But he nods, and I step forward to the middle of the loose semi-circle the team is standing in.

"Listen, I know there are some rumors going around right now. You guys can gossip about me all you want, but I'm not interested in hearing opinions from anyone here about decisions I make off the field. We're playing Glenmont on Friday, and I have no intention of losing that game. I also fully expect to become state champions again this year. That's all you should need to know. You boys willing to help me out with that?" I look around the group of guys assembled before me, meeting each pair of eyes unflinchingly before holding my hand out in the middle of the circle.

There's a slight pause. Chris is the first to hold his out as well, followed by Charlie and Adam, then Josh, and I let out a sigh of relief as the pile of appendages grows to include every guy on the varsity Alleghany football team. "Let's go Eagles!" I shout, and it's loudly echoed around me.

"All right, then," Coach Blake intervenes. "Usual teams, boys. Get lined up."

I start to follow the rest of the team when I hear my name. My stomach sinks. I was hoping he'd let it go. "Yes, Coach?" I turn back around.

"That was quite the speech, Cole."

"Sorry, Coach. I know you hate any drama on the team. Seemed necessary to address this bout head on, though."

"I've noticed a real difference in you this season, Cole. You're more mature. More focused. Now, I'm in the business of coaching champions, not listening to gossip, but I wouldn't be too concerned with where whoever may have inspired that change lives. And it's up to you whether you are. Just my pair of pennies. Now, get out of here."

"Yes, sir," I reply. I was steeling myself for a lecture about dragging the team into my personal life, and now I'm reeling from the implications Coach Blake just made. And the confirmation gossip about my love life has spread to the Alleghany High faculty along with the students.

I jog over to Chris's side. "Thanks for backing me up there," I tell him. "Sorry I got short in the library."

He shrugs. "You were right. As long as you don't let it mess with your game, it's none of my business what you do off the field. Even if it involves a girl from Glenmont."

"Chris. You're one of my best friends. It's not that I—" I sigh. "It's always been complicated with her. Right now, I don't even— I don't even know where to begin."

Chris nods slowly. "If you want to talk about it, I'll listen. I can't promise I won't tell you to get over it and move on, but I'll listen."

"Thanks, Fields."

"Any time, Cole."

It's a relief to clear the air with Chris. The other source of contrition in my life? Much more convoluted. Worse than not knowing if I want to fix things after our talk this morning, I'm not even sure if things between me and Maeve are repairable.

CHAPTER TWENTY-THREE

MAEVE

Ironically, my last name, one of the primary obstacles in my ill-fated relationship with Weston Cole, is what safeguards me in the hallways of Glenmont High.

I'm followed by rampant stares and whispers everywhere I go, but no one has been bold enough to ask me about the rumors directly.

The exception is Brooke, who drags me from Calculus all the way to the lunchroom on Tuesday and plants me at one of the corner tables. I'm incredibly grateful Thanksgiving is on Thursday, so I only have to make it through the rest of the day.

"Start talking, Maeve Stevens. Right now," Brooke instructs.

I watch Sarah enter the room, look over at our usual table, and then make a beeline over to the new spot Brooke chose.

"Talk about what?" I ask, playing dumb.

"Oh, I don't know…" Brooke taps a finger against her chin. "Oh, I *do* know! Maybe about how the entire school thinks there's something going on between you and Weston fucking Cole?"

I roll my eyes at her dramatics. "What do people think is going on?" I ask carefully.

"Susan Andrews told me she saw him in the parking lot yesterday morning. And the general consensus seems to be the two of you got into some sort of screaming match at the soccer field?"

Sarah plops down in the seat next to me. "What did I miss?"

"Maeve was just about to clarify whether the rumors about Weston Cole are true," Brooke supplies.

"Of course they're true. I video-chatted with him in her bedroom last week."

I close my eyes in anticipation of Brooke's reaction. "You what?" she screeches.

"I went over to Maeve's. Her mom was there and mentioned Maeve had been at my place the previous night. She hadn't, so I confronted her about it, and she finally told me. I didn't believe her, so she called Weston. He was actually shirtless for part of it, and I mean, I don't normally go for the jock type, but he looked, I mean, he looked really good. I—"

"I'm right here, Sarah," I interject.

"Sorry. I got sidetracked."

"I noticed," I state. "You also forgot we were going to keep that little interaction between us?"

Sarah has the good sense to look slightly abashed. "Right. Sorry."

"You told Sarah, but you didn't tell me?" Brooke asks, outraged.

"I wasn't going to tell anyone!" I reply. "Sarah found out by accident, and I asked her not to say anything." I send her a quick glance to emphasize my point, and she gives me a sheepish look in response.

"Whatever, we'll get back to that. So, you did get into a screaming match with Weston Cole yesterday?" Brooke gets back on track with her original interrogation.

I cringe. "It wasn't a screaming match, exactly... I'd characterize it more like a loud conversation."

Brooke swats my words away like an irritating fly. "I couldn't care less how you're characterizing it. What was it about?"

"I've been—um, I kind of had a thing. With him."

"You had a thing. With Weston fucking Cole?" Astonishment blankets every word and lingers on her face.

"Uh-huh." I try to act nonchalant as I pull my lunch out of my backpack and start eating my turkey sandwich.

Brooke appraises me carefully. "You. Maeve Stevens. Miss Perfect, Straight A's, Rule Follower, Student Council President, Soccer Captain had a *thing* with the Alleghany quarterback?"

"Yes." I take another bite of my sandwich.

"How—how did you even meet him?"

"Uh, at the Alleghany party Maggie brought me to." Our freshman year tête-à-tête is not something I'm willing to share.

Brooke nods as though she's come to some brilliant realization. "Oh, is that what the 'loud conversation' was about? You told him you were some girl from Fayetteville then and he figured out the truth somehow?"

I scoff at her assumption. "No. He's always known who I am. And our conversation was about Matt kissing me at the Alleghany field on Thursday."

"That was you?" Sarah gasps. "Everyone's been trying to figure out who that was."

"Fantastic." I take another bite.

"Damn, Maeve. You've got things going with both Matt and Weston Cole? If I weren't so horrified by the Weston Cole of it all, I'd almost be impressed," Brooke comments.

"There's *nothing* going on between me and Matt," I clarify. "He caught me off guard, and Sam had the brilliant timing of capturing it on camera and sending it around. The only person I have feelings for is Wes, but that's especially complicated right now. Ergo, the 'loud conversation.'"

"Wes?" Brooke catches. "Wow. I guess people haven't been exaggerating about the Weston Cole charm after all."

"There's a lot more to him than that," I snap.

"You're awfully defensive of someone you were screaming at yesterday."

"It's not just his fault things between us are a mess. And...I'm in love with him, okay?"

Brooke looks at me with pity. "Oh, Maeve. He fed you that line?"

"It wasn't a line," I respond tersely. Sarah stays silent, and I can't help but glance at her. She's the only person who's seen us interact. Did it seem false to her?

"So, you didn't sleep with him?"

"I'm not discussing it with you," I tell Brooke stiffly.

"That's not a 'no,' Maeve."

"You're right. It's an 'I'm not discussing it with you.' If you want to ask me questions about him, fine. But it's not helpful for you to pick apart my relationship—"

"Relationship?" Brooke cuts me off. "I'm trying to keep you from getting more hurt, Maeve. He's Weston fucking Cole! He's a total player! I could list ten girls I know he's hooked up with."

"And I'd hardly say you're in a position to judge them, or me," I reply. "Wasn't it just a couple months ago you were begging me for details about how he looks in person? You ask Maggie about him every time we see her!"

"I think he's hot, yes! And I was teasing Maggie about him because I never thought she would ever hook up with him! Even now that she lives in Alleghany. And I'm not judging you, Maeve. You know I've done plenty of stupid stuff, and you're one of my best friends. I'm just trying to get you to see reality, since apparently you've lost touch."

The bell signaling the end of lunch rings, and I stand, packing away my mostly untouched lunch. "I'll see you guys at Chase's tonight."

I slink into English. Damn Mr. Thompson and his attempt to be innovative and seat us alphabetically by first name instead of last.

Matt is already in his seat. I give him a hesitant smile, meeting his gaze for the first time since Thursday. I haven't known how to act around him, but I feel guilty for avoiding him, especially after Liam's sulking comment last night.

"Hey," I greet him like it's any ordinary weekday. He doesn't reply, but I watch a muscle jump in his jaw. "Come on, Matt, I thought we were friends."

"We *were* friends. Before I knew the guy you were talking about was Weston fucking Cole."

"Look, I'm really sorry if I hurt your feelings—"

Matt scoffs loudly, and I belatedly realize this was probably not the best place to start this conversation. Mr. Thompson is still writing quotes out on the board, so the entirety of my English class is eavesdropping on our conversation.

"You didn't 'hurt my feelings,' Maeve. I'm disappointed in you. Even if he weren't from Alleghany, Weston Cole is a total asshole. All he cares about is playing football and getting laid."

"You just described a lot of teenage guys. Including yourself," I retort.

Matt's face flushes an angry shade of red. "Just don't come crying to me when you fall for his charms, and he drops you for the next challenge. All I'll have is a big fat told-you-so."

I bristle. I'm sick of people assuming I didn't know what I

was getting into with Wes. That he somehow charmed me sense-less. That I wasn't an equal participant.

"Well, you can save your breath, because I 'fell for his charms', and he still stuck around."

It doesn't take long for me to regret my hasty words. Not only because I've just inadvertently implied—actually more like loudly announced—to my entire English class that I've slept with Weston Cole, but because Matt's crushed expression makes it pretty clear I was right before. I did hurt his feelings by turning him down, and this latest revelation is salt in the wound.

Thankfully, Mr. Thompson chooses this moment to call the class to attention, and I look away from Matt's angry, crestfallen face.

The rest of the day drags. I endure two more classes of stares and whispers, and then a long soccer practice of side glances from my teammates. I head straight to Sarah's house from practice. Maggie, Brooke, and Sarah are all there already.

Maggie berates me for not telling her about Wes and then fires all the same questions at me that Brooke did at lunch. Her reaction is less disapproving, but she's just as astounded by my reve-lations. The exception is when I reveal I encountered Wes again after the kitchen at the party this summer.

"I'm sorry. What did you just say? When you 'went to the bathroom' you were actually kissing Weston Cole? Un-freaking-believable," she muses. "The one Alleghany party I take you to…"

Brooke asks her if there are rumors about me at Alleghany High, and I hold my breath as I wait for her answer.

"Uh, yeah," she informs us. "It's Weston Cole. People gossip about his lunch choices. Everyone's talking about Maeve showing up at the party on Friday, and Wes going to Glenmont High."

"Did you see him today?" I can't help but ask.

"Once. In the hallway," Maggie tells me.

"Did he look mad?"

"He didn't look thrilled," she responds. "No one at school will say a thing to his face, but I'm guessing he's going to take some heat from the football team."

I say nothing in response. Maggie leaves at eight, saying she has an "Alleghany commitment."

Neither Brooke nor Sarah bother to ask for more details, and I don't need to. I already know where she's headed. Tonight is the Alleghany Athletics ceremony Wes told me about a few weeks ago. The reason he had to reschedule his trip to Lincoln.

I shower in Sarah's guest bathroom, and then change into a pair of dark skinny jeans and a loose, light gray sweater.

We arrive at Chase's house to find the party is already in full swing. Sam usually hosts the parties after football games, but Chase lives in Glenmont's most upscale neighborhood, and has parents who don't seem to mind housing hundreds of drunk teenagers, so he ends up hosting most of Glenmont High's more notorious get-togethers. The start of Thanksgiving break is a classic blowout.

I walk through the entryway and toward the kitchen, hesitantly, even with Brooke and Sarah on either side of me. None of the Glenmont football players besides Matt have said anything to me about Wes directly, but I know there's still plenty of speculation swirling.

"Shots, ladies?" Chase asks as we enter the kitchen. He's converted the corner breakfast nook into a makeshift bar and has sprawled out along the booth with an expansive array of alcohol spread before him.

"Hell yes!" Brooke agrees, unsurprisingly. "Five-day weekend!" She downs the alcohol.

"I'm good," Sarah replies, which is also predictable.

Brooke and Maggie have always been the wilder half of our quartet. Sarah and I have always trodden with more caution.

But I threw that into disarray a while ago.

"I'll take one." I hold my hand out.

I feel Brooke and Sarah's eyes on me.

"Maeve, are you sure that's a good idea?" Sarah asks cautiously.

I don't answer Sarah. I down the chilled liquid, making a face at the taste as it burns its way down my throat.

"Let her have some fun, Sarah. She's had a rough few days," Brooke says.

The roughest.

"What else do you have?" I ask Chase. He grins.

CHAPTER TWENTY-FOUR

WESTON

"Yo, Cole, you in?" Chris calls as we head out to the parking lot.

"Yeah, sure," I respond, loosening my tie as I head toward my car. "I'll meet you there."

I'm glad I drove separately since my parents bailed on the awards ceremony early for an "important work event." I'm guessing that wasn't entirely accurate, based on the hard set of my mother's mouth all night, but for once I'm not focused on my parents' fucked-up relationship.

I've got my own to worry about.

Just as I climb into the driver's seat, I feel my phone vibrate. I pull it out, expecting it to be Chris asking me to pick something up on my way over.

It's not. It's her.

My pulse quickens as I unlock my phone. It's been radio silence from Maeve since I showed up at her soccer practice. Based on the rumors swirling around Alleghany, I'm guessing there's some speculation about us flying around Glenmont now, too. I don't want to be, but I'm curious about what she has to say.

It's gibberish. *JI muss uou.*

I think it's entirely nonsensical at first. But, as I study the jumbled letters more closely, I realize that's not true. She sent me a garbled version of *I miss you.* And there's only one reason I can think of why she would have sent me an error-ridden version of it. I tap her name, but her phone rings and rings without her answering. I try again; same result.

"Damn it." I slam my palm against the steering wheel, trying not to imagine all the possible scenarios she could be in right now. Drunk for the first time. Alone, at the lake, with another guy… "Fuck!"

I open the location sharing app. She still shows up, so she hasn't blocked me. And she's showing up at a house in Glenmont. I'm tempted to take another swing at my steering wheel. I know I'll never forgive myself if I go to Chris's right now and something happens to her, no matter how angry I still am.

It doesn't take long to plug the address into my GPS, and then I start driving.

Belatedly, I wonder if I should have asked Chris or Charlie to come with me. Our make-up game against Glenmont is in three days, and I'm about to show up at one of their parties looking for Liam Stevens' sister. I've never even interacted with anyone from Glenmont besides Maeve outside of football before.

I know other guys who have gone to parties in Fayetteville, but I'm the Alleghany quarterback. I don't have the luxury of anonymity. The only high school party outside of Alleghany I've been to is the one my cousin threw my freshman year. Where I first met Maeve.

I cross the boundary line into Glenmont and drive another ten minutes before I park haphazardly in front of a large, white, Colonial-style house. I can hear music playing loudly inside as soon as I climb out of the car.

I don't bother knocking; I just walk inside.

There are only a few people standing in the front entryway when I enter the house, and all three of them stop talking and stare as soon as they see me. I keep striding forward, into what I quickly realize is the kitchen. The crowded room falls silent when I enter it, but my gaze is fixed on Maeve.

She's leaning against the marble kitchen counter, laughing loudly with a brunette girl. I can't help but drink in the sight of her as I walk over. She's drunk, no doubt about it, but she also looks happy. Carefree. Her blonde hair is loose, and the light gray sweater she's wearing is hanging off of one shoulder.

The shift in the kitchen's atmosphere eventually reaches her, and she turns toward me right as I stop a couple of feet from her.

Startled green eyes meet mine.

"Wes," she breathes. "What are you doing here?"

"You texted me."

"I did?" She looks bewildered.

"You did," I confirm.

"And you came?"

"Nothing gets past you, Stevens." Her brunette friend laughs. "Come on, let's go."

"I don't want to leave yet. I'm having fun." She giggles, as if to emphasize just how much fun she's having.

"No, you're not. You're wasted. Let's go, I'm supposed to be somewhere else right now," I urge impatiently. I can feel stares boring into my back, and I'm anxious to get out of here.

Ire flashes across Maeve's features. "I don't need you to babysit me, Wes."

"Well, I don't see anyone else volunteering to help you sober up."

"I don't need anyone's help! I'm having fun, okay? I'm just trying to have some fun."

"This isn't how you have fun, Maeve. This isn't you."

"It isn't? You already decided I'm a slut; might as well be a lush now too, right?" Spite dances in her green eyes.

Fuck. I close my eyes and count to ten. "We're not having this conversation right now."

"Why? Because we're in Glenmont? On my home turf? They all know already, anyway. I even told my English class we've had sex because Matt said you would dump me once you got in my pants."

I hear a few gasps behind me, and I rake my fingers through my hair, tempted to just toss Maeve over my shoulder. Of course she'd be a belligerent drunk.

"I said we're *not* having this conversation right now, Maeve Elizabeth Stevens." I level her with a hard look, and she finally shuts her mouth.

"That was your only one," she reminds me.

"I know."

She studies me, and then asks, "Did you win?"

For one moment, I think she's asking about the staring match we're locked in. Then I realize she's finally noticed what I'm wearing. I hate that she remembered.

"Yeah, I won."

"I knew you would," she says softly, and the tender expression on her face is worse than when she was talking about our sex life in front of half of Glenmont's senior class. "I'm proud of you, Wes." Something shifts in her expression. "I'm really mad at you, but I'm proud of you, too."

"Not exactly thrilled with you at the moment either, Stevens," I respond. Turning toward the fridge she's standing next to, I open the door and pull a bottle of water out. I unscrew the cap and hand it to Maeve. "Drink this; we're leaving."

"I don't want to leave," she replies petulantly.

"We've covered that. But you're drunk, and I'm not leaving you here like this."

"So you're the only one who's allowed to get drunk and kiss other people?"

At this point, you could hear a pin drop in the kitchen, and it's ironic, really, how we've gone from no one knowing anything about our relationship to acting as live entertainment for dozens.

"We're not discussing this here, Maeve. I didn't come to fight with you. I came because I was worried. Please, just let me take you home."

Some of the confrontation finally drains from her posture.

"What the hell is going o—oh. What are you doing here, Cole?" Liam Stevens chooses this moment to enter the silent kitchen. His voice is carefully measured, but there's a slight edge to it. Liam's eyes shift to Maeve, giving away the answer to his own question. He knows. Either she told him, or Glenmont's gossip mill did.

"I'm taking Maeve home," I state, copying his emotionless tone.

"I'll make sure she gets home, or one of her friends will. Maeve can leave whenever she wants to. She doesn't need you bossing her around."

"Well, seeing as you didn't even notice she's wasted, I don't have a whole lot of confidence in your ability to do that," I retort.

"Maeve's not—"

"Yes, she fucking is, and you of all people should not have let that happen!" I'm quickly losing my temper.

"What are you insinuating, Cole?"

"You know there's a reason Maeve doesn't drink, right?" I ask Liam.

He pales. "She told—"

Thankfully, Maeve finally decides to be agreeable. "It's fine, Liam," she tells her twin brother. "I'll see you at home."

She whispers something to her friend and then starts toward me. She stumbles slightly as she does, and I automatically reach out to steady her. Rather than move away, she leans into me. Liam's gaze bounces between us.

"I thought you were in some big rush, Wes?" she adds pointedly when I don't move.

I snort. Normally I appreciate Maeve's spirit, but I'm not in the mood right now. "Don't start, Stevens."

She rolls her eyes at me and starts toward the doorway, swaying slightly.

"Jesus Christ," I follow her, placing my hand on the small of her back to help steady her. "Where's your jacket, Maeve? It's freezing out."

"Don't have one." Maeve smirks up at me as the material of her thin sweater slips further down her shoulder. I sigh before pulling off my suit jacket and settling it on her shoulders.

"Let's go."

She comes with me willingly, and no one else in the house says anything as we head out the front door and down the walkway.

"Nice parking job," Maeve comments as we reach the curb. My car is crookedly angled against the cement divider.

"I didn't think I'd be here for long."

"You should have known better," Maeve replies.

"Yeah, probably," I admit. She's stubborn sober.

Maeve heads toward the passenger side and fumbles with the handle. I sigh and follow her, opening it easily. She doesn't climb right inside, though. She leans against the side of the car and stares at me.

"I'm sorry. I know I said some shit in there I shouldn't have."

"You're drunk. That makes people do stupid stuff."

"Yeah, it does," she replies sadly, and I know we're not just talking about her anymore. We're talking about me, too. "I just wanted to try to forget for a while. But I didn't. All I thought about was my dad...wondering what he was trying to forget. And you. I think about you a lot."

"Maeve..." I start, not sure what to say. Not sure what to even think anymore.

"Do you still not believe me?"

"I don't know," I whisper. But I think I do know, and that's terrifying in its own way.

Maeve nods and finally climbs in the car. It's been my goal all along, but suddenly it's the last thing I want her to do. I expected her to fight my words, to force me to tell her why I still think she cheated on me when everything since I saw that photo has pointed to the contrary. But she doesn't. She just accepts my half-answer.

I guess it's true what they say. The opposite of love isn't hate; it's indifference. And that's exactly what Maeve's blank face conveys as she pulls the door shut, leaving me standing on the street. Alone. I walk around the car and climb into the driver's seat, shutting my own door to block out the cold chill of the night air.

We sit in silence for a moment. I feel like I need to say something else, but I don't know what. I don't know how much I can give her.

"I thought you were in a big rush? I'm assuming it's to get to some party?" Maeve finally asks. Her voice is quiet and emotionless.

She's right, that was my primary goal in dragging her out of there as quickly as possible. And if the amount of buzzing my phone has been doing is any indication, my absence has definitely been noticed. But the thought of drinking beer with my teammates, dodging questions about the blonde sitting next to me, and shrugging off eager girls has rapidly become an unappealing one.

"I'm not walking home, so if you want to get there sometime soon, then you'd better start driving."

I almost laugh. Instead, I turn on the car, and the rush of warm air from the vents fills the silence between us.

"I need directions," I admit to her.

It's bizarre, considering all that we've shared, both the good and the bad, that I've never been to her house. I have no idea where she lives.

Maeve laughs, and I wonder if she's thinking the same thing. "Take a right at the end of the street. It's eight houses down. The yellow bungalow."

"You live one street over?"

"Uh-huh," Maeve replies. "You going to make me walk now?"

"No, I'm not going to make you walk, Stevens," I assure her as I start driving along.

It doesn't even take two minutes to reach her house. It's homey. Quaint. Charming. Not where I would have pictured Liam Stevens living, but its cheerful color and inviting style fits Maeve. The windows are all dark.

"Your parents already went to bed?" I ask Maeve in surprise. It's only just after ten.

"No, they're gone for the night. My mom had some realtor conference in the city, and they're spending the night at a hotel."

"Oh. Do you need help getting inside?" I offer, even though I know it's a monumentally stupid suggestion, especially since her parents are gone.

Thankfully, she shakes her head, although I also experience a rush of disappointment. Just another dip on the rollercoaster of contrary emotions Maeve Stevens elicits in me.

"I'll be okay," she promises. "The water helped." She holds up the almost empty water bottle for my inspection.

"Okay. Drink some more when you get inside," I instruct.

"Unless—did you *want* to come in?" she asks tentatively as she shrugs off my suit jacket.

I tighten my grip on the steering wheel. "That's a bad idea, Maeve."

"It's just sex, Wes."

"It's never been just sex with you, Maeve."

She doesn't say anything else, she just climbs out of the car and shuts the door behind her. I sit in the driveway until I see her disappear inside, and then reverse and start driving toward Chris's house.

Emotions swirl within me, and I'm not sure which one is most dominant: anger, annoyance, or regret.

I park in Chris's driveway and head inside. The greeting I receive here is a stark contrast to what met me in Glenmont.

Instead of silence, I hear cheers.

Rather than a pair of wary green eyes, I've got dozens of girls trying to get near me. Evidently, they've taken the rumors about me and a girl from Glenmont as an invitation to become even more aggressive.

I brush past most of the people greeting me and head into the kitchen.

"Where the fuck have you been, Cole?" Chris asks as he comes over to me. "I thought you were coming straight here from the banquet. It's been almost an hour."

"I got side-tracked."

There's no chance he won't hear I was at a party in Glenmont earlier, but I have zero interest in divulging that information right now. The suspicious glint in Chris's eyes makes me think he suspects the truth.

I don't really feel like drinking, but I head to the fridge and grab a can of beer to crack open. Not drinking will raise more questions than sipping this for the rest of the night will. I lean against the counter next to the fridge, warring with myself.

Finally, I pull out my phone. *You feeling okay?* I text Maeve.

She replies immediately, which I'm grateful for. *Like crap but the world stopped spinning.*

I smile despite myself. *Drink more water.*

*I already drank a ton s*he tells me. After a minute, *I'll drink more.*

"So, Maeve Stevens, huh?"

I look up from my phone to see Natalie leaning against the kitchen island across from me.

"What do you mean?" I ask carefully.

She rolls her eyes. "It's all over school, Wes. The girl you have feelings for? It's Maeve Stevens, right? God, I should have put it together when she showed up at Josh's after the Glenmont game. You're not one to back down from a challenge, I'll give you that. Liam Stevens' sister? I mean, I get why you would go there, but her? I thought Maeve Stevens was a loyal goody two-shoes."

"You don't know anything about her, Natalie."

Natalie appraises me. "Maybe not. But she'll always be a girl from Glenmont. You're a decent guy, Weston. Don't fool yourself into thinking it was anything more than a fling." She pushes away from the counter, and the smile she gives me isn't a mocking one. It's a resigned one. She strolls away.

My phone vibrates in my hand. I look down to see Maeve's sent me a photo. It's of her, with two full water glasses on the table next to her. Her hair is damp, and she's wearing a sweatshirt.

My sweatshirt.

And I'm more confused than ever.

CHAPTER TWENTY-FIVE

MAEVE

Thanksgiving is a mostly silent affair in my house.

My father's focused on the rescheduled game against Alleghany tomorrow night. Liam hasn't talked to me since Wes picked me up from Chase's party a couple of nights ago. I'm too caught up in my own thoughts to contribute much. And my mother either has worries of her own, or picks up on the antisocial atmosphere at the table and remains mostly silent as well.

It starts raining just after we finish our meal. Despite the cold, wet weather, my father and Liam head out into the backyard to go over plays for what must be the millionth time. My mother busies herself in the kitchen storing all the leftovers, and I snag the sedan keys and head outside.

I drive around town for about fifteen minutes before finally admitting my destination to myself.

His car is already there when I arrive. Somehow, I knew it would be. I pass the cabin and follow the now familiar path to the same fallen tree where I first encountered Weston Cole.

If only my freshman year self had known what she was in for

as a result of trying to hide out at that party. The scary part? I don't think I would go back and change it. Any of it.

The log comes into view, and I trace the lines and curves of the familiar figure sitting in the darkness. The rain patters against the few stubborn leaves still clinging to the branches overhead. The wind soughs, swirling the air and whipping my hair.

I know he must have heard my approach, but Wes doesn't say anything as I take a seat on the damp bark next to him. He does glance over at my choice of outerwear but doesn't comment on it. Or worse, ask for it back. It's stupid, but I want him to see I'm not ashamed to wear his sweatshirt. That it's not tainted from that night at Alleghany's field.

"Thank you for coming on Tuesday night. And I'm sorry for how I acted. To be honest, I don't remember parts of it, but Brooke assured me I said some stuff I definitely wouldn't have sober."

"You don't need to thank me, Maeve. Or apologize."

"Still, thank you. I needed you. And you came."

"I'm sorry about kissing Natalie. No matter what I thought you'd done, you were right. It was a shitty thing to do."

"It's okay," I reply. It still smarts, but I don't know what else to say. What his apology means.

I'm worried he did more than just kiss her later that night, but I don't know how to ask him.

Don't know if I want to know the answer.

He looks over at me. "No, it's not okay, Maeve. I should have believed you about Crawford. I *do* believe you. I just—this wasn't supposed to mean this much, you know? You were right. I got scared. *You* scare me."

Silence stretches between us, as impenetrable and thick as the dark woods surrounding us.

"How was your Thanksgiving?" I finally ask.

Wes lets out a short laugh. "Not great. Yours?"

"Quiet. Liam's not talking to me."

"He was calmer than I expected. At that party."

I sigh. "I told him about us. Or that there used to be an us. After you showed up at practice. I knew there would be rumors, and I thought it would be better if he heard it from me."

Wes doesn't say anything at first. "It's always going to be there between us, Maeve. This stupid fucking rivalry. I'll always be from Alleghany, and you'll always be from Glenmont. Your brother will always resent me. Your father will never like me. Our friends will never get along. We live fifteen minutes apart, but it might as well be fifteen thousand miles. We were fooling ourselves, thinking this could ever work. I'm sick of sneaking around. I'm sick of wondering if I should tell you something. I'm sick of lying to my friends about where I've been."

Tears begin sliding down my cheeks, and I hope it's dark enough he can't tell. Because he's saying we're—I'm—not worth it.

And I thought we were.

I think he is.

I want to throw his past words back at him. Tell him he shouldn't allow other people's opinions to define us. Call him a coward again.

But I'm so tired of fighting. Fighting and losing.

I stand and brush the damp forest debris off my leggings. "Good luck tomorrow, Wes." I mean it. I don't want Alleghany to win, but I don't think I'll ever be able to wish Wes won't.

I turn to make the trek back to my car.

"What did he say?"

"Huh?" I glance back at Wes, but he's still staring straight ahead.

"Liam. When you told him about us."

I'm brutally honest; I've got nothing left to lose now. "He was surprised. That you'd commit—to me. That you'd even care Matt kissed me. I told him he doesn't know anything about you. And then he asked what you'd told me about the Eagles. And I told him you've never asked me the same thing about the Stallions."

Wes says nothing in response. I turn to go again.

"You know, this wasn't just your problem, Wes. You kissing me didn't exactly make my life easier. But I'm still glad you did."

This time, I leave him sitting on the same mossy log where we first spoke two and a half years ago.

We've come full circle.

The following morning, Liam and I are eating our breakfast at the table silently when my father enters the dining room.

"I've got Crawford, Peters, and Williams coming in early to watch some extra footage, Liam. Finish up eating, I came up with a new play last night I want to run through."

Liam nods, dutifully scooping up the last of his eggs.

"Why aren't you coming to my game, Dad?" I don't realize I actually said the words out loud until he and Liam both look over at me.

"What?" my father asks, looking startled.

"I asked why you aren't coming to my game," I repeat.

"We're reviewing film," my father replies. "We're playing Alleghany tonight, Maeve. You know how important this is."

"Yes, I do," I acknowledge. "But you don't seem to get how important soccer is to me. You've spent every waking moment for the past few months preparing for this game, but you can't spare two hours to come to my last high school soccer game?"

"Maeve, of course I was planning to go. But that was before the game got rescheduled for today, and now there's a conflict in the schedules. I didn't have any control over the thunderstorm last week, or when the game was moved to."

"The game didn't get rescheduled for the same time as mine. *You* scheduled this film review at the same time."

"Maeve, this is my job! I'm sure Alleghany isn't taking the day off reviewing film. You can't expect me to just because of your game."

"Well, it would be nice if I could expect you to act like you have two kids, not just one," I retort. "We may be twins, but we're not interchangeable."

I stride into the kitchen, not bothering to wait for his response.

I've never said anything to my father before because I knew it wouldn't make a difference, just like it didn't now, but I underestimated how freeing it would be to let my father know exactly how I feel about his blatant favoritism toward Liam and football.

The feeling of satisfaction fades when I realize exactly who I want to tell about this. The person who inspired me to say it in the first place. The boy who broke my heart last night.

I put my spoon and bowl in the dishwasher and head upstairs to get ready for my game.

Liam appears in my doorway about twenty minutes later, hovering uncertainly. Things were already tense between us, and my outburst during breakfast has added extra layers of awkwardness.

"Good luck," he finally says.

"Thanks," I reply, tying off one side of my French braid.

"Liam!" my father bellows from downstairs. "Let's go."

Liam disappears into the hallway. I finish braiding the other half of my hair and then gather up my gear and head downstairs. I run into my mother on the front porch, just back from showing a house.

"You're headed to the game already?" my mother asks, glancing at her watch.

"Yup."

"Okay, I've got to make a quick stop at the office to drop these keys off, but I'll see you at the game, all right?" I'm guessing the reassurance means she already spoke to my father.

"Okay," I respond, heading toward the sedan.

The crowd of people at the field is unexpected. I've become accustomed to having about the same number of spectators as the roster of players on a basketball team. Last year's final was an away game, so fans were especially limited. Thanks to our superior season record, we're hosting Clayville today, and a vast majority of the hundred or so people gathered around the field are wearing Glenmont's signature shade of maroon in support.

I drop my soccer bag off at the team bench. My teammates greet me with nervous smiles that don't help to alleviate the butterflies fluttering in my stomach. I don't usually get anxious before games, but this is it. The final one. The one that really matters. Coach Bloom beckons me over.

"Ready, Stevens?" she asks.

"Absolutely," I reply, projecting as much confidence in my voice as I can.

Coach Bloom smiles at my response, but I think she sees through it, at least a little, because she squeezes my shoulder once before nodding toward the field.

"Run them through the usual," she instructs me. I nod once before heading toward our end of the field. My teammates follow me without prompting.

I'm halfway through leading the warm-up stretches when I see him. He's wearing all black and a baseball cap in an obvious attempt to look incognito, but it's definitely him. I'd know those broad shoulders and that confident stance anywhere. What I don't know is what he's doing here.

"So, am I crazy, or is that Weston Cole at our soccer game?" Becca whispers from her spot next to me as we shift to sitting on the grass in order to stretch our hamstrings.

"You're not crazy," I reply.

Rather than serve as a distraction, Wes's presence buoys me as the game starts. Just like the last time he showed up to watch me play, I want to impress him. Make this worth his while.

It's probably not the healthiest mindset considering we just officially broke up, but it serves me well on the field. It's also the perfect antidote to the nerves niggling in my stomach. Brazen confidence washes them away.

I score the first goal of the game ten minutes in. After that, Clayville doesn't stand a chance. We're unstoppable. Becca scores right after halftime, and I make a second goal fifteen minutes later. Clayville tries, but they can't stop our momentum.

The final whistle sounds, and I'm swarmed. My ears ring with the screams and shouts of my teammates as we unite into one celebratory mass. The first thing I do when we detangle is glance at the spot where Wes was standing. He's gone, and I try not to let the ache of disappointment infringe on the happiness bubbling inside me.

We line up for the familiar handshake, and as soon as Clayville's team departs, our spectators pour on the field. My mom is the first to reach me.

"Congratulations, Maeve! I'm so proud of you!" she tells me as she gives me a big hug.

"Thanks, Mom," I reply, hugging her tightly.

Sarah and Brooke reach me next, both vibrating with excitement. Sarah grabs me first. I'm hugging Brooke when Maggie comes bounding over.

"Maeve! I'm so sorry I missed the game. Practice ran long, or else I would have been here sooner. Congratulations!" She gives me a big hug.

"Practice ran long?" Brooke asks when we pull apart. "You must miss the Glenmont squad. We didn't even have practice this week."

Maggie groans. "You have no idea. We were supposed to coordinate with the football team to prepare for tonight, but apparently their captain's meeting got moved and no one told us. Natalie made us stay late to make sure we're ready. I swear, if the season wasn't almost over, I'd be tempted to quit."

I wasn't sure if Brooke and Sarah saw Wes here, but the glances they both give me following Maggie's words confirm they did.

Because we all know who the captain of Alleghany's football team is.

"What? What did I miss?" Maggie asks, tracking the direction of their stares.

My father and brother chose to watch football film instead of coming to my game. My mother was fifteen minutes late thanks to her "quick stop" at the office. And Wes moved the Alleghany football team's meeting on the day they're playing Glenmont so he could be here. For me.

I'm not sure whether to laugh at the irony or start crying.

"Not what. Who," Brooke replies. "A certain quarterback who apparently moved his entire team's pre-game meeting so he could watch Maeve kick some ass."

Maggie gasps. "Weston Cole was here?"

"You just missed him," Sarah adds.

All three of them look at me. I shrug. "I have no idea why he was here. He dumped me last night. Again. Still. We're done."

Brooke scoffs. "Yeah, right."

"What? You're the one who said he's a player, and I was stupid to get involved with him."

"That was before I saw you two together. Weston Cole is seriously smitten with you. He came to a Glenmont party to help you because you sent him a drunk text. Do you know how many guys I've sent drunk texts to? A lot. I don't even know. How many do you think have shown up to see if I'm okay? That I do know. Zero."

"He knows I don't usually drink. I'm sure he just felt obligated. It's not like he could text you or Sarah and check."

"It seemed a lot more like love than obligation. I was doubtful when you told us he said it. Because it means a lot more to act like it. I hadn't had a chance to see it. But he does act like it, Maeve."

One of my teammates rushes over to grab me for a group picture, and I say goodbye to my best friends. Honestly, I'm grateful for the interruption. I thought I'd finally settled where Wes and I stand.

Him coming here? Brooke's words? Sends things back into a disarray I'm not sure if I'm equipped for.

An hour later, I sit on my front porch stairs, sipping on a mug of steaming tea. The door opens and closes behind me.

"You want to tell me what's wrong, Maeve?" My mother takes a seat next to me on the top step and gives me a searching look. "You should be thrilled after winning that game. You were incredible."

I sigh. High school students aren't the only gossips in this town. She'll likely hear it eventually.

"I have feelings for someone…inconvenient."

My mother nods once. "Weston Cole."

I look over at her, surprised. "How do you know that?"

"Call it a mother's intuition." I raise my eyebrows. "And I may have found an Alleghany jersey with his name on it under your bed a couple weeks ago."

"Yeah, I should probably burn that."

"What happened?"

"We broke up. First because of a misunderstanding. But then, he said it could never work between us. That he was sick of lying and sneaking around."

"So, why don't you stop doing that?"

"That's the point. We have."

My mother laughs. "No, I mean stop lying and sneaking around. Let people know you're a couple. Who cares what they think if the two of you are happy?"

"Mom. He's Weston Cole."

"He's also the boy you have feelings for, right?"

"Yes," I admit. No way am I dropping the l-word right now.

"That sounds more important to me than a high school rivalry. Your brother and father will get over it."

"I'm not so sure about that. Besides, he doesn't want me anymore."

"Did he say that?"

"He said the rivalry will always be there. Between us."

"So show him it won't."

"I don't know how to do that. *If* I can do that." I look down at the steam curling from my mug.

"Yes, you do."

CHAPTER TWENTY-SIX

WESTON

I'm one of the first guys to arrive at the bus. I lean against one of the bleacher supports, staring out at our home field. It's been cleaned, but I can still picture the horseshoes scattered all across it. At least the live version didn't include Maeve kissing another guy.

"Cole! You ready to kick some ass?"

I turn to see Chris bounding toward me. He's filled with the energy and enthusiasm I should have. I'm ready. I'm confident. But I'm not enthused.

"Absolutely." I return my gaze to the grass.

"What's going on with you now, Wes?"

"Nothing. I'm fine." My voice is hollow. I'm wavering again, and I hate it. I thought I'd feel relief when I told Maeve it was over last night. But all I've experienced since then is regret.

Chris studies my face, and I see the exact moment it dawns on him. "This is about her. I thought you said it is over."

"It is."

"But you don't want it to be?"

"I don't know."

"Wes, you promised the team you would have your head on straight when it comes to this game. This is Glenmont we're playing!"

"I know. I'm ready for the game," I assure him.

"What are you guys doing over here?" Charlie asks, lumbering over to the bleachers.

"Just discussing how Wes is letting Maeve Stevens get inside his head." Chris doesn't hesitate to throw me under the bus, and I glare at him. He shrugs.

"I am not, for the record," I tell Chris emphatically as Adam joins us.

"This have anything to do with why our meeting earlier was mysteriously moved to a time that didn't conflict with the Glenmont girls' soccer game?" Adam questions.

I didn't expect anyone to put together the real reason I changed the time. "You're keeping track of the Glenmont girls' soccer schedule?"

"Caroline mentioned it to Josh."

"Huh." I employ my usual non-answer.

"I heard they won," is Charlie's contribution.

"Yeah, they did," I reply unnecessarily.

"And…did you talk to her?" Chris asks.

"Of course not."

"Why not?"

"Uh—because we just broke up?"

"Was Crawford there?" Charlie asks.

"Not that I saw."

"He's probably going to make another move on her, Cole."

I'm seriously regretting ever filling my friends in on what started the strife between Maeve and me. Because Charlie's words prompt a new pang of regret. And make me glad I'm about to be in a position to cream Crawford along with the rest of Glenmont's team.

"Let's go," I say, turning and striding toward the bus. We're the final players to board. I take the same seat I always do at the very back, and then we pull out of the parking lot, headed toward Glenmont.

The absent excitement finally appears. Not because I'm growing closer to the game, but because I'm growing closer to her.

Glenmont's parking lot is packed when the bus pulls up. We file off one by one. Coach Blake doesn't say anything as I pass him to lead the team out onto the field, but he claps me on the back.

When we appear on the field, it's to a barrage of boos. Alleghany fans are out in force, but they're no match for the packed home crowd. The demeaning sound fuels me the same way it does at every away game. Adrenaline pumps through my system.

It's expected: the noise, the crowded stands, the electric atmosphere.

What's not expected? The solitary speck of royal blue among the sea of maroon comprising the Glenmont side.

I freeze as soon as I see it. I never asked for my extra jersey back after the night we first had sex. I would have bet money it hadn't survived through the tumult of this past week.

And yet there Maeve Stevens sits, wearing my blue jersey in a sea of Glenmont fans. She's seated only a few rows back from the field. I can see my number emblazoned on the front from here.

Chris lets out a low whistle as he comes to a stop next to me. The rest of the team keeps walking, although there are a number of glances back at me. "That's one hell of a gesture, Cole."

Maeve's choice of attire is drawing plenty of attention from both sides of the field. I see Liam Stevens glancing between us. Matt Crawford is giving me a death glare. And I'm still stupefied. I can't believe she did this.

"So…you standing here like a statue is not exactly inspiring confidence you're ready for this game," Chris adds. "She's probably going to regret wearing your jersey if you're too busy imitating a figurine to actually play."

The zeal and zest I've been missing all day finally appears in full force. "Oh, I'm ready, Fields." I give him a confident smirk as I start to jog toward the bench.

The face-off with Liam Stevens and Matt Crawford for the coin toss is awkward, to say the least. Even the referee looks uncomfortable with the palpable tension as I call tails. Especially when the coin doesn't come up as the heads Stevens called. It's a small victory, one that will likely end up being meaningless in the grand scheme of things, but it's a win, nonetheless.

Rather than the blind rage that possessed me the last time we were on this field, I'm exhilarated. It's not a feigned air of indifference, the way I've played games in the past. It's genuine. I'm enjoying myself.

Based on the grim set of Liam Stevens' mouth, he can't say the same. I don't think I've ever seen him smile. He's got an almost militaristic persona on the field, and Glenmont follows every command with perfect precision.

I'm not surprised when they cap off a series of meticulously plotted plays with the game's first touchdown. They're meticulous, but they're also predictable.

Loud cheers resound around the field as I stride out with our offensive unit. Not for me, they're residual applause for Glenmont. I even catch Liam Stevens with a slight grin. The sight doesn't bother me.

Out of everyone in Glenmont, I get why he hates me. Especially now.

I'm also confident they won't be ahead for long. I mutter the play I want to run to Chris as we take our positions on the field. We break our starting stance, and Glenmont's doing its damnedest to get to me. I only have seconds. My eyes find Chris, right where I told him to be.

This split second is why I love playing football. Why I love being the quarterback. I started out as a receiver, and I was a good one. But once my coaches realized I could throw, I was shifted to quarterback. I've retained the uncanny ability to know exactly where the ball should go, though. Where I would need it if I were the one about to run. My finger finds the sweet spot between the laces, and I let the weathered leather fly. It spirals through the air in a deadly arc. Deadly, because it lands in Chris's waiting arms, and travels in them to the end zone.

Hello, momentum.

Our kicker makes the extra point, and we're tied. The blue side of the bleachers is jubilant, and I don't look at Glenmont's side. I haven't since the game began.

Glenmont can't manage to generate anything offensively, despite their best efforts. They slow us down, but they can't halt us completely. We score two more touchdowns before the final whistle blows.

It's eerie, how one side sits silent while the other erupts. I'm mobbed. My jersey is yanked, my facemask is grabbed, my helmet is clanked against every one of my teammates'.

They're acting like we just won the state championship, and I know for many of them, this is an even sweeter victory. It's a testament to the power of Alleghany's rivalry against Glenmont. With the exception of me and a couple other guys, all my teammates grew up coming to Alleghany High games. They spent their middle school years watching Coach Stevens' team trounce ours. Hearing about how Liam Stevens was coming and Glenmont would be unstoppable. We just ensured that never happened.

We halt our celebrations for the time-tested tradition of shaking hands and repeating the mantra of "good game." It's a ritual I respect, but right now it feels a little bit like forcing the same poles of two magnets together. The hatred emanating off Glenmont's team feels tangible, choking the air between us as the two lines start to move.

Suddenly, I realize the hand I'm shaking is Liam Stevens'.

"Good game," I repeat to him. He says the same, but keeps gripping my hand, holding me in place. He opens his mouth like there's something else he wants to say, but he thinks better of it.

He closes his mouth and lets go of my hand. I grab the next Glenmont player's hand. Which happens to belong to Matt Crawford.

"Good game," I say again. He mutters it back to me, looking like he'd rather tell me something much less complimentary.

As soon as the last two players shake hands, the cheerleaders come off the track to join our celebration, and several of them give me hugs, including Natalie, making me hope Maeve isn't watching. Then, parents start to appear as well. I'm in the midst of a second detailed discussion of my first touchdown pass with a teammate's father when I spot a familiar figure making her way toward me.

Mr. Baylor departs with one final pat on the back, just as my mother stops in front of me.

"Mom," I state. "What are you doing here? Aren't you supposed to be in the city? With Dad?"

"I turned around and left as soon as we arrived. I should have changed my plans as soon as your game was moved. It's just—I felt like I needed to—"

"I know, Mom. I know why you go with him," I say, so she doesn't have to.

"I know you do, Wes. And I hate that you do. I hate that your relationship with your father has become what it has. I stayed with him for a lot of reasons, but the primary one has always been to keep our family intact. But it hasn't felt that way for a while."

"That's not your fault, Mom. It's his."

"He's embarrassed, Wes. He knows you judge him for it." I open my mouth, but she continues. "I'm not defending him. He deserves judgement for some of the choices he's made."

"He hasn't done much to fix things."

"Your father wants to be someone you look to for advice and support, Wes. He knows he's not, so it's easier for him to not be present for these moments than to be here and for you to ignore him." I start to talk, but my mother holds up her hand. "I'm just sharing with you what he told me. But you're right. That's why I told him earlier if things don't change, I'm done. The way things are right now, they're not healthy for any of us. I should have done it a long time ago, but I was worried. Worried the affairs would come out. Worried about you. Worried your father might just leave. And I'm sorry I didn't do it sooner."

"You don't have anything to apologize for, Mom," I assure her. "It's a shitty situation."

For once, she doesn't correct my foul language. Instead, she lets out a teary laugh and pulls me in for a tight hug. I squeeze her back.

"I'm so proud of you, Weston," she tells me. "You're a better person than either your father or me, and I couldn't be more grateful you're my son."

"Thanks, Mom," I mutter past the lump in my throat.

She pulls back, looking equally emotional. "Enough heavy

stuff! This is a celebration. Go be with your teammates, and we can talk tomorrow, all right?" She gives me a wide smile.

"Okay," I reply, grinning back.

"And be home before curfew," she instructs, sounding more like her usual self.

"I will be," I promise.

"Good." She gives me one last hug and then disappears into the crowd.

I finally let myself look for Maeve. My teammates are packing up their gear, eager to return to Alleghany and celebrate. Unlike most of our away games, we never bother to change here.

A line of blue jerseys is already headed toward the bus that's loitering along the curb, just past the bleachers. The stands are half-empty, more so on the Glenmont side. It's hardly surprising; I doubt many of their fans were willing to stick around to watch our celebration.

I thought she might, though.

"Cole, you coming?" Adam calls from halfway across the field.

"Yeah," I reply, swinging my bag across my shoulder and starting toward the bus. The bleachers hid how crowded the parking lot still is. Glenmont may not have wanted to watch us celebrate on the field, but they certainly stuck around.

Parents, cheerleaders, and players all wearing maroon mill about. Which is probably why "We Are the Champions" is blasting from our bus. I'd bet money Charlie was the one who put it on. He's always been obsessed with Queen. I toss my bag in the luggage compartment under the bus and start toward the stairs.

"WES! Wes!" I turn to see Maeve jogging toward me.

There's a group of maroon-clad students standing behind her with an open gap in their circle, staring after her with wide eyes. She slows to a walk, and then to a stop a couple of feet away from me. She plays with the hem of my jersey, which she's tied off to the side to compensate for the fact I'm six inches taller and at least eighty pounds burlier than she is.

"Um, hi," she finally says. Her blonde hair is messy, and her green eyes are timid. It's a stark contrast to her bold greeting a few seconds ago, which attracted plenty of attention. Scrutiny I can still feel on us.

"Nice jersey. I wasn't aware you're an Eagles fan," I state.

It's stupid, but I can't think of anything else to say, and the silence between us is starting to drag. I need some cue from her as to what she wants, and she's giving me nothing.

Maeve takes a deep breath. "Wes. I live in Glenmont. *I* play for Glenmont. I've been rooting for the Stallions for as long as I can remember. Because that's what you do. You cheer for your home team. And you hope they win. Plus, my home team is coached by my dad, and it's led by my brother. My friends play for and cheer for my team. But you don't. And that's made things confusing. Because—you—Wes, I'm wearing an Eagles jersey. But not because I'm an Eagles fan." She rolls her eyes to emphasize how asinine my comment was. "Because it's your jersey." She takes another deep breath. "It would have been really easy not to wear this, Wes. Way easier. The way saying things will never change is easy."

I flinch slightly at her pointed reference to my words last night. "But you wore it."

"Yeah, I did."

"I was worried you might not choose me," I admit. My mother and I are more alike than I realized. "If you had to take sides. I didn't want to know what you'd do. And didn't want you to have to choose. Ending things fixed that."

"I know you meant what you said about the rivalry. But, I also thought you didn't want people to know we were in an actual relationship. That you felt trapped because people were starting to find out and you wanted to go back to being with a different girl every weekend. That I was the only one clutching onto us." Maeve tells me quietly, dropping her gaze.

"Maeve, all I did was kiss Natalie that night. And it was only because you showed up, and I was still so mad, and I didn't know how to handle it. I haven't slept with her, or anyone else since that night I first kissed you."

"I think I would have forgiven you. If you had."

Vulnerability seeps across Maeve's face, and I think of the first time I looked at her, how she told me she could never forgive cheating, and I told her the same.

I know what the admission means to her.

What she's really trying to say.

"You won't ever have to," I promise.

"I won't?" Her voice is hesitant. Hopeful.

I reach out and use the material of my jersey to pull her closer. "You won't," I murmur.

Maeve kisses me first. In the parking lot of the Glenmont football stadium. With most of the town watching. Wearing my jersey.

And it feels better than winning the game.

CHAPTER TWENTY-SEVEN

MAEVE

"I don't really think the coffee table needs to be wiped *again*, Mom. It's not the President coming to visit, it's just my arch nemesis," Liam remarks caustically from his spot on the coach.

I peek back from my spot in the armchair by the window to watch our mother give him a sharp glance.

"I know you're not thrilled about who our dinner guest is this evening, but you will not like the consequences if you are anything less than polite tonight, Liam. Understand? Football aside, this boy is important to your sister, and he is welcome in this house."

Liam grumbles something under his breath that I doubt is an agreement.

After the game last night, Wes went off to celebrate with his teammates. He offered to skip it or have me come, but I wanted him to have his moment. Plus, I had two unpleasant conversations waiting for me at home. Liam didn't say much when I told him I've gotten back together with Wes. My father was even more inscrutable. My mother said she's happy for me.

This morning, I woke up to a loud argument. The gist? My

mother wanted to invite Wes over for dinner. My father was less than enthused about the idea.

I entered the kitchen just in time for my mother to tell my father that "our daughter's happiness is more important that a grudge" and to tell me to invite "Weston over at six." I expected Wes to have some ambivalence about the idea, but he accepted the invitation immediately.

Wes's Range Rover pulls into my driveway, and I leap up from the armchair I've been perched in for the last hour, even though it's only just six now.

The grandfather clock next to the fireplace chimes, and Liam rolls his eyes. "He's probably been parked around the block, waiting to pull up exactly at six."

"You're annoyed he's on time? Seriously, Liam?" I question as I head over to the front door.

I open it as soon as I hear his steps on the stairs, and Wes gives me a smile that makes my stomach flutter. He looks at ease, but he's dressed up somewhat. Aside from when he picked me up from Chase's and his birthday, I've only ever seen him in athletic apparel. Tonight, he's wearing a pair of dark wash jeans and a gray sweater that hugs his muscular chest. He's clutching a bunch of flowers.

"Hey," he greets, leaning in and giving me a kiss.

"Hi," I reply, beaming up at him. I know I have a dopey grin on my face, but I don't bother to hide it. This moment feels surreal, and I'm determined to enjoy it.

"You must be Weston," my mother says, appearing in the front hallway.

I step aside and shut the front door so she can greet him.

"Yes, I am. It's nice to meet you, Mrs. Stevens," Wes replies. "These are for you." He holds out the bouquet.

"Thank you, these are lovely!" my mother exclaims. Unlike

my father and Liam, this is the first time she's ever seen Wes in person, up close at least. I can tell she's taken aback by how good looking he is.

Liam comes and hovers in the open doorway between the front hallway and the living room.

"Hi, Liam," Wes greets graciously.

"Weston," Liam grits out in a much less amicable tone. I send him a glare, and my mother does the same.

"I'm going out to help Dad with the grill," Liam announces.

Despite the chilly temperatures outside, my father decided to grill the chicken for dinner. I know it had a lot less to do with his claim it tastes better, and a lot more to do with the fact it means he can escape outside.

"I should put these in some water," my mother says before heading into the kitchen, flowers in hand.

"This your attempt at a Van Gogh?" Wes asks me as she disappears, peering at the framed painting of a star-filled sky on the wall.

"What gave it away?" I ask wryly. "Does it not look like the original?"

"It looks like a fresh take on it," Wes offers with a dimpled smile.

"Smooth, Cole."

"I've got game, Stevens."

"Oh, I know," I mutter. We wouldn't been standing here if he didn't. Based on his grin, Wes heard me.

"Dinner's ready," my mom says as she re-enters the entryway. "Are you two ready to eat?"

"Sure," I reply. Wes nods.

For the first time since he arrived, he looks a bit nervous. I'm guessing it has to do with the one member of my family he hasn't yet seen tonight. I give him what I hope is a reassuring smile, but to be honest, I have no idea what to expect from my father. He's rarely verbose, and he's been even more reserved around me since my outburst yesterday morning.

Me bringing a guy home is uncharted territory.

Me bringing home a guy from Alleghany? It goes against the rivalry he's been an avid supporter of since his childhood.

My father and Liam are already seated at the table when we enter the dining room. I know it's a purposeful move, a show of solidarity between them. I know it's not lost on Wes or my mother, either.

Wes walks over to the head of the table, where my father is sitting. He holds out his hand. "It's nice to meet you officially, Coach Stevens."

I hold my breath as my father studies Wes's offered hand. Finally, he stands and shakes it. The air leaves me in a whoosh.

Wes rounds the table to take his seat, and I sit down next to him. My mother settles at the head opposite my father. The only sound in the dining room is the clink of metal against china as we pass the dishes containing dinner around the table. I heap my plate with grilled chicken, salad, rice, and roasted vegetables.

"Dinner is delicious," Wes compliments as we eat.

"That's very sweet of you to say, Weston," my mother replies. Liam lets out a quiet snort that earns him a harsh look from our mother.

The room descends into silence again, and I keep stuffing my mouth with food so I don't choke on the awkwardness. I risk a glance at Wes. I wouldn't blame him if he was about ready to bolt from the room. I'm surprised by how at ease he looks.

"So, Weston, how is your senior year going?" my mother asks, breaking the silence.

"It's going well, thanks."

"Do you have a favorite subject in school?" she continues.

I'm tempted to roll my eyes at her lame question, but I resist. I know she's just trying to help. Liam doesn't do the same, and I frown at him as Wes answers.

"Probably English. I've always loved to read."

"Really?" My mother grasps on to the tidbit. "I was an English major in college. Any favorites?"

"Shakespeare," I toss out between bites, and Wes grins.

"I like novels too. *To Kill a Mockingbird* has always been a favorite," he tells my mother.

"I'm impressed you find time to read with all the other activities you have going on," she replies, tactfully avoiding any mention of football.

"I tend to read on the bus to away games," Wes responds. "It helps me get out of my head."

"That's nice," my mother responds. "I'm sure you'll miss it now that the season's over."

She realizes her mistake at the same time everyone else at the table does, but Liam is the one who corrects her.

"He's from Alleghany, Mom. *Their* season isn't over." His voice is dripping with derision.

Silence falls again as my mother scrambles for a way to navigate the topic back to safer waters. She settles on me.

"Did you hear about Maeve's game yesterday?" she asks Wes. Before he can answer, she continues on a detailed, embellished description of the game.

Finally, I intercede, embarrassed. "Mom, he knows. He was there."

"Oh, well, that's…" my mother scrambles for an adjective that won't be an affront to the two people at the table who chose not to attend my game. She settles on "nice."

"Weston, what are your plans for college? I assume you're going to play football?"

Of course football is how my father would choose to enter the conversation. But he's talking, which means we're not sitting in silence. His voice is neutral, not antagonistic like Liam's, so I don't intervene.

"My dad went to Lincoln University, and he's always wanted me to attend there as well," Wes replies. My father's eyebrows raise slightly in response to this information, a subtle acknowledgement he's impressed.

Lincoln is known to be one of the most competitive universities in the country academically, and it's revered for its football program in particular.

"That's a worthwhile opportunity," my father acquiesces. It's the equivalent of a ringing endorsement from him. "I assume they've shown some interest?"

"They made an offer," Wes replies. "But I'm still weighing my other options. Like Arlington. Coach Phillips spoke very highly of you, sir."

I thought the enmity in the room hit its peak when Liam last spoke. I was wrong. The tension in the room ratchets up to that of a taut string about to snap in response to Wes's casual words. Liam's the one who snips it.

"You're looking at Arlington? Are you fucking kidding me?"

"Liam," my mother admonishes. My brother doesn't say anything else, but he glowers, first at Wes, then at me.

"Lincoln's program is higher ranked." I'm surprised my father is the one who breaks the strained silence. To disparage his alma mater and the team he used to coach, of all things.

"Yes, it is," Wes agrees. "But Arlington is Maeve's first choice."

I stare at him, stunned. Surprised he realized that, and even more shocked he's factoring it into his own future plans, especially given the recent upheaval in our relationship.

"It is?" my father questions, looking at me.

"Yeah, it is," I admit, looking away from Wes and cutting my chicken. "I applied to lots of places, though."

Dinner doesn't last much longer, and it's mostly filled with my mother and Wes talking. I chime in a few times, but my father and brother are silent.

"What time is it?" I ask my mother as soon as we all finish eating.

She checks her watch. "Almost seven."

"Wow, we'd better get going," I tell Wes, looking at him meaningfully.

He catches on quickly. "You'd better hurry up and change, Stevens. Then we can get moving."

I give Wes a clueless look because we didn't actually make any plans past dinner. I was thinking we could escape my house and go to the cabin. What am I supposed to change into?

"Change?" my mother asks. "Where are you two headed?"

"Mini golf," Wes responds.

"That sounds fun." My mother stands and starts collecting the dishes. "Better dress warm, Maeve. It's chilly out."

"Okay, I'll do that," I say, standing. I shoot Wes a look to make sure he really meant it, and he just gives me a serene grin.

I head back out into the front hallway and up the stairs to my room. I pull off the blouse I was wearing and start pawing through my closet for a cute sweater to change into. There's a knock on my door just as I've pulled one over my head.

"Yes?" I call out, expecting it to be my mother, checking up on me. It's not. It's Liam. And based on the agitated expression on his face, he hasn't come to apologize for his moody behavior at dinner.

"What is it, Liam?" I ask impatiently as I grab my winter coat out of my closet and shove my phone in the pocket.

"He's considering Arlington?"

I sigh. "I guess so. He didn't tell me."

"Yeah, right," Liam scoffs. "He's only considering playing at Arlington because of you! Over *higher-ranked* programs!"

"Liam, I get why you're upset. I know you've always wanted to play there. But I only just applied. I might not even get in, and a lot could change between—"

"Maeve, your grades are perfect, you're student council president, and you were captain of a soccer team that just won state for the first time ever. You're going to get in, and he's going to follow you there, and I'm going to spend another four years stuck in Weston Cole's shadow."

"You don't know that! We've never even discussed going to the same school. A lot could change between now and then. There's a good chance he'll change his mind and end up going to Lincoln to please his dad."

"He announced to Mom and Dad at dinner he's choosing a school based on where you go, Maeve. That doesn't sound like someone who's going to change his mind."

"I don't know what you want me to say, Liam," I reply. "I'm sorry you're upset, but this isn't my fault."

"Of course it's your fault! Every other girl in Glenmont manages to stick to the guys in town, and *my* sister is the one stupid enough to fall for the Alleghany quarterback? Do you have any idea how embarrassing this is for me, Maeve? How much shit the team is giving me?"

I can feel it coming. The moment Wes was talking about. The moment where I have to choose.

"I'm sorry you feel personally attacked by the person I fell in love with, Liam," I reply. "But I won't apologize for it. And it would be nice if you could just be happy for me rather than tossing insults. And also tell your team to shut up about my love life."

"Oh, that's what I'm supposed to say when they make comments about my sister sleeping with the enemy? 'Shut up'?"

"It's none of their business."

"You made it the entire school's business, Maeve! As soon as you got involved with a guy from Alleghany. I mean, any guy would have been bad enough, but Weston fucking Cole?"

"Why do you hate him so much?"

That question pulls Liam up short. "You're joking, right?"

"No, I mean it. Aside from the rivalry. Why don't you like him?"

"He's a jerk."

"Which you know from…what? All the quality time you've spent together over the past few years?"

"No. I've heard stuff, okay?"

"So you believe every rumor you hear?"

Liam's face hardens. "I doubt they're all lies."

"But you don't believe me when I say he's a good person, and he makes me happy? I mean, Liam, you're upset because he wants to go to the same school as me. I get why you're threatened by that, but it might not be all bad. He could help—"

Liam snorts. "I don't need help from Weston Cole when it comes to football."

"Fine. But if you're asking me to pick you over him, I won't."

Fresh betrayal streaks across Liam's face at my words. He strides out into the hallway, and I hear his door slam shut a few seconds later. I finish getting ready and head downstairs.

My father and Wes are standing in the entryway, talking. To my immense shock, they're both smiling.

"Ready?" I ask Wes, coming to a stop beside them.

"Yup," he confirms.

"Weston was just telling me you run drills at the track every other night," my father says. "I was thinking I might come with you tomorrow night, if that's okay?"

I stare at him, gobsmacked. Now that my season is over, I wasn't planning on training tomorrow night, but I'm not about to dissuade my father from something I've hoped he'd do for years.

"Um, yeah. Sure," I reply.

"All right, then," my father responds, as though the two of us making plans is entirely normal. "You two have fun tonight."

"Thank you, Coach Stevens," Wes replies respectfully.

I simply nod, too surprised to say anything as we head outside into the cold winter air.

"Was I hallucinating back there?" I can't help but ask as Wes backs out of my driveway. "Or did my dad just offer to run drills with me?"

"Nope, that's what I heard too," Wes confirms, smiling over at me. He looks pleased with himself, and I'm immediately suspicious.

"Did you say something to him?" I ask.

"I may have mentioned I thought he should pay a little more attention to what a star athlete his daughter is when he said he regretted missing your game yesterday."

A lump grows in my throat. "Thank you."

Wes shrugs. "I was just being honest. No need to thank me." He pauses. "You were upstairs for a while."

"Yeah. I was talking to Liam," I admit.

"I thought I heard some yelling."

"You did."

"Do you want to talk about it?" Wes gives me a concerned look.

"No," I respond. After a moment, I add, "I chose you."

I can feel Wes's eyes on me. "I'm sorry, Maeve. Sorry you had to."

"It's not your fault," I tell him. "I don't have any regrets."

Wes smiles at me as we pull into the parking lot of Alleghany's mini golf course. It's twice the size of Glenmont's, but I'm still amazed it's even open this time of year. Unsurprisingly, it's mostly empty.

We're about halfway through our game when I notice that change. More people start arriving. Alleghany High School students, to be specific. I get my first taste of what it must be like to be Weston Cole as people keep walking past us, trying to appear like they're not staring. Unsuccessfully.

"Is it always like this?" I ask Wes as one girl passes us for the fourth time.

"Pretty much, and it's only going to get worse," Wes cautions me. "Do you want to leave?"

"Not until I beat you," I inform him.

My burst of bravery falters at the sound of a male voice behind us. "Well, well, well. Maeve Stevens and Weston Cole. I feel like I'm watching one of those unlikely friendship animal videos."

I turn to see Chris Fields standing with two other guys who I know are on the Alleghany football team.

Wes sighs. "Guess I'm not entirely surprised you three have nothing better to do on a Saturday night than crash my date."

"Catch up, Cole," Chris says. "The whole school's here."

"Maeve, these are the people I sometimes claim as friends. Adam, Chris, and Charlie." Wes points to each guy as he says their names.

"Hey, guys," I greet. Charlie is the one who spoke first, so I focus on him. "What's your favorite video?" I ask him.

"What?" he replies, looking confused.

"Of the unlikely friendships."

Charlie laughs. "No idea. My little sister watches them. Why, what's yours?"

I don't miss a beat. "The horse and the bird."

He stares at me for a moment as the meaning sinks in. A slow smile starts to spread across his face until he's grinning widely. "Damn it, I might actually like you, Maeve Stevens."

I'm surprised to realize the feeling is mutual. Not just about Charlie, but all three of Wes's friends. Once we stumble through the initial awkwardness, it's shockingly easy to see them as three normal high school guys rather than the embodiment of the town and team I'm meant to hate. They banter and joke with each other easily as we finish the rest of the course. Despite the stares we're receiving, no one else approaches us, and I'm grateful. I left my comfort zone when we crossed over the Alleghany town line.

I beat Wes by one point, and he doesn't hesitate to remind me I said that was within the margin of error. I expect him to take me up on my offer of a rematch, but he doesn't.

He says goodbye to Charlie, Chris, and Adam, tugs me over to the window to return our clubs, and then tows me to the parking lot. I barely have time to wave goodbye to his friends.

"Someone's a sore loser," I remark as we climb back into the car. "I wasn't going to tease you about it. Much."

Wes laughs as he turns back onto the road. "That's not why I wanted to leave. I thought of somewhere else I wanted to show you."

"What did—"

The rest of my question dies when Wes pulls over to the side of the road. Up ahead, I can see the thousands of twinkling lights Alleghany wraps around the pines framing the beach on their side of the lake each year for the holidays. It's a beautiful view from Glenmont's side of the water, but even more stunning up close.

"Wow," I breathe. "It's gorgeous."

We walk hand in hand onto the sand. We're not the only people here, but I'm too fixated on the dazzling display of lights to focus on anyone else. Except for Wes.

"Did you mean what you said at dinner? About going to the same college?" I ask as we walk along the beach.

Wes doesn't blink an eye at my abrupt subject change. "Yes," he replies immediately.

"That's good to know," I respond, smiling widely.

They're the same four words he spoke before he kissed me for the first time, and I know the reference isn't lost on him when he leans down and kisses me again.

I've kissed Weston Cole dozens of times by now. Hundreds. Maybe thousands. But I still experience the same dizzying rush I did the first time. The flood of heat. The sizzle of lust. The way the world disappears.

We pull apart and sit side by side in the sand. For the first time, we're not confined to the small Fayetteville stretch by his uncle's cabin. We're out in the open, where anyone can see us. And we're not alone. But it feels like we are.

I lean against Wes's side, and he draws me closer.

We're a living contradiction of the Alleghany-Glenmont rivalry. Because we disregarded it. Overcame it. Faced it. To most people, that wouldn't mean much. For anyone who's never lived in either town, it probably wouldn't mean anything.

But to Wes? To me?

We know it means we can survive anything.

EPILOGUE
WESTON

I'm nervous.

I don't really *get* nervous, which sounds arrogant. But the situations that incite nerves in most have always inspired confidence in me.

Playing in front of a sold-out crowd of hundreds of thousands? No problem.

Being interviewed on national television? Piece of cake.

But anything involving Maeve Stevens has always affected me differently. Still does, even after five years together.

She's the only reason I'm driving past buildings that have become familiar. We've eaten together at the Italian restaurant on the corner. The real estate office where her mom, Stephanie, works is a couple of buildings down.

I pull off at the gas station that bookends the final block of Glenmont before the downtown section turns residential. There's a middle-aged man on the opposite side of the pump, fueling his Volvo. I give him a small nod of acknowledgment before unscrewing the fuel cap and swiping my card.

The digital numbers tick away, rising right along with my anxiety levels. There have been good moments in Glenmont. But mostly, this town represents a division between me and the one person I hate to be separated from. Coming here has never felt like coming home, just an inescapable inevitability.

The rivalry between Glenmont and Alleghany is alive and well. Maybe stronger than ever. Everyone who said Maeve and I were idealistic to think our relationship would ease any animosity was right, for the most part. Our friends and family came around a while ago. Most of our towns never did, and never will. At least half of the cars I've passed since crossing the town border have had *Beat Alleghany* bumper stickers affixed to the back. Sports divide just as decisively as they unite. And when it comes to small lake towns in Connecticut, that division is a permanent tradition Maeve and I didn't have a chance of overwhelming.

We've lasted a lot longer than anyone thought we would, and that's a victory in itself. It's also a lesson—the world changes you far more than you'll ever change the world.

Philosophical musings pair well with the unfamiliar nerves in my stomach. Both make me feel uncertain.

"Excuse me."

Reflexively, I glance toward the source of the sound. The same man is still standing on the opposite side of the pump, now looking straight at me. I can guess what he'll want to talk about, but I say "Yeah?" like I've got no idea. If my car wasn't running on fumes, this definitely isn't where I would have chosen to stop for gas.

"You're Weston Cole, aren't you?"

"I am." I smile at him, wryly. *Called it.* "You a football fan?"

"I'm a *Glenmont* football fan."

"I figured."

The man eyes me suspiciously, like he was expecting more opposition to that statement. "San Diego, right?"

"Right," I confirm.

I'm not expecting the fact that I'm now a professional football player to do anything to sway this guy toward looking at me with anything more inviting than a scowl, and he doesn't disappoint. His expression stays stoic as he nods. Loyalty—the real, residual kind—isn't impressed by clout or fame. Not that I have much of it —just more than the average twenty-two-year-old. Four years at Lincoln, several Bowl appearances, a solid showing at the Combine in February, and I was selected as a first-round draft pick for the San Diego Sharks.

"You headed out there soon?"

"Next week."

The man nods, not looking like my travel itinerary is of any interest to him. "My wife is from the Bay Area."

All I can come up with to say to that is, "Nice." I was bracing myself for a more aggressive response.

The pump shuts off. I return the handle to its holder and screw the cap back on.

"Have a nice night."

I only make it a few steps toward the car door before he speaks again. "Would you mind signing this?"

I turn around.

My expression must convey my surprise, because he shrugs before holding out the receipt the pump spit out. "Might be worth something one day."

I scoff as I take the offered pen and paper, scribbling *Beat Glenmont* above my signature in a small rebellion on behalf of the blue jersey I wore in high school. "It'll be worth a lot more than something, soon."

271

The man scowls when he sees what I wrote. But it's weaker than it was before, lacking the same degree of animosity. It's harder to hate up close.

"Thanks," he mutters, managing to make the appreciation sound begrudging.

I nod before climbing back in my car. I respect him more, for not capitulating or acting like a fake fan to get on my good side and score an autograph.

The drive from the gas station to the Stevens' yellow bungalow only takes a few minutes. I park along the curb, rather than pull into the driveway. In the time it takes me to turn off the car and climb out, Maeve appears.

It's been nearly seven years since the first time I saw her, the summer after freshman year. I've seen her a thousand times since. But it still hits me square in the center of my chest, every damn time.

Maeve walks down the front steps wearing a light blue dress. It's short-sleeved and just *short*, and I know it will be the source of some complaints about being cold before the end of the night. June nights on the east coast are a long way from tropical.

She plays it cool for the first couple of steps, then starts to jog. It feels like milliseconds and days before her warm body collides with mine.

I inhale deeply, breathing the familiar scent of her shampoo and perfume. Absorbing how it feels, having her back in my arms.

Maeve clings to me, and it's the first thing to alleviate my nerves all day. It's a confirmation I needed, knowing she's missed me these past few weeks as much as I've missed her. It's one thing to exchange those words on the phone or via text. It's another to feel them seeping out of someone.

We stand like that for a while, before Maeve loosens her grip enough to tilt her head back and make eye contact.

"Hi." She smiles, and I tug on one of the curls in her usually straight hair in response.

"Hey, Stevens."

"You're here."

"I'm here."

There's an unsaid *for now* at the end of both of our sentences. It hovers like an invisible cloud signaling storms to come.

Maeve and I have never had a plan beyond being together. After we officially started dating in the middle of our senior year of high school, we were happy to sneak off and spend time together alone.

College decisions were difficult. Lincoln made the most sense for me, and Arlington was where she wanted to go. We were undoubtedly the only two with any confidence we were strong enough to spend four years going to school hundreds of miles apart. And we wavered too, especially the summer after freshman year.

And now, a month after graduating college, we still have no plan.

I'm moving to San Diego next week to get settled before training camp begins. Maeve moved home after graduation and is applying to jobs. Her degree is in education. She's hoping to teach and to coach soccer—somewhere. Ideally, San Diego. But I haven't asked, and she hasn't offered.

California is farther than I was hoping for. About as far from Connecticut as you can get. But I didn't have much say in the matter. The excitement surrounding the draft was quickly drowned out by the flurry of finals and goodbyes and graduation and moving. Maeve and I haven't had a chance to talk—really talk—in weeks. Nothing about my future is certain. I could get injured the first week of camp. Traded at some point. I'm not so much asking Maeve to consider a life in San Diego; I'm asking her to mold her life around mine, to make her decisions fit with my goals. It's selfish, and it'll directly affect the one person I want to support, not limit.

That's the reason my stomach feels nauseous with nerves and the tiny box in my pocket feels like it weighs a hundred pounds. Because I know this is a commitment I'm ready for, but I'm not sure if Maeve is. We've spoken of our future in absolutes, but vague ones. She changed her major twice before deciding on education. I had no guarantees when it came to football until my name was called. Not wavering on wanting to be together is one thing. The logistics of having that remain a certainty are another.

"You look tired," Maeve says, brushing a finger across my cheek.

I lean into her touch. I'm more than tired—I'm exhausted. The bone deep kind fueled by stress and uncertainty, not just the physical toll of long days and little sleep.

"I am," I agree.

"It's too bad the timing with your mom's trip wasn't any better."

"I'll be fine." I'm basically running on pure adrenaline, anyway.

Today was the earliest I could leave Michigan, after packing up the off-campus house I shared with four football teammates. Tomorrow, my mom is leaving for a river cruise in Italy with Dean, her boyfriend. He seems like a decent guy, based on the limited time I've spent with him. I'm not sure if it will ever not be weird, seeing my parents with other people, though.

For all the judgments of my mom for staying with my dad despite his repeated infidelity, I never fully considered what them leading separate lives would look like.

From an objective standpoint, it's reassuring and inspiring. They're both happier and healthier for it. But as the little kid who watched his parents laugh together, I'm not sure it will ever feel right.

I don't know if I believe in soul mates or destiny or fate. But it's been easy to entertain the possibility, since I met Maeve.

Her hand drops from my face, brushing my neck and then sliding into my hair. I got a haircut for graduation, so the strands are shorter than usual. "I can drive, if you want."

"Nuh-uh."

Maeve huffs. "Is this about the bunny? Because I—"

I cut her off with a kiss. She melts into me, not even attempting to finish her sentence. The last time Maeve drove my car, she nearly swerved into the guardrail trying to avoid a rabbit. We laughed on an adrenaline rush and then I told her she wasn't allowed to drive my car anymore.

Any thoughts or worries flee as our kiss deepens. Maeve has always had a calming effect on me. The first time I met her, I shared a secret I'd never told anyone else.

Around her, I feel lighter. More relaxed. Stressors seem like manageable problems.

Maeve's hands slide from my hair to wrap around my neck, pressing every inch of our bodies together. I pull her bottom lip between mine, and she lets out the throaty little moan that never fails to affect me.

I take a step back, pulling her with me and pressing her up against the side of the car.

Soft and gentle turns greedy and desperate. Lust blazes a heady trail through my body. I love kissing Maeve Stevens, and I don't get to do it nearly as often as I'd like. It's always with some looming deadline, with both of us knowing one is leaving. Eagerness and frustration pour into our kiss as Maeve sucks on my tongue.

A throat clears. Nearby and loud.

Maeve looks dazed when we move apart. I smirk at her flushed cheeks and lidded eyes before looking at the source of our interruption.

Liam doesn't look like he wants to punch me out, which is a lot further than I thought our relationship might ever come, to be honest.

Setting aside our prominent roles on opposite sides of the rivalry, I'm dating his sister.

I'm not sure which of those offenses bothers Liam the most— my Alleghany address or my relationship with Maeve. By some miracle, we've become friendly.

Proposing to Maeve might erase away goodwill that victory gained. But I don't focus on that, because I'm anxious enough. Kissing her was a nice distraction, but now I'm suffused with nerves again. I give Liam a smile and a nod, dropping my hands from Maeve's waist.

Liam glances at his sister's disheveled appearance and then gives me an unimpressed look on par with the man at the gas station. "I should have gone with Mom and Dad."

"John and Stephanie already left?" I ask.

He nods. "They headed out a couple of minutes before you got here."

"Okay. Let's go." I head for the driver's side. Maeve climbs into the passenger's seat and Liam gets in the back.

"I was ready to go ten minutes ago, before you two started making out," Liam grumbles, but there's no real irritation in his voice.

"I haven't seen Wes in *weeks*," Maeve tells him.

"Yeah, yeah," Liam says.

"How is the new place?" I ask Liam, as I pull away from the curb and head toward Fayetteville. After graduating from Arlington, Liam moved to Boston and started working at an engineering firm.

"It's small and expensive," Liam replies. "But it's nice, being in the city."

I glance at Maeve. She's staring out the window. I have no idea what she's thinking. We've been together for a long time. Longer than Liam and his girlfriend, who just moved in together. Logically, I know that every relationship is different. Natalie and Liam's path forward as a couple was clear after they both graduated.

The factors Maeve and I have to consider are complicated. We're at a crossroads we've kept pushing further and further away. Eventually, we'll have to decide whether and how to merge paths, or else just keep drifting apart. Physically, and maybe in other ways as well.

The driveway is full when I pull up. I end up having to half park on the grass in order to get off the road.

My mom sold our house in Alleghany about a year after the divorce was finalized. She ended up renovating and moving into my uncle's cabin in Fayetteville, which sat empty most of the year, splitting her time between here and New York City, where her boyfriend Dean lives.

The lawn is crawling with people who are filling plates from the buffet that's set up, sipping drinks, and socializing. We're some of the last to arrive.

Tonight is meant to roll a lot of celebrations into one—graduations, the draft, new beginnings, the start of summer. It's a massive mix of people. Most of my friends are here, along with their parents. There's a healthy representation from Glenmont, too.

Chris comes right over as soon as he sees me. We text a lot, but this is the first time I've seen him in person since I was home for the holidays. He smiles at Liam, hugs Maeve, then turns to me. We've been best friends since we were fourteen. The past eight years have been filled with plenty of speculation about what my future in football might look like. Seeing him, knowing at least some of those goals have come true, is a special feeling.

Maeve and Liam drift toward the center of the party, giving me and Chris a chance to talk. He peppers me with questions about San Diego and training camp until we hear my mom announce dinner has been served.

Chris claps me on the back and says we'll talk more later. I walk over to where my mom is standing, waving at Stephanie and John Stevens as I pass them.

My mom is standing with Natalie's, setting bowls of pasta and salad out next to the trays of meat already on the table.

"Hey, Mom."

She spins, a wide smile stretching her face as she sets down the bowl she was holding and throws her arms around me. "Wes! The drive was okay? You didn't hit any traffic?"

I shake my head. "No, it was fine."

"Everything fit in the car?"

"Yeah. All good."

My mom took a bunch of stuff back after graduation and the house I lived in was fully furnished. All I had to load this morning were a few suitcases.

"Sorry to interrupt," Natalie's mom says with a smile. "Catherine, did the buns get brought out?"

My mom glances around. "No, I think they're still in the kitchen. Let me just finish arranging all of this and then I'll head inside and grab them."

"I can do it," I volunteer.

My mom gives me a grateful look. "Top of the fridge."

"Got it." I head for the front door, smiling back at the familiar faces I see.

I'm accustomed to the changes in the cabin. But it's still strange, walking inside and seeing the different furnishings. New furniture and changes to the wall decorations. But the most disconcerting sight is my dad standing in the living room, his hands shoved in his pockets as he stares out the window toward the lake.

I debate for a second, then walk over to him, stopping a couple of feet away.

"Mom changed a lot, huh?" I aim the words at the window I'm facing.

He doesn't speak right away. "Yeah," he finally responds. "She did."

"I wasn't sure if you'd gotten here yet." It's the closest I'll come to admitting I looked for him when we arrived.

"Just came in to use the bathroom."

I say nothing to that. I certainly don't mention the obvious detour.

We stand side by side, staring out at the woods in a building that's hosted some of my happiest memories. Vacations with my parents when I was younger. Falling for Maeve when I was in high school.

The silence between us is weighted, but it's not uncomfortable. I've never been shy about expressing my resentments. The past isn't malleable. It remains solid, unchanged by current feelings or events that have taken place since. But he's still my dad, and he's continued to show up. Even at events like this, when he's forced to face his mistakes. He's shown up, and that means something.

Means a lot.

"Hard leaving Lincoln this morning?" my dad asks. At one point in time, I'd take his question as an affront. A not-so-subtle *told you so*. Lincoln was where he went, and some of my complicated feelings toward my dad got transferred to the university. I loved my time there. Thrived there, just like he said I would.

I let him be proud, instead of taking offense.

"Yeah, it was," I answer. "Nice to be back home, at least for a little while." Although Fayetteville is even less of a home than I considered Alleghany to be. I'm not sure if the descriptor qualifies, but it's the closest fit. "San Diego will be a big change."

Out of the corner of my eye, I catch my dad's slow nod. California isn't close to Florida, either, which is where he ended up after the divorce. "It will be."

"You planning to visit?"

I glance over, and he meets my gaze for the first time.

"Of course."

I nod. Half-smile. And then words I wasn't planning to say— to anyone—spill out. "I'm going to propose to Maeve." I glance over one shoulder, checking to make sure no one else has entered the living room since I did and overheard what I just said. Still empty.

Even once the words left my mouth, I'm shocked they did. My dad and I haven't been on the sort of terms where I tell him secrets or ask advice in a long time.

"Good," is my dad's reply.

I raise a brow in response. "You're not going to say I'm too young?"

He smiles, a little wry and a lot uncertain. "Would you listen to anything I said?"

We've exchanged some heated words over the years about

allowing me to make my own choices, which I assume is what he's referring to.

"I've thought it through. It wasn't a rash decision." I'm not looking for his approval. But part of me feels obligated to say that.

"I'm sure you have. I'm relieved, honestly."

"Relieved?"

"I know things between me and your mom…well, I'm happy to know we didn't ruin your faith in love, I guess." My dad shifts beside me, then sticks his hands in his pockets.

He's set me right up for a snarky comment about how I'm different than he is. How *I* would never cheat on a significant other. But I'm sick of it—the strife. Holding a grudge is exhausting. So, instead, I just say, "You didn't."

My dad glances over. "I don't think you're too young, Weston. You're a good man, and you'll make a great husband."

Something lodges in my throat. All I can manage is a nod before my dad turns around and walks back outside. I stand there for a minute longer, looking at the trees and replaying our interaction, before I head into the kitchen to grab the buns.

The next few hours pass in a blur of catching up with people I haven't spoken to in months, some for even longer. Most of my old teammates from Alleghany High are here. I answer many of the same questions over and over again.

Once it's dark out, some of the parents depart. Chris and I build a fire in the fancy fire pit my mom had installed. Maeve, predictably, goes inside to borrow one of my sweatshirts once the sun drops and the moon appears.

When she returns, I grab her hand. "Wanna go for a walk?"

Maeve studies me for a second as she tugs at the strings of the hoodie with her free hand. "Yeah. Sure."

A few people glance our way as we head for the tree line, but most are too busy talking or eating dessert to pay us much mind as we walk into the foliage that separates the cabin from the lake.

Gradually, the lights and sounds from the party fade as we grow closer to the shore of the lake. The knot of anxiety in my stomach tightens. Talking to my dad helped—shockingly—but I'm still nervous. Not because I don't think Maeve really loves me or because she doesn't want to marry me, but I know she values her independence. And I'm worried if I ask and she says no, it'll leave a lasting mark on our relationship, like a stain that won't fully wash out.

I'm so lost in my own thoughts I stumble when Maeve pulls to a stop. She shines the light from her phone on the foliage surrounding us, so I can see her lean over and brush a few leaves off the surface of the bark.

Maeve glances back, her skin pale in the harsh light. "Remember this?"

I squeeze her hand. "Of course."

"We haven't come here in ages," Maeve says, brushing a few more stray leaves off the fallen tree where we first met.

"I know. I miss it."

She arches a brow. "The tree?"

I laugh as I pick at some moss with my free hand. "That version of us."

"We were strangers."

I shrug. "Things felt simpler."

"Yeah," Maeve replies, softly. "I guess they were."

I tug on her hand, pulling her deeper into the woods and closer to the shore. I can hear the water lapping against the strip of sand that encircles the lake. The moon is rising now that the very last streaks of pink and orange faded, sending muted light glimmering and refracting across the smooth surface.

Maeve glances between me and the lake. "I'm not going

swimming, if that's your plan here. This—" She gestures to herself. "Took a while."

"Trying to impress someone, Stevens?"

"You, mostly."

There's a naked honesty—a vulnerability—to her response that makes more teasing a non-option. I tip her chin up, forcing her to look at me. "Maeve. I don't see anyone but you."

"Right. I'm sure all the girls trying to get your attention are easy to miss."

I almost smile at her dry tone. "I don't see anyone but you," I repeat.

Rather than reply, Maeve kisses me again. There's none of the gentle teasing that started our kiss earlier. She's kissing me like she needs me more than oxygen. Hands rove. Our tongues tangle. And it's not until I end up sitting on the sandy ground and she's straddling my lap that I realize Maeve intends for this to go further than kissing.

I pull away. "Maeve, baby, that isn't—I wanted to talk."

Maeve leans back, running a hand through the blonde hair I missed as she mumbles something that sounds a lot like *That's a first.*

I grin, but nerves wash it away fast. All of a sudden, I'm panicked that everything about this is wrong. That there should be candles and I should be wearing a tux and I should have more to offer her than a rookie contract with no guarantees. And that the prelude for these four words shouldn't have been feeling her up in the moonlight while we fend off mosquitos.

"Wes?" Maeve prompts, signaling I've been silent for too long.

"Yeah. Sorry. I'm just…nervous."

Maeve looks surprised. Because she knows I don't get nervous, usually. Because she knows *me*, and that offers a modicum of comfort that no matter how the next few minutes go, we'll be fine.

She clears her throat before asking, "Nervous about what?"

Now *she* sounds nervous, so I'm definitely fucking this up.

I inhale a deep breath. "We haven't talked much about what comes next since I was drafted. And I know that San Diego is far, and not what you wanted, but—"

She bites her bottom lip. "Wes…"

"I just want you to know that—"

"I never said that I didn't—"

We continue to talk over each other for a few seconds. As soon as there's a pause, I blurt the words that have been percolating in my mind for weeks. Months. Years. I'm not sure how long after meeting Maeve I knew she was the one, but it wasn't very long. "Will you marry me, Maeve Stevens?"

She stares at me. Blinks.

More staring.

More blinking.

I swallow. "I love you, Maeve. I'm *in love* with you. I have been since—I don't even know when it started. Maybe when you brought me to that drive-in movie. I just know I haven't stopped, and I'm never going to. And I don't want you to give up anything for me. But I *do* want you to know I want you with me. Now and always. If you're not ready to get engaged, if it's too much, too soon, that's okay. I'll keep asking until you say yes or tell me to get lost."

There's a pause that might be seconds but feels like hours. "You aren't going to get on one knee?"

"You're sitting on it," I say, scrutinizing her expression.

"Poor planning, on your part."

I smile, hesitantly, as I scan her expression. "I wasn't expecting you to maul me as soon as we got down here."

Maeve rolls her eyes. Then she meets and holds my gaze as she reaches into the pocket of my sweatshirt. "I was going to leave this in here and see if you found it, but then I got worried your mom might wash it first."

I glance down at the piece of paper, covered with black text. It takes me a minute to absorb enough information to tell what she's offering me. It's a one-way ticket from Hartford, Connecticut, to San Diego, California.

"They still have paper plane tickets?"

"No. I downloaded a template online and printed it out. Seemed more romantic than sending you a screenshot."

She pauses. I glance up from the ticket.

"I—I wanted you to know I mean it. That I want to do this. Live with you. Be with you. I'm not giving up *anything*, Wes. I'm getting everything I ever wanted. And…" She smiles. "I really want to marry you. So, uh, yes. You don't need to ask again, and I'm never going to tell you to get lost."

It feels like my chest is getting cracked open. But it's not painful. It's letting in lightness and happiness and all the giddy emotions uncertainty has held back these past few months.

I was thrilled when I got drafted. Playing professionally is a dream of mine. A rare accomplishment. But this feels like a bigger moment. Maeve Stevens choosing me is more pivotal than a bunch of guys in suits scrutinizing my stats. My life with her will stretch much longer than my football career, even if I'm lucky enough to play for more years than most.

And it doesn't fully feel real. "Yes?" I say, on the off chance I'm hallucinating.

She nods. Smiles, and it spreads into a grin, then a laugh. "Did that really just happen? Are we really engaged?"

I realize I missed a step. I reach into my pocket and pull out the small black box.

Maeve's green eyes widen to a comical size. "You already got a ring?"

"I've had it for months," I tell her. "Just been waiting for the right time. And now—" I open the box and slide the diamond ring onto her finger. "Felt like the right time."

Maeve twists her hand to side to side, studying the new addition to her left hand. "It's beautiful."

"So are you."

She makes a face. "That was cheesy."

"It's not cheesy if it's true."

"No one has said that. Ever."

"I just did," I reply, tugging at one of the strings of the sweatshirt she's wearing.

Maeve leans forward, so our foreheads are touching. "I love you, Wes," she whispers.

The first time she said those three words to me was a few hundred feet away, in the cabin that's seen the good and the ugly of my family's history. I feel the same thrill now that I did then. Some words retain their value, no matter how many times you say or hear them.

"I love you too," I whisper back. It feels right, talking quietly under the moonlight, even with no one else around. "Thank you for sitting on that tree, even after you realized who I was."

It's funny how the Alleghany-Glenmont rivalry—once a seemingly insurmountable obstacle between us—has been diminished to a reality that just exists. How hate can turn to love, and strangers can become people you can't imagine living without.

Maeve and I feel bigger than it now, despite the rivalry's longevity. It's no longer a force that could break us. I don't think there's *any* force that could break us.

I feel Maeve smile, her lips so close they brush mine as she talks. "Thank you for kissing me, even after you realized who I was."

And then we're kissing again, lost in the familiar haze of each other. Where time stands still and moments mean more. Sitting next to the lake that separates two towns and united us.

THE END

ALSO BY C.W. FARNSWORTH

Four Months, Three Words

First Flight, Final Fall

Come Break My Heart Again

Famous Last Words

Winning Mr. Wrong

Back Where We Began

Like I Never Said

Fly Bye

Serve

Fake Empire

Heartbreak for Two

For Now, Not Forever

Friday Night Lies

Tuesday Night Truths

Pretty Ugly Promises

Six Summers to Fall

Real Regrets

Left Field Love

ABOUT THE AUTHOR

C.W. Farnsworth is the author of numerous adult and young adult romance novels featuring sports, strong female leads, and happy endings.

Charlotte lives in Rhode Island and when she isn't writing spends her free time reading, at the beach, or snuggling with her Australian Shepherd.

Find her on Facebook (@cwfarnsworth), Twitter (@cw_farnsworth), Instagram (@authorcwfarnsworth) and check out her website www.authorcwfarnsworth.com for news about upcoming releases!

Printed in Great Britain
by Amazon

40138398R00169